The Navigator

By Steve Dyster

To Jill and John,
best wishes, SD

North Staffordshire Press

Newcastle-under-Lyme

Staffordshire

i

The Navigator

ISBN 978-0-9935783-2-8

First Published in 2017

By

North Staffordshire Press

Brampton Business Centre

10 Queen Street

Newcastle-under-Lyme

ST5 1ED

I'd like to dedicate these stories to Emma and Ed for giving me the opportunity to write and for their love and support. Thanks, too, are due to Larry the Lurcher for getting me out of the house on rainy days.

Contents

Acknowledgements

There have been lots of people who have guided me in the process of getting from page to print. So, my thanks go to Malcolm Henson and Emma Lockley at North Staffordshire Press, who offered encouragement and asked lots of important questions. The covers and illustrations are by Fox Hat; Emily's suggestions and advice are much appreciated, as well as her work.

Author

Born in 1960, Steve graduated from Sheffield University with a degree in History and a hangover. After training as a teacher at Swansea University, he spent many happy years as a high school teacher before becoming a geriatric dad and househusband. Always a keen cyclist and walker with a love of the landscape and the past, he worked in schools in Stoke-on-Trent for seven years, promoting cycling. Now he spends his time developing www.sevendaycyclist.com, writing and taking Larry the Lurcher for walkies. Steve is married to Emma and has one son, Ed.

Preface

All I know of the following tales is that they come from two pieces of paper and a good deal of research. The former reveals very little and the latter even less. The stories and the attached papers came into the hands of my uncle some years ago. He was a collector of all sorts of odds and ends. I suspect that these particular items were gathered during the nineteen-fifties, when canal travel eased his mind after the experiences of war. Many of his papers were sent, upon his death, to the Essex County Record Office. These particular ones were not included in his instructions.

Beyond this little is known about these tales, except that they revolve around the experiences of one Job Carter. The accounts were created some time after his death. It is unclear when that exactly was, but he clearly lived a long life, since he was born in the seventeen-eighties and was nearly a hundred years old when he passed away. He had spent much of his life as a boatman on the canals, before stabling his horse for the last time and settling down to enjoy his retirement with his third daughter and her husband.

It seems that the names have been changed by whoever collated those stories. In one of the accounts Job Carter claimed to have served at the

Battle of Trafalgar, but there is no record of him; Jagland and Carter, Doddrington and Oaktree appear in the census records, but the other details do not fit and none of the others can be identified. There is no possible Doddrington to be found in Crockford's, either. Also, the geographical location cannot be pinpointed, although the South Midlands seems most likely: Northamptonshire, Warwickshire, North Oxfordshire and Buckinghamshire. However, anyone who cruises the Grand Union, as it is now known, or the Coventry and Oxford canals, or any of the others in the region, will know that old cottages with walled gardens close to the canal are not unusual; unfortunately, most have not survived.

Research may reveal more and I cannot say that I have looked under every stone, not even some of the largest and most obvious ones. Perhaps that appears lazy to some, but there is a danger that what some of Job Carter's descendants always thought may be true: he might simply have made it all up. His relatives may have been divided over this, but some were sure he was a storyteller. There were one or two who took his tales at face value, or nearly so. A couple of these tales include an aspect which draws upon the old man's life, but centres on the lives of his descendants.

The papers have never been published, but some preparation has been done, including a good deal of sentimental scene setting. There is no harm in this, although the stories themselves do not all fit in with the sunshine and scent of honeysuckle endings. Who it was who did the little preparation that has been done is unknown, though the manner of presentation varies meaning it may well have been a joint effort or an assembly of recollections by grandchildren and great-grandchildren. The many ways in which the family relationships are described confirm this.

A few of these tales have lengthy introductions, some have none; whilst some are told in the present, others are set as recollections around the fire in winter or in the shade of a tree on a summer evening. While others are clearly far-fetched. It is hard to believe that Napoleon really sent a force to blow up a Midland canal tunnel in revenge for the defeat at Trafalgar. Equally, at least one of the stories fits in well with known historical events described by an observant traveller in the early days of that huge growth of industry that created the Black Country.

It is clear that Job Carter had a lively time of things. Some might find it barely credible that he was as sober and such an unwilling participant in the revels of Mr. Nat Jones, his first skipper, as he likes to make out. Though it must be noted, that if Job was as determined to offend his thoroughly Victorian daughter and her allies as he seems to have been, it is hard to believe that he would not have made more of every opportunity available. As a man who had his habits formed long before the dead hand of Victorian decency was laid upon him, it is quite likely that he had lived a long time before morality, values, the landscape and attitudes were revolutionised, and that he witnessed some of the pains of the birth of modern England.

Time Line

Oct 1760   George III "Farmer George" becomes King.

1765   Josiah Wedgwood and his acquaintance James Brindley (described as The Duke of Bridgewater's Engineer) meet at The Leopard Hotel, Burslem, to discuss a canal through The Potteries to the Mersey.

1769   Hannah Ball opens a Sunday School, amongst the very first.

1772   James Brindley, engineer and canal builder dies.

1777   Trent and Mersey Canal (The Grand Trunk Canal) opened.

Mid 1780s   Job Carter. The Old Man, is born.

1780   Sunday School Movement begins in earnest.

1787   Maylebone Cricket Club formed, becoming the guardian of the Laws of Cricket first codified in 1747.

1790   (Coventry and) Oxford Canal opened.

1792   The Dudley Canal tunnel opened, giving direct access from the Black

Country to the River Severn. Since 1772 it had been possible to reach the Staffordshire and Worcestershire Canal via the Birmingham Old Main Line Canal. The story about his Grandmother and the Wooden Leg, clearly predates this by a couple of decades, at least.

1799   Religious Tracts Society founded.

May 1803   War with Napoleonic France recommences.

March 1805 Blisworth Canal Tunnel signals completion of the Grand Junction Canal.

Oct 1805   Battle of Trafalgar. Death of Nelson.

1814   Impressment of sailors (the "press" or "press-gang") falls into abeyance, though remains legal.

June 1815   Battle of Waterloo.

1816   Paddington to Camden section of the Regent's Canal opened. The remainder, to Limehouse, opened in 1820.

Jan 1820   George IV becomes King.

1829	Metropolitan Police formed. Before this watchmen and constables were responsible for keeping the peace and arresting criminals, however, there was no expectation that they would investigate crimes.
June 1830	Swing Riots commence.
June 1830	William IV becomes King.
1831	To escape his creditors, Jack Mytton flees abroad.
June 1832	Great Reform Act becomes law.
Dec 1832	William Cobbett becomes MP for Oldham until his death in 1835.
1832	City of London Police formed.
August 1834	Poor Law Amendment Act leads to the Workhouse system becoming compulsory, though never introduced in some major cities.
1834	Thomas Telford, civil engineer dies. Jack Mytton dies in a debtors prison.
June 1837	Victoria becomes Queen.
Dec 1843	Charles Dickens' "A Christmas Carol" first published.
1845	Shropshire Union Canal & Railway

company formed. Interestingly Carter uses the term "The Shroppie" when he must have known the canals he followed when he met Jack Mytton (in Class) by other names. The Shropshire Union was an amalgamation of canals that developed out of a failed plan to link the Mersey, the Dee and the Severn and other canals, such as what we know as the Llangollen and Montgomery Canals.

1847   Carlo Gatti arrives in England, widely credited with making the first ice-cream generally available to the public.

1854-1856   Crimean War, during which Florence Nightingale became famous.

1858   The Netherton Canal tunnel opened. The last to be built on the UK canal system.

Mid 1860s   "The Smoke" becomes slang for London. Thus, the tale recounted in True Love must have been told in the 1860s or 1870s, presumably when Carter was "getting on a bit."

1870s/1880s Job Carter, the Old Man, dies.

Introduction

The year 2016, when the finishing touches were put to these stories, was a year in which we heard much about those whom modern day society and economic forces were leaving behind. The British vote to leave the European Union, the election of Donald Trump, the popularity of more extreme political forces were all laid to this cause. In the world of the twenty-first century, no less than the twentieth, change upon change flows like the Niagara Falls with no sign of slowing. Globalisation, technology, the death of traditional industries in many western countries, social media with its huge sweep across the world replacing face-to-face interaction with neighbours and colleagues…the list is almost endless.

But change is not new, even if the race has become a headlong steeplechase with many followers hopelessly behind the main event. Change, continuity and their impact are complex concepts. Even tougher is the relationship between change and "progress." Simply put, we all love our village pub and our high street shops, but we still do most of our shopping on-line or at the supermarket and stock up with beer to drink whilst watching the telly.

"The Age of Progress"; "The Age of Improvement"; "The Age of Revolution"; all epithets given to chunks of that period of British History that runs from the late eighteenth century to some time around 1900. Huge change occurred in almost every aspect of life, from fashion to manufacturing, agriculture, manners to religion, communications to social attitudes. Economically, the standard of living rose – though often haphazardly and with numerous casualties – though there's some debate about quality of life. Whatever the outcome, the process was, for many, painful. People have always been left behind, sometimes to catch up, sometimes not.

These stories really came to me when thinking about the past and present and how easy it is to laugh at the stick-in-the-muds, the unenlightened who could not see change as good and who could not keep up with the leaders of the race. "Luddite" is, these days, a general term used to describe some fogey who does not use the latest technology; my son is no doubt baffled by my use of a mobile phone mainly to make phone calls, receive email and texts, rather than do all the other things that this wonderful piece of equipment could allow me to do.

The "Luddites" of history did not like machinery. In the early nineteenth century, they went on wrecking sprees to destroy newfangled equipment in the textile industries. Their deliberately ignorant actions were dealt with by the authorities, industry moved on and the folk who acted in the name of "Ned Ludd" are consigned to memory as a bunch of stupid thugs; people who did not like technology. If they were asked, perhaps they would have pointed out that the new machinery was destroying their world, the trade they had known for generations and their place in the social order, worse, it was taking away their livelihood, leaving their children hungry and their future uncertain, to say the least.

The "Swing" rioters and rick-burners of 1830 may have said very much the same. Bad harvests and threshing machines took away the farm labourer's winter work at the same time as bread prices climbed, fueled by the Corn Laws which prevented, between 1815 and 1848, imports undercutting the price of home produce. At the same time, amongst the powerful, attitudes to poverty were changing; the Poor Law Amendment Act of 1834 was the culmination of the process. The Workhouse Act aimed to make the treatment of the poor consistent across the country (it failed), to make poverty unattractive (as if it had been), to ensure that those who went into the workhouse were seen as feckless and deliberately idle by those outside and that those on the breadline at any particular time, would do anything to keep out of the hands of the Guardians. That many filled up with single mothers, the blind, simple and aged seemed to be of little concern. At the same time, Vagrancy Acts made it hard for many to seek work away from their homes.

Compassion was not lost for the individual respectable poor of a village or town, but the notion that the God-given order of society - itself very much a concept under long-term siege - came with God-given responsibilities was slipping. The manor houses of the sixteenth and seventeenth century gentry had often been close to the homes of everyone else in the village; as the eighteenth and nineteenth centuries progressed, it was not just their park walls and long driveways that put greater distance between man and master.

Even so, the big industrial towns brought a freedom - albeit at the cost of disease-ridden courts, foul air, and filthy water - from traditional authority that the farm labourer could only dream of. London continued to dwarf other cities, but some of its glamour - began to be mimicked by other towns and cities as their population swelled. Higher wages - often - radical ideas, societies, debate, Chartism, Unions, glitzy pubs and down-at-heel drinking and gambling dens; sport, boxing for example, where all classes of society might meet. Fear of revolution, demands for reform, cheap beer, vigorous commercial activity, all effected those who held authority and sought to preserve it and those who followed less blindly than they had done before.

In his diaries, the Reverend Thomas Holland, vicar of Over Stowey, Somerset, paints a lively picture of rural life. Lamenting hikes in food prices - he often sold the produce of his glebe lands to the less-well-off below the market price - he blames the farmers and the middle-men of the commercial world for the suffering of the poor. Yet this work ethic, the prosperity and energy of commerce drove much of what happened in the nineteenth century, from some of its wars to the improving standard of living that many experienced. Growing wealth could convince even the lower levels of society that to be poor was a deliberate act due to fecklessness, but it could also give access to the new morality of evangelical Christianity and the most moral monarch Victoria. Fox and Pitt may have been eight bottle men; Gladstone and Disraeli were most certainly not.

When Job Carter rebels against temperance and abstinence; when he expresses sympathy for the heathen folk of Birmingham assailed by religious tracts; when he ponders on the future of his friends on the canal boats; when he declares that his Grandparents were just as much married as if they had been wedded in a church, he is really just being left behind in a changing world, though those driving the changes – and often benefitting most from them – would describe the conservative rebellion of those who would resist as dangerous and revolutionary.

Some of the stories are based upon real events. Old Moses or Moey and the sale of his wife is recounted in several Black Country sources. Wife Sales were viewed as a disgrace by the "improving" middle-classes; however, EP Thompson has shown quite clearly that most of the sales were no such thing. In an era when the forces of authority failed to serve the burgeoning industrial settlements, those without access to law or religion, took measure into their own hands. Thompson points out that it is clear that "buyer" and the "goods" were usually acquainted, that the "transaction" was pre-arranged and that the degrading symbols of halter, auction, exchange of money and beer, were the same symbols used to make any "market" transaction "legal" and, most importantly, publicly witnessed. Degrading for the woman no doubt to the modern eye; painful, most likely; but for "the lower orders" a practical exercise using their own traditions and symbols rather than those unaffordable legal proceedings of their masters. May be worthy of condemnation, but understandable. "Rough Music" or "Riding the Stang" was another way in which marital relations were regulated by the community.

Other stories are set against a background of historic events, more or less well known. Hostility between the Anglican Church and non-conformists such as Baptists, Congregationalists and Independents had been present since the reformation, though were no longer enshrined in punitive laws directed at the latter. Then came the Methodists in the eighteenth century to further stir the pot. The Baptists were traditionally very strong in Northamptonshire and Leicestershire. Another story is set against the background of the Swing Riots, whilst the case similar to that of Samuel Farmingham can be found in the records of the Old Bailey.

Naturally, canals feature a good deal. The Grand Union and Trent and Mersey canals, amongst many others were the arteries of the industrial revolution before the advent of steam-hauled locomotives and the immense rail system that spread across the country. Of course, there are still some goods carried on the canals today, but the leisurely passage of today's craft bears little resemblance to the hub-bub of canal life in the early nineteenth century.

While much of the detail in the stories fits well with reality, there are some anomalies that may, I guess, be excused because they were not seen as essential. Crews were usually of three in the early days, though two-man operations were not unknown and were much cheaper. Nor did things remain static over Job Carter's lifetime. In the early years a boatman's family did not inhabit the boat, they were left at home on the bank; as competition from rail grew and times got harder, whole families came to inhabit the boat.

Georgian and Victorian society did not really like the idea of ordinary people moving freely about the country, especially when they had a reputation for heavy drinking and pilfering goods, though neither was as extensive as the shocked "chattering" classes believed. Even so, in the 1840s the Grand Union Canal Company went so far as to instruct its employees to take the names and details of any boatmen judged to be drunk. By the end of Carter's life, the full force of reform and improvement had been unleashed on the boatmen and their families. Though laudable in many ways, these efforts to bring "progress" to the canal people were based upon the oft-held principle that "those people are not like us and, though we have made no effort to understand their opinions and practices, we are determined that they should not remain in ignorance and will make them more like us whether they like it or not."

Prejudice, bigotry and fear of the different, might be within us all. Many of the intolerant, cruel and derogatory attitudes of the past are, hopefully, disappearing - though they are far from gone. Yet, if you had told Job Carter that his grandfather and grandmother were immoral, that Mr. Happy was dirty, or that a bellyful of beer was not just what the doctor ordered after a long day in the field or at the workbench, he would have told you that all those folk were just making their way in a tough old world and doing it according to their lights, rather than yours, made them none-the-worse.

Carter certainly claims to have met some interesting folk; one can only assume that the man on his "way to Ireland" in Slippery Fellows is none other than Arthur Wellesley, later Duke of Wellington, though as Carter had a sack over his head he could not be expected to make a precise identification. William Cobbett, tory-radical, was a man of many talents and much knowledge, best known today for his books "Cottage Economy" and, most famously, "Rural Rides." The latter describes his observations while travelling through the agricultural country of south and east England. A thorough supporter of the ordinary folk whom he believed had been swindled out of land, duped by paper money and made beggarly through dependency, his solutions and theories hark to the past. He, too, was, in some ways, being left behind.

The most bizarre individual in the accounts is almost certainly Mad Jack Mytton of Halston Hall. After failing to get a degree at Cambridge, possibly due to the 2000 bottles of port that he took with him, but more likely because he just was not interested in such slow stuff as studying, he had a brief military career, before returning to his native Shropshire to live life to the full. With a pack of hounds and plenty of cash, he is reputed to have owned around 150 sets of hunting clothes, nearly 1000 hats and to have fed his favourite pets on steak and champagne. His favourite horse was known to loll about in front of the fire, have free range of the house and was frequently invited into rural cottages on cold days. Mytton was not unpopular and could be wonderfully generous, going so far as to give prizes to children in Dinas Mawddwy if they were able to roll all the way down the hill in the village. Other exploits included deliberately upsetting his gig so his passenger would know what it was like and setting fire to his nightgown in order to cure his hiccups. This last act took place whilst in exile in France: he fled his creditors in 1831 or 1832. And there we have the problem with our story.

Class is the one story that does not quite seem to match the facts. Carter seems to have done most of his work on what became the Grand Union Canal and the Trent and Mersey and canals to which they linked – the exceptions being in "Oh Taste and See" and in "Class." And that is the issue. The cut that links Middlewich, on the Trent and Mersey, with Barbridge, on what became the Shropshire Union was not opened until 1833. Mytton was in exile, returning to die in prison in 1834. Halston Hall could have been reached from the Mersey, using the Ellesmere and Chester Canals. However, it would have been an extraordinarily long and expensive business involving a voyage on the Mersey estuary – hard enough for any small boat, but unfeasible for an unpowered narrowboat. Maybe he and the boy wandered away from his normal haunts and worked on the Ellesmere and Chester Canals for a stint? Perhaps he met Mytton at that time and confused the event with a later journey made after the opening of the Middlewich branch. It is just possible that Mytton returned to Shropshire in 1833, before his creditors caught up with him and he was incarcerated in the King's Bench Prison. This is unlikely as Mad Jack was, by this time, in seriously declining health, far from the hearty devil-take-the-hindmost character described in the story. We have no way of telling.

Equally his memory often seems sound enough. The Battle of Trafalgar in 1805 should be well-known to us as it would have been to people of his generation, to whom Admiral Nelson was not just a Hero, but The Hero. Then Blisworth Tunnel was badly built, especially in its middle sections, though poor quality was not helped by an unusual dip in the clay that forms most of the hill through which it runs.

So, Carter lived in a time of change beyond his ken, the powerful made laws and wars, the rich and wealthy led and the rest followed, some resisted, others made the most of things, some were despised and others exalted, some got drunk and some abstained. And that's sufficient history.

Slippery Fellows

Though his working life was spent in the gardens of the Great House, Mr Jagland liked little more than to potter in his own patch and tend the flowers that were confined to the narrow beds along the walls. His ever-prudent wife had set aside most of the garden for vegetables and a few fruit bushes, as well as the apple trees that kept a corner of the garden always in shade. He tended the "food plants", as he thought of them, but he did not love them. He loved the honeysuckle and the old roses, the pinks, even the silver pennies and golden guineas that grew in the hedgerow. In the greenhouses and the ornamental gardens of the house he had learnt how to care for the latest discoveries from distant parts of the Empire: new botanical specialities without which any garden of the eighteen-seventies would be unfashionable; fussy items that were carried in and out of the warmth as the seasons demanded. By contrast, his borders were made for the summer season. A summer of native flowers with a timeless scent that filled the evening air; dewy blankets of blooms that brightened his morning in the early light.

He was a man of, what he thought to be, tradition. As head gardener to Sir Sidney Hollingsworth, he might chide the under gardeners and the gardener's boys when they mistreated a precious specimen, but his heart precluded any sincerity in his strictures. The result of this was his ferocious reputation in protecting the delicate that was thoroughly undeserved. Like many countrymen of his generation he knew his place and had an innate respect for the Great House and its denizens. On his first day of employment as a gardener's boy some fifty years before, he had found his place in the great scheme of things. He knew that whatever he thought, there were those who knew better and there were those who did not, but were to be obeyed. At one time he had been quite subservient in his attitude: his marriage had changed this. He became subservient to a greater force, his new wife, whilst his introduction to his father-in-law showed him that knowing your place was not the same as being a slave, however, he did like to know his place, and everyone else's. Life was simple, provided that people kept to their positions in the great structure: Sir Sidney in his "castle", Mr. Doddrington in the Vicarage, Mr. Jagland in the garden. Problems arose, not so much when someone aspired to betterment, but when their airs rose above their graces. Even more awkward situations occurred when those high up the social scale expected more than they should from those lower down it. He would talk happily with Sir Sidney about the gardens, but he would never publicly voice approval or disapproval, let alone talk on any other subject with his employer. He would have thought it unfair of Sir Sidney to expect him to. To be fair to him, Sir Sidney never did, for he knew, how things should stand. Nor did Sir Sidney think he knew plants better than Mr. Jagland.

That morning, with the dew still on the grass and October in the air, he stood looking at his favourite fruit tree. At his elbow, leaning more heavily than he needed to on two stout sticks, was his father-in-law.

"I heard her telling you to dig it out. You'll have to do it one of these years."

Mr. Jagland sighed heavily. "Seems a shame, though. Won't rush it."

"But she likes a garden that produces – and she does know how to cook well enough when it does."

The old man was right. It would have to go and be replaced by something more productive. "Flavour's good."

"But it don't produce. I'd keep it, but then she's my daughter and not my wife."

"Sir Sidney has some fine plum trees up at the House. Provided he's asked, he's happy for the men to have some bits. I'll see what I can graft. Still be a shame to see this go."

Once again, the Warwickshire Drooper had produced little and shed what it had too easily. "Maybe a more sheltered spot would better suit it."

"Best find another good old English plum. All that stuff up at the House comes from all over, don't it?"

"Sir Sidney has a wide collection of all things. He loves his gardens, says it relaxes him."

"Damned if I know what he has a need of that for? Quarter Sessions four times a year, season in London, season in the country, take the waters in Leamington or one of those German places."

Springing to the defence of his employer, Mr. Jagland pointed out the old man's errors. "He's always off up to London at odd times and back at even odder ones."

"I used to go off to London with a boat full o' coal. And I went at some hours of the day – all of them. That was work. Going to London ain't work for him: wasn't all work for me, I'll tell you…"

"'Course you did. You were a boatman, he's not."

"No, that's why he don't go there to work."

"'Course he does. Gentlemen are different. They don't have their piece work or their hours. He don't go up there with a load of coal."

"Do him good, if he did."

"Serves the people, he does, by keeping them where they belong and deciding what is best done."

The old man looked blank. "A servant? Best?"

"Yes, of us. Don't you twist it: you know what I mean well enough. And he is working now, at the House. Now, don't say a word. There's all sorts of folk up there at the moment; German, French, Italian. All sorts. All gentlemen and their ladies, of course, but from all over."

The old man found anything ordinary worth looking at and the extraordinary still fascinated him, rather like the first look down a telescope had made him look twice and want to take it apart.

"I was in the garden the other day, inspecting the plants. Terrible, these damp days we've been having. Good to have some sun. Sir Sidney comes up and asks me if I would show this gentleman round the gardens. Well, there's few things I like more, as you know, so I was more than pleased."

"Prospect of a nice tip, too?"

"Not at all." Mr. Jagland had accepted a small gratuity, but would never seek it out. "The gentleman was introduced as Monsieur Lavallitot, no less than a member of the French government. And most..."

"I knew a time when we fought to keep them fellows out."

"Well things has changed, old timer."

"But has they? Slippery men they are. You should keep your ears open when you're round them bushes. You'll hear low voices in one of those summer-houses. Handsome reward you'll have for saving Britannia. He'll be studying our defences, mark my words. One morning we'll awake and find ourselves ruined."

"Dah! Your imagination is a phenomenon, for sure."

"Imagination, say you?"

"Yes, imagination, for I know you aren't cracked. Be practical. Simple fact is that anyone who wanted to invade us has to come by sea. We are as far from the sea as anyone can get on this island. Now, forget your fancies, because you have my point already." In case he had not, Mr. Jagland proceeded with unerring logic. "The Royal Navy must be overcome and there is no power on earth can do that, but if they were foolish enough to think they might, they would want to know about our docks and our coastline. That is miles off, so no man would come here to look at our defences because there aren't any. So, I'll hear no secrets in the summerhouse because these gentlemen are not here to plan an invasion and because there are no defences here." The old man seemed to be silenced by the force of the logic.

"You're a clever man and you reads the paper, so you must know what goes on. But here's a thing. No defences here, you say, because we have the navy. Well, what better place to attack us? Hold before you say more, my lad. I know, because it's been thought of before, but few people know it. The Duke of Wellington did and so did Lord Grenville, and so did I."

"What have you to do with them?"

"Well, just after I escaped from the navy, after Trafalgar…"

"I haven't the time…"

"Trafalgar, I found myself back here and back to my old work. I was a bit old for a boat boy, but I was needy, so Nat Jones was pleased to have me back and I was glad to be back with Nat. I thought I'd get me own boat one day, or rather skipper someone else's. Those years was busy ones. Though we all thought we was safe after Nelson blasted the Frenchie's to bits, there was still war in full swing. We carried gunpowder and all sorts to be taken to the army, and we was up and down like nobody's business. The new tunnel was opened up so we had a quicker way. Didn't like the thought of that powder though, 'specially as Nat Jones was such a man for his baccy. Now we'd been down to Paddington and was on our way back. We had a few bits-and-bobs on board, but some of the return cargo was human. You don't get that now, what with the railways and that woman that was murdered a while back. But back then you got a lot of folk getting a ride home. We had one that trip."

Mr. Jagland listened as he pulled weeds. He knew better than to interrupt, let alone question.

"Nat was happy and called it a right good turn-up. He'd had a bit o' bad luck up town, having met a man he'd wagered with a few weeks back. Since he'd flashed a bill or two to impress some ladies sitting nearby, but had been spotted, he had to pay the shot and couldn't claim he was bang out of money. Half-sucky he was. Cleared the boat, we had, and needed refreshment. So he paid over his owings and I took him off. See, I had me wits about me. Never liked being round London with money in my pocket. Old Nat never had the sense to keep it hidden. Put him to bed at The Castle and back to the boat late next morning, though he protested that a gentleman such as himself should have treated those girls. I told him his Masters would appreciate having more of their money and his poor old wife would be happy to see him home sooner. I thought the Masters'll prefer men with a bit about them."

"But what did you know? I haven't all day."

"Rush, rush, rush. If you want to learn about the defence of your liberty you must not hurry, but digest slow."

Mr. Jagland looked down at a small weed, sighed and lifted it dexterously by the tiny leaves. A little one will become a big one if you fail to get the root.

"So, we got back to the yard and there was this chap wanting to head back our way. Nat was eager to get him aboard and get off afore someone else offered him cheaper conveyance. I was cautious. Lots of scuffle-hunters around in those days, saying they was after work or a trip and watching out for easy pickings when your back was turned. So I told Nat that we should know something of him or he'd be off down the towpath as soon as we got the other side of Uxbridge. But he was the skipper and told me to keep an eye out if I wanted. A little after we were on our way with this fellow sitting by Nat chatting away like his long lost brother. Very well spoken he was, thought it an odd thing for a gent to hitch a ride on a boat when he could have an inside seat on a coach."

"True, a bit odd, but hardly worth a fuss," commented Mr. Jagland. Then, more directly, "and I still don't see what this all has to do with my liberty."

"Odder things have happened, thought I," continued the narrator, ignoring any hint to come to the point, "until we reached Black Jack's and went alongside a boat called the Victorious. Nat knew the skipper, but what I noticed was that there was a young chap who looked at our fellow and met his eye. No word did they say, but I knew that they was acquainted. It was a look that said 'say nothing'. Straightway the fellow on the other boat speaks up. Well-spoken as our chap he was. Looked at me, as if to see what I was thinking. Froze me stiff that look did. Warm work through a lock, but I felt a chill. Still the other skipper was pleased, said his lad had run off in London, or been press-ganged. He said he'd find it rich as he hadn't liked a windy day on the cut. Yes, thought I, I'd been pressed and emptied me guts before we'd reached the sea. Good job that he'd picked this fellow up the old skipper said, earning his ticket he was.

"This old skipper was a butty of Nat's, so we went together a little way, mooring up a bit early so we could try our luck for sustenance in Rickmansworth. These two young fellows saying they was by the wind, having been at sea, and would stop behind and save what was left in their purses. Nat was never one to lose the chance to fraternise with one of his old butties, so he was happy and off we went. He and the old skipper renewed their acquaintance in the manner of the day and were soon oiled to the point of garrulousity, garrulity, whichever. I was quiet. The old skipper asks me if I'm not thinking of running off to sea too; all the young men of fashion wanted to emulate Lord Nelson. Nat tells him I had only just got back from a jollification with the Hero himself. And damn lucky I didn't end up the way he did, says I. I said I was heading back for a sleep. I left them and walked to the boat.

"I stood on a bridge and looked down the cut. The moon, playing hide and seek behind the clouds, was shining straight along the water and stayed for a moment. Away ahead a lock gate was touched by silver as wind-stirred water ran with light and was then dark once more. A little group of oil lamps glowing in the darkness showed we'd been joined by others. When I got near, I counted six boats in all. I couldn't read the names or whose they were, but there were six, including ours. The lights I'd seen were on the back two boats. I stole past them on my toes. Why I wanted to sneak about I could not say, but there was something odd about it all and I've always trusted my guts. There were murmuring voices as I went past and the odd laugh. I crept up to our own boat where all was dark: so much for keeping an eye out. I expected he'd had some of the cargo away and we'd not see hide nor hair of our passenger again. I pulled open the little door that opened into the cabin as quiet-like as I could. For one moment the moonlight lit the interior: all was in place, including Nat's medicine. I went down to the bow, not wanting to peep into the cabin of the other boat unless I had to. Besides, our guest was to bed down there. I stuck my head in. I could make out the few boxes and sacks we carried but could see no sleeper, nor hear snoring. Quiet one, thinks I. Mind everything looked to be in place. Perhaps he's gone for a wander. I often used to go of a night to help the farmer save his crops from the rabbits. Nice plump bunnies. Mind, not the sort of thing a gent would do.

"At that second I was gripped around head and chest, a palm over my mouth strong enough to push me teeth out backward. Now, I was in the fitness of youth and I'd served at sea. Hoisting all those sails gave you muscles and I was lithe enough to run aloft with the best of them. But this was a grip that would not let go. The strong man, whoever he was, lifted me off my feet and swung me around, face to face with another man. I say face to face, but the moon was at his back and his hat was pulled down over his eyes. I glanced around with darting eyes and shook: I caught sight, ever so briefly, of the thin, silver line of a knife-edge gleaming in the moment it took the clouds to hide moonlight.

"You still listening? Now he recognised me, his eyes flashed bright with rage. 'Jew,' he said or 'dew,' or something like it. Made no sense to me at that moment. Mind, I still feared a knife in my heart. Then he turns all calm and says, 'It is you, my brave boy.' He sounded pleased to see me. The grip went loose and I was set free. The bruiser who'd pinned me was none other than the chap from our boat. I quickly stepped aside, in case I needed to bolt for it. But they was as nice as pie. No sooner had I told them what a pair of damned ruffians they were, then they were apologising most genteel. They had thought I was a robber, they had wanted to protect good Mr. Jones' cargo. Yes, I thought, you're a pair o' downy old birds. I wonder what you're up to? But I kept that to myself.

"I still reckoned they were villains, but what they were up to I couldn't fathom. They told Nat and the old skipper all about it and they laughed. Now, Old Nat was a grand man, a better friend to me there never was, but I thought he liked these fellows with genteel accents a good deal too well. I still wondered why they were on a boat and why they'd nearly stuck me in the guts. If I'd seen some thief on a dark night I'd have shouted to scare him and then given chase. Mind, I suppose I was a bit wary – not many folks have had a musket ball in the arse and if they had they might not be so ready to take on what they don't know. But there we are, they were probably harmless enough. It came to mind that they may be a couple of toffs seeing how far they could get for a wager – the swells put money on anything then, and lost most of it.

"Next morning we set off with the others. Now, these other four were packed, with gunpowder, bound for Liverpool. Seemed another oddity – after all we'd just been taking a cargo of the same the other way. The swell on Victorious explained that it was probably wanted for Ireland – the French, he said, saw Ireland as a backdoor and wanted to stir up rebellion. Well, seemed sensible. We'd seen some of those old Irish Navvies build the canals: struck me Boney had misjudged them: 'twasn't powder they needed, just a few flasks of whisky at the end of a week of going without and they'd take on half the army.

"Now you're saying to yourself, gentlemen don't wave knives in the faces of folk on a dark night. Well, they did then. Poor old Charlies – watchmen – had a terrible time when the swells were heading home around dawn. Tip their sentry boxes over and give them a thrashing. I'd seen it happen when I was up in London. So, it all seemed possible. Nat was right. Maybe the cold nights had been aggravating me war wound: affected my brains, he said. French sharpshooters were renowned they said: killed Nelson and found the seat of my intelligence.

"No, I was coming round to thinking that these two puffed-up ruffians, mocking a man who'd fought to save their bacon, could only be our own English aristocrats. That's Eton and Oxford for you. But while I wondered less about them, I thought more on those other four boats. It wasn't that they bore powder, after all, there was a war to fight, nor was it that they were taking it in the opposite direction to us, for you can't expect the army and admiralty to act normal-like. Our warriors' heroic deeds have often been in the face of adversities created by their superiors. No, what set me pondering, as I plodded along with the horse, was that they were all full-grown men – none of them were boys, youngish chaps – and I was unusual in being a second man on a boat in those parts – and they never said but a few words all day. They travelled with us. That night they moored-up alongside, but they avoided your looks and stuck to themselves and never had nothing to do with us. Well, except with the two toffs, who seemed to get something from them every now and again, even if only a look or a word. More than the rest of us got. Ask them about their horses, women, beer, home and you got nothing out of them more than a grunt and a growl that told you to keep your distance.

"I kept it, too. Didn't need their nonsense. I used to love those days. I was on the old side for it, but I still feel the breeze of an autumn day with the clouds scudding across a blue sky can't be beat. The harvest just about done and the ploughmen setting about their work, followed by flocks of birds, turning over the stubble and changing the season as they went. You see nature starting to bed down for winter, the last of another year, yet you know it'll soon return. I'd not have cared to be a ploughman, but I wouldn't have mind turning me hand to farming. All that wonder – won't argue with Doddrington or Ashton about that, I even like the Harvest Home – and all you have to do is pass along quietly, labour hard and it's yours.

"We didn't get so far that day. Well, there's locks all the way and you had to wait and wait and take your turn. Gets up to some height along there – not so you'd know it unless you're working the lot of them – what was it? Four hundred feet and something? Don't matter really, but I like to remember if I can. Then, of course, you had to work down again. More locks – seven at Marsworth alone. Well, we was so slow that day that Nat said we should moor up by Aldbury. Seems he had been walking in another man's shoes, as they used to say, in that place and fancied taking a look to see what, or who, was about. Now the old skipper was not too bothered and the silent foursome had nothing to say as ever, but the toffs were all for pushing on. I was for stopping, and I told them they'd be too if they'd been putting their back into as I had. But they had been egging us to move along all day long. The poor old lock keepers along the way had got right earful. So they went on and on. Yes, I was right, I thought, they've got some kind of steeplechase-wager, except on a boat. Anyway, it seems that Nat had come to wonder if her husband might not be at home, so he obliged them by heading on, with the others following. Nat told them that the keepers would not let them down at that time, but when they got there the toffs ran ahead and had words with the keeper. I imagine that money opened those locks for us and as dark fell, I was again shoving and heaving. We pressed on a little further, but Nat said they'd kill the poor old horse if they didn't stop and they wouldn't go nowhere without the horse for I was, he said, too idle to haul the boat. The gentlemen seemed happy. They even sent out for some gin that night. The lock keepers lad fetched it. Bloody gut-rot it is too, so I had none, but all the others took their fill.

"Since Nat hadn't fraternised the night before, we were off at first light, egged on by the toffs who was after winning their wager. It was still breezy, so there was none of that lovely mist that hangs on the fields cutting the trunks from the boughs and floating the Church Towers on a sea of white: no spider's webs, hung with drops of dew, in the hedge rows. It was a chill morning and I pulled my coat on.

"And so we went along. We left the hills behind. Champion country, I've heard farmers call it. Big neat fields, hedged and level: even the copse and cover set out by human hand. Mile after mile we passed teams ploughing away and carts going back and forth with the product of the harvest. Storing stuff up. No, I couldn't have been a ploughman: at least I lead the horse somewhere. To be honest, I always found that stretch on the dull side. Past Great Brickhill, things get better, I say.

"Any road, I was drifting off, thinking how pleasant and gentle it all was – 'specially compared to being at sea – when our little flotilla passed under a bridge. It was one of those brick bridges they built to take a little road from nether to beyond. On this bridge was standing a man. Well-dressed, holding the reins of a horse, and staring at me, from between a hat, pulled down, a high neckercher and high stiff collars of his coat. It was as if his head was in a box. By the time we were under the bridge he'd come down to the path and asked me if I knew where we were. I had a bit of an idea, but not that much, the country away from the canal being unfamiliar. So, I told him what I thought and he questioned me to see how sure I was. By this time, we'd gone some way from the bridge and he said he might as well walk on with me. I didn't mind that.

"Quietly spoke fellow he was. He didn't whisper, but you had to listen hard to pick out his words. He was asking all sorts of things about me, the boat and where we had been and what we carried. When I mentioned the people we had with us, he became most attentive. I told him what I thought of the two who spoke genteel, but hadn't dressed to match. He looked and said my observation did me credit. As for the men on the other boat, he took another look and said that they looked like a surly bunch to have for companions. I told him they were no companions of mine and Nat's, though the human cargo seemed to get on like a house on fire with them.

"He looked concerned. 'You don't seem to care for any of them', said this chap. 'Not by a long chalk.' 'Why not, though, you look like a sociable sort of fellow.' 'I'd say so, but warrant it, those men are not trustworthy.' 'Come, come, fellow,' he says, 'You mustn't be hard.' 'Hard is it? I have reason, enough,' says I. 'And what reason have you for suspecting them of something?' So I recounted my tale.

"Then, out of the blue, he asked me straight how Trafalgar had suited me. That set me right back on my heels. I asked him how he knew about that, but he didn't answer. He went straight on, and asked me why I had got out of the Navy and if I hadn't jumped ship and why? But he didn't even wait for an answer, just paused long enough to see my jaw drop. I could have had bosun's mate, or even bosun and then who knew what, he told me. I tried to butt in, but he wasn't having it and, in all honesty, I was stumped for what to think or say. He told me how I had been well thought of by the officers: great shame I hadn't stuck to the sea."

Mr. Jagland grunted in affirmation.

"Good. Paying attention still?" Perhaps the Old Man should have been a schoolmaster.

He continued, "I stood in silence. A yell from Nat brought me round and on we went. This cove as seemed to know all about me, held his hand up to hush me. All the time he continued in his low tones. He told me that he was going to take me into his confidence. I told him I didn't care to have that privilege, as gentlemen have such odd notions of what an ordinary fellow should be about, but he went on anyway. He told me how I was right about suspecting our companions were not what they seemed. I butted in about wagers and so on, but he frowned, and told me to listen carefully to him. I told him I'd do nothing to hinder them, if he were the man they'd wagered with. As for the other boats I wanted nothing to do with them at all. Then in a cool voice he says, 'But you will and you will do as I ask, because you are a loyal Britisher.' I didn't like the sound of it and he must have noticed, but here was a man with authority. 'The Admiralty will not appreciate it if you do not and you wouldn't want the press gang searching you out again, would you? Next trip to London, down at the Limehouse, who can tell what might befall a poor boat boy on a dark night...I know there's no pressing now, but there are special exceptions to the best of rules...' So, as you see, I had no choice, didn't want to be off on the briny again. Not even to protect our liberty.

"Then he went on to tell me a likely tale, as I thought. He started by explaining that he was in the employ of King George, or rather, his ministers. I thought I was done for – fighting the French had been bad enough, being in with our own government men was a worse prospect. So I asked him what the likes of His Majesty's officers were doing sneaking about on towpaths threatening His Majesty's loyal subjects. He ignored this and took me back to that night when our toff friend had nearly had his knife in my guts. Now he says, you're right when you say they are gentlemen, naval officers they are, brave and daring men – and dangerous. What had his word of surprise been? Not 'jew' or 'dew', no, says he, neither of those. Where I was wrong was in supposing they were

English gentlemen. 'Dieu'. These brave gentlemen were Frenchie's, by God. I wanted to ask him things, but he said that there was a bridge ahead and he would have to leave me. He told me that he'd been sent to follow them when word had come that they had arrived in England. It had taken time to pick them up, but he was in no doubt they were into some kind of devilry, but what he hadn't been sure of. Then he found out about these other boats, with their silent boatmen and their supposed cargo of gunpowder. Now they must be aiming to blow something up, but the exact target was not clear to him. 'Must be Weedon Barracks', says I. 'Could be taking it to traitors in the cotton towns up north', says he. Then I told him what I'd thought about the boat being too high in the water to have a full cargo of powder. He asked if I was sure, so I told him we'd just taken a load down to London on our last trip.

"He puffed his cheeks, then went on as the bridge approached, 'There's a troop of dragoons on their way from the other side of Northampton, when they'll arrive I do not know. I hope they put their best hooves forward, but until then we have to watch these Devils like hawks. I'll never be far away, but you must be my eyes and ears on the boat. Now...'

"He was just about to mount up and go. 'Hang on,' says I, 'there's enough lads in these fields and on the boats, we'll come across to knock the stuffing out of a few Frenchie's. Blast me, we'll...' But no says he. That would not do. His Majesty's ministers wanted to keep it as quiet as possible, no explosions and no common folk involved. The Dragoons would be sworn to secrecy he said, and, as he mounted up, so was I.

"He cries out nice and loud, 'Thank'ee my boy. Here's sixpence for your trouble. To the right and then, at the wood, turn to the steeple and keep straight?' With that he tossed a coin to me and turned his horses up the slope to the road. 'Thank'ee', I muttered. Sixpence for sitting on a powder keg with a bunch of Frog desperadoes, who didn't like the look of me and had nearly spiked me in the belly already.

"As we went on, I thought he must have been up Crispin's Hill – or escaped from it. Mind, in those days it was hard to tell with some young gentlemen. All sorts they got up to. Eight bottles a night men, some of 'em was. Far cry from the likes of Sir Sidney. Last treat up at the house I got was a glass of porter! One glass. Any road, gents back there were less for sobriety and all for devilry. I'll tell you about the time I met Squire Mytton, one day, but that's bye-the-bye for now. So, I couldn't help thinking that this young sportsman was putting me up to something. A friend of our toffs, I reckoned. That was my first thought, but I knew it couldn't be.

He knew too much and all he said fitted with what I'd seen."

My son-in-law was getting agitated. "So come on, old timer, what were they after? I have to get on with something useful." He knew the reprimands that would come his way if he had not done what was required in the garden by the appointed time. In any case he'd lost track of why he was listening in the first place and what led to this far-fetched tale.

"This is useful: instructive for generations to come. I'll tell you, even Sir Sidney should hear this tale, I mean account, if he thinks he can put any trust in those foreign fellows, even if they claim to be gentlemen. So, don't rush. Now, it was not long before one of the Frenchie's, the one who had nearly crushed me in a bear-hug while the other made his mind up not to skewer me, comes trotting along and catches me up. He only wanted to know who the chap was and what he had wanted. So I told him about him wanting directions and how I'd set him right. That wasn't good enough of course, he wanted to know what we'd talked of while we walked along and wasn't it strange that a gentleman on a journey spent so long talking to a boat boy when he could be pressing on? Thought quick I did, so I told him, I didn't know about up at Oxford, but hereabouts it weren't such a strange thing for a gentleman to talk with a labouring man.

And it wasn't. I remember the swells and the nobs mixing with the common folk around the boxing ring and on the race courses. Sporting days back then sportsmen all.

"So he gave up and changed the subject. He asked me about whether we would make Stoke Bruerne soon. I said we would and not a moment too soon, as we'd had another long old day. I pointed ahead as the first lock came into sight. When we passed all the locks we found the usual thing at Stoke. Nowhere to moor. So we pushed on to towards the tunnel. As we got close a couple of men on the towpath called out that they'd leg us through for five shillings. That was extortion because it was late and they were meant to have finished. Nat asks the Frenchie's if they want to push on, but I said no, I didn't want to be leading the old horse over the hill that night. One of the Frenchie's says that we must spare the horses and we can push on tomorrow, so Nat tells these leggers to go to Hell for their five shillings.

"As we moored up near the tunnel mouth, it was nearly dark. The wind had dropped and in that cutting it felt as still and as quiet as a tomb. Not a bird sang the last tune of day, not a bough swayed. And there was no-one else about, except a figure on horseback riding up the track that climbs gently by the tunnel and goes over the hill. A retreating shadow, the shape merged with the ever-closing dark and was gone from view. I know you, I thought, and wondered if any of the others had seen. I looked round and there were our French friends talking closely and looking toward the tunnel. Had they seen that figure? Had they recognised it? If they had, what would they do, for they must be suspicious? Where were the Dragoons?

"We ate some dinner. When we were done, our Frenchie says he has a treat for us and brought out a bottle of brandy, pulls the cork and hands it round. Nat was ever so pleased and drank deep, but I said I would have none of it. Nat stared in disbelief and the Frenchman became all persuasive. Still I told him that I would have none of it. So Nat tells me to head off and buy a couple of shillings worth of gin. Now, of course, I was unwilling to let those men out of my sight, though what I thought I'd do if they tried anything I had no idea. But Nat was two swigs of brandy along the way and was a very persistent man. So, I had to go. I ran back to the village; the inn was full and I got impatient and demanded the gin. Never does to be argumentative with serving girls: she refused to serve me. So I spoke gently to her and sure enough she fetched the gin and off I went. Fast as I could, back along the towpath. I thought to myself that there was nothing they'd get up to that could do any harm while Nat was there. So I slowed to a walk.

"I walked along in the silent darkness. When I got back to the boats, I saw how wrong I had been, for two of them had gone: the two that had looked too light in the water. I shouted for Nat. Not a sound. I jumped down into the cabin and there he was, snoring fit to bust, flat out. They've done for him somehow, I thought, Nat could hold his own on the bottle with any man. Next to him, slumped on his shoulder like the best of friends was the old skipper. I shook them both, but all they did was splutter, so I left them.

"Of course, the question was what were the Frenchie's up to and how had they got those old boats anywhere. They hadn't gone back down towards Bruerne, so they must be in the tunnel. I raced as fast as I could move to the tunnel portal and listened. I could hear a gentle lapping echoing down the tunnel, with what sounded like a muffled oath every now and again. They were going through. I hoped those Dragoons were waiting at the far end. Then a thought struck me, what if they weren't going through, what if they aimed to set a charge in the tunnel. No, how could they fire it? They couldn't, unless one of them stayed there and they didn't seem the sort of desperate men that would die unnecessarily. No, it couldn't be. They must be making a break for Weedon Barracks.

"All this time, I'd been wondering if that fellow on the horse would get me taken back to sea. So, having convinced myself that the Frenchie's weren't going to blow themselves up in the tunnel, I decided I would swim after them. At least, that way, I'd be able to say that I'd done my duty. I been through before on a boat and I liked swimming anyway. So I slipped into the water and tried to make progress into the dripping blackness as quietly as I could. Chilled to the bone in no time. Every now and again I stopped to listen. There were wooden boards along the side, to help guide boats through, so I clung onto that. Freezing it was, so I kept moving. All the while I could hear them ahead: distant and muffled, then clear and closer. I was catching up. Idle Devils, I thought, but then I'd never legged, never have since either.

"At about that moment my arm caught on something, a thin rope. I tugged it and it gave a little before being pulled hard in reply. The sound of an oath and a babble of French came clearly. Then there was a flash and a bang and the fizzing graze of lead ball across my cheek. Quick as anything I let out a cry and a gurgle and hung on tight and silent. There was a chuckle of satisfaction. Lucky shot they were thinking.

"So, there I was in the dark, cold, shivering, petrified and pretending to be dead. And all the while there were those brigands up a head. The cold must have made me slow. For after a few minutes I realised the voices were still as loud: they hadn't moved. There were fewer words, but more grunts, until there were just two voices, then silence. Now they hadn't moved away and faded, they had just disappeared. Dead quiet, dead dark and I'd no idea what was going on.

"Remember that I'd had a musket ball in the arse at Trafalgar? I knew that graze was nothing to worry about. Only good thing about being shot once – you know what it's like. Sounds foolish, but there's many a man who'd be less willing to send his fellow men to war if he'd had a musket ball in his rump when he was a boy. So, I decided that I'd go and see what had happened to those voices.

"I swam gently ahead. It didn't take more than thirty long strokes before I nearly ran into stern. Right over to one side of the tunnel the boat was. I reached across and there was the second. The boats lay side-by-side. I struggled to raise myself up. Hard thing it is, trying to be as quiet as possible, just in case there was still a Frenchie with a knife aboard. I pulled myself round to the side of the boat, using the wooden rails to help. I peeped over and froze. There was my old mate with the knife, halfway down the hold. How he hadn't heard me I still can't comprehend. But he hadn't. He was bent over something and was concentrating on whatever it was. Perhaps that was why I hadn't caught his attention. He seemed to be alone. The others must have swum off.

"I couldn't see what he was up to properly. He had a tiny lamp, but it only shed light where he was looking. Must be why I hadn't seen it in the dark. Then there was a flash of fire and I saw him set light to a fuse. My God, I'd been right. They'd set a charge in the tunnel. Well, I'd not get away if she blew. Nor would he. Wrong again. He scuttled sharpish across to the other boat and climbed into a basket, tugged at a rope which seemed to hang down from the tunnel roof and started to rise.

"A shaft. He was being lifted up one of the old shafts. I knew these were desperate chaps, and our enemies, but I admired their bravery and intelligence. I didn't admire it long, mind you, just long enough for him to disappear completely. I could never swim back in the time I'd got. I fancied myself being shot out of the tunnel like a grand cannon ball from a vast gun. Then panic made me do the only sensible thing. I hauled myself up onto the boat, rushed towards the fuse and tripped. I smacked my head on a trunk and leapt up as my hand burned sharply. As it turned out I needn't have rushed. Clever chap, a long slow fuse: he'd given himself time to escape. He'd given me time to foil the plot, even if I had fallen and smothered it by accident. I was happy as anything, a hero! Nelson of the canal, thought I. There'd be a reward. The thanks of the King.

"I came back to this world with the sound of guns discharging above, immediately followed by the basket and its occupant smashing through the timber frame of the hold. I ran across to deal with him before he could get his wits about him. No need, he was dead: his back snapped in half. I sat down next to the corpse and suddenly felt very tired. I pulled some canvas round me and fell asleep in the knowledge that I was freezing cold, had blood dribbling from my skull and that there was nowhere to go, but I weren't about to be blasted to Kingdom Come.

"How long it was that I lay there I could not tell. I only awoke when I heard a voice calling down the tunnel. I looked round and saw lights coming close. On the bow stood the man on the horse, without his horse. 'Brave lad,' he said, asked how I fared and said we'd best go and find a warm fire and some brandy. He gave a few orders to the Dragoons. 'Get everything clear before first light. Secrecy. Not a word: nothing to be left of the night's entertainment.' With that he lead me, struck dumb with amazement, along two boats and onto a third. Slowly it moved back towards the tunnel mouth. Those Dragoons legged well. 'Good men, turn their hands to anything, learned that a couple of days ago, when we realised we might need to get ourselves through a tunnel on a barge.' They did well, legging was hard and dangerous and not just brute force.

"He told me to strip and gave me dry clothes. By the time we emerged from the tunnel, I was dressed neatly and wrapped against the cold night air. I asked the time. It was about an hour to first light, he told me. 'Your boys'll need to get a move on to be clear,' I said. 'They will, besides, nothing happened last night,' he replied. 'It may not have on your part,' I got angry, 'but I saved the tunnel from...' 'I know,' he said, 'I know, it will be noted, but remember nothing happened here in the same way that you never jumped ship last year.' Slippery fellows they are, whatever side they're on.

"We reached Pegasus. I wanted to go and check Nat was alive, but the man said his people had seen to that. A potion mixed with his brandy meant that Nat and the old skipper would sleep happily for a good while yet.

"Short of the village, by a little bridge, the boat moored-up. We moved quickly across a grassy orchard and entered a house through a porch. Inside a fire roared and candles flickered, the smell of devilled kidneys in a pan, spitting on the fire, a bottle on the table, bread and cheese and...so I took no second invitation to weigh in.

"As I ate, the man says to me that he owes me some explanation of what had happened that night.

He told me how the Dragoons had been coming over Blisworth Hill and come across some of the French around one of the ventilation shafts. It seems that these men had been using a block and tackle to hoist a basket up the shaft. Figures emerged, silhouetted as they came over the parapet. One of the French had called that the last man was now on his way up. At that point the Dragoons had attacked and the unprepared French had fought hard for a few minutes, but were no match for our lads. The last one must have fallen back down the shaft, so we knew he was dead. 'Nearly landed on you, did he?' He didn't seem too concerned, but went on, 'good job you had smothered the fuse already – you did smother the fuse, I presume? Yes, we expected to hear a big explosion. No doubt, sir, you saved the day.' And that was about it. No promise of reward, just a sideways remark that all the French had died and only loyal men knew some of what had gone on and that it would be 'remarkably unfortunate' if anything were to befall such fine fellows, amongst whom he counted me.

"With that he sent me back to the boat as if there'd been no desperate men abroad that night and no fearful shivering in the darkness deep under the ground. Somehow, I knew that I hadn't heard the last of him, though I half hoped he'd never drag me into such wild escapades again.

"Well, Nat and the old skipper slept for a good long time that morning. The sun was well up when they awoke. Their heads were soon cleared by the fact that the other boats had disappeared, but once they'd got over that they seemed happy enough. Nat asked me what I'd been doing since dawn. After all, 'I was fraternising over some brandy, but you had none,' he said, and looking at the old skipper, 'Just like these young fellows, lay about half the day even with a clear head.' I kept quiet. For days I had the feeling that every word was being listened to by a cool-headed man on horseback standing on every bridge.

"Our next few trips were up to the Potteries, so we kept clear of London. This kept Nat out of the way of too much temptation. I didn't mind either. The further I was from France, the better. It was a few weeks before we went back to London, carrying trunks and boxes for some Milord. When we reached Paddington and saw the carts, lots of it there was, taking the load off to wherever it was bound, we headed off to The Castle. A jolly place that was, a lot of the best of society assembled there. Then to the Blue Posts and next we ended up at a place called Crane's, or some such thing. Now we weren't drunk, but we weren't sober, but Nat was having a rare old time with some old lasses and a few old acquaintances. I'd drank a good deal more than I wanted and went out into the yard to get a bit of air. Now, as I passed the foot of the stairs a man steps out in front of me. I went to push past him, but he blocked me, a sack was pulled over my head and I was lifted off the floor. By the sound of their footsteps I knew I was being taken up the stairs. Any cries I made were muffled and any struggling was clapped tight hold of. I'd had my fill of muscle-bound assassins, I thought.

"I heard a door close and I was set on my feet. The sack was pulled off and I had my liberty. I made a dash for it, but the room was well-lit with a group of wealthy gentlemen arranged around the fire in armchairs, glasses in hand smiling at me. I turned to look round: there by my side was the horseman on the bridge.

"It took me a while to take it all in. 'Well, my man, you have done old England proud, have you not?' A hook-nosed gentleman had started to speak. 'Indeed he has, Sir Arthur, I expect you would like to be taking such a resourceful fellow to Ireland when you take up your new duties.' 'I hope your Lordship will be calling me to a command before I have set sail to Dublin.' 'Indeed, you may hope. But you, my fellow, the nation owes you thanks for your brave deeds and it is my happy duty to offer them to you on behalf of His Majesty's Ministers and His Majesty, King George.' I was struck dumb, but managed a forelock tugging thank you, My Lord. 'I understand you have seen service in His Majesty's

Navy,' he winked at the man standing next to me. 'How would you like to be bosun aboard a man o' war and nothing to be asked of the last year or so? Let us say your unfortunate injury placed you in difficulties?' I didn't answer.

"Another fellow pipes up and says, 'I'll wager the rascal would sooner have a purse of sovereigns for his trouble. Go to sea, when there are saucy wenches a-plenty to be found at home, I wouldn't have had had I not been sent by my father! Trouble with being a blasted younger son of...' 'It is well not to be indiscreet, sir', the second speaker chips in to prevent any indiscretion. Then he says, 'Well, if that is all done, let us begone.' He looked me in the eye and asked, 'Have you anything to say?'

"Too right I had. Here was all this thanks and not so much as a sixpence or a word of what it had all been about. So, I spoke up and asked him to tell me what the Frenchie's had been up to and why it had to be a secret and what I was to gain from it.

"There was a general chorus to the effect that I was an impertinent rogue who deserved a whipping had I not served so well, mixed with laughter and a bit of hurrahing for the free-born Britisher. However, the tall, curly-haired chap they referred to as My Lord, waved them to be quiet. He then proceeded to answer. 'Firstly, after his defeat at Trafalgar Bonaparte seemed not to concentrate on military matters, but he was in his heart intensely disappointed at such a blow to his plans and prestige. Moreover, he was set on attacking those whom he felt had betrayed him by being defeated. The two officers who lead the expedition were equally determined to regain the Emperor's confidence. Thus they set out to destroy a thing of prestige – and of some strategic importance. That they failed is partly due to you, for which action you have received the personal thanks of some of the most eminent men in the land, and, if it were made public, you would undoubtedly be lauded by the whole nation. However, that will not be. Imagine how the reputation of the Ministry would suffer were it known that the French had penetrated to the Heart of England by canal boat. Resignations would be called for and the ability of our Kingdom to defeat the French, as we will, would be severely shaken. All the country has thanked the late Lord Nelson for preserving us from invasion: a noble tar, they call him. How would the Ministers fare were it revealed that whereas his Lordship had overcome the French and Spanish Fleets, a year later the French had pierced our defences and calamity had only been prevented by the actions of a boat boy? No, it must remain a secret. As for your reward, you have the honour of foregoing ostentation and amongst those who do know you will be honoured in the years to come: you will not be forgotton, though' – and here he winked – 'your past might be.' Well, I thought, at least I'm a live hero.

"With that, I was ushered out. Gratitude of the nation didn't buy more liquor, so I was off to the boat. Damn Bonaparte: great man? No. If he had been he'd have known that in the middle of the Blisworth Tunnel you could pull the bricks out by hand. Shoddily built, except at the ends. Saved me a lot of worry and his men a lot of trouble, had he known that. Telford, another Great Man, said it was a magnificent feat of building. Great men all round, I warn you, watch out for them; right or wrong they're always right. Slippery fellows all, I tell you."

"Well, good job you finished there, for I have work to do."

"Back up to the house, are you? Take care and note what you hear behind them shrubs."

True Love

"He stared at me with weary eyes. He'd said all this before. He may even have said it to Nat, years back. 'Now, I know you've been up and down the navigations of the Midland parts of this land with Nat Jones since you were but a lad, but listen to what I demand of my Captains so you don't fall foul of my standards. You'll be well paid, but I expect a good deal by way of return.'

"The Master had been laying down the law for half an hour. It was the same length of time since he told me that he'd heard I was a resourceful and trustworthy fellow and, though he doubted me for my youth, he would give me all encouragement. Then he ranted on as if I were the idlest most foolish, good-for-nothing who'd ever done him a disservice. That was Master Watkins all over. Not that I blame him, they were his six boats and he made his livelihood with them. Carting and wharfage were his business too. It was 1815 and I was a skipper, like Nat, but, as Watkins hoped, not too much like Nat.

"No, Nat was no longer his ideal. He told me straightforward-like, though I knew him and Nat to be on amiable terms. 'I can hardly conceive of a more ruffianly mentor for a youth,' – I was nearly twenty-eight – 'than Nathaniel Jones. A fine boatman, but not a business head. My temples grey and the brain inside my skull pulses on each occasion I think of him with my money: I could tremble with despair. How often have I had to dig him out of a hole dug by and for himself by handing over too much of what should have been mine to innkeepers and tavern wenches? A skipper in my employ must be careful of the boat and the cargo and those men under his control. His job, nay first duty, is to ensure that all the goods are safely loaded on board, protected during their journey and delivered whole and complete. No a-little-bit-here-and-a-little-bit-there carrying on. All the cargo that is indented for is to be unindented for too, with all dockets, papers and bonds pertaining thereunto to be kept safe and sound and handed over to myself along with monies, especially the monies. The good name of George Watkins, Boatmaster, is to be protected as is the paintwork, such as it is, and all items appertaining to the boat along with what hangs off it or on it. That is your chief charge and will meet all my need, for in the course of maintaining a good name comes all that is reputable in the commercial life. No chiselling, neither, my lad. I'll not have that. Your boy's to be kept in order and worked hard. And beware, for I know every lock-keeper, toll collector and landlord up and down the waterways and I will, you may rest assured, hear of any improper goings-on to the detriment of my good name. The boat is more important than the boy and the cargo, especially if it's for a Lady or Gentleman, is more important than you. If it is coal or salt or some such commodity then it still is to arrive entire, without deductions made for the purpose of beer, ale or any other needfuls that should come out of your own pocket. Not that I expect a hardworking man and his boy to be without beer and spirits to fortify them against the elements, which I know can blow alarming cold, but be sure you can always do your duty to my good name.

"Now, where was I? Items appertaining to myself? Yes. Sobriety? Treatment of the boy? And as a final word, have a pull on this flask and shake hand, my lad. Brandy, from a boat bound for Nottingham. An example it is that I do not want to hear of you following: top the barrel up with water he will. If I were his Master I'd...' He wiped his mouth with the dirty cuff of a shirt that extended well beyond the length of the arm of his coat. 'Benjamin! Get here my boy. Here's the manifest for Hardy. Take it to him and tell him to hand it to Mr. Lewis with the compliments of Mr. Watkins. He's to ask after his health - slow payer, frail man - and see if he can see his way to pay up sooner rather than later, for I hate giving business to the lawyers. Tell Hardy that he should charm Mr. Lewis with our best wishes on his health, but on no account to become too vigorous in his efforts to gain prompt renumeration save he is finished off with a fit of apoplexy.'

"He rubbed his nose between his finger and thumb. 'A trial it is in the world of commerce. You do your best to make mine an easy life and I shall be pleased. Now, there's a load of packages, parcels, chairs, tables, bedsteads and paraphernalia for My Lord FitzHarley. You're to go to the wharf near Chedborough Castle, where you'll receive it – mind you check every piece against the manifest, for these nobs are very Devils for making a fight of every farthing, especially if they can prise it from the grasp of an honest man of commerce. Paddington, London is where you should hand it over to Henry Tompkins, Carrier and Wharfinger. He's a warehouse there, but if there's no-one about send the boy to The Leopard in Holborn, where he has some stabling and he'll see you right. He'll stable the horse for you too, but knock a quarter off his third offer before you take him up on it. The goods is needed for His Lordship's London establishment, but it may well be a day or two before you can unload it, so you'll have to wait. Understand me?' I nodded. 'Now, see Mr. Harrington in the booth, he'll stake your journey and mind you look after it. You'll find yourself with a good deal of money on this trip, especially in London. Now I want no Nat Jonesery when you're there. Try evensong at St. Paul's – I know you're not a Baptist, so there's no objection to it on those grounds, but you're supposed to be a Christian.'

"Those were my instructions – and I did see St. Paul's, though not for evensong and not with consequences Mr. Watkins would have relished – not since it was his money that was at risk: mind his boat was safe and his good name had to look after itself, not for the first time. As for Nat, well how he and Mr. Watkins rubbed along so well was beyond me, though I doubt the Master hadn't been up to a jape or two with him in their younger days. Nat as my teacher? Well, on this trip, I don't believe I could have had better – years of keeping an eye-out while he went large in the smoke at the end of a voyage had taught me most of what I thought I needed to know."

"'Must say, my lad,' the Master went on, 'that old nag you've laid your hands on is no ornament. Are you sure he'll go beyond Braunston? Hope you parted with not too much of your wherewithal? I see you have all the harnesses nicely done up. Must have cost a pretty penny. Keep in mind that George Watkins is your kindly uncle in all this and he'll do a very decent rate for a young chap such as yourself, seeing how you are just setting out on your venture. No? Well, you'll know your circumstances better than I. And you'll steer. Don't want that boy demolishing the locks and causing the company to send me unwelcome letters. Nat said you know the ropes and can steer as well as lead the horse. Quite. Now, get to work.' And that was it.

"I'd best tell you about my boy. John Facey. Too handsome by half to lead an old nag of mine, I thought. Still, if he couldn't use his looks to find a better way of earning his bread that was his affair. Besides, he was a hearty sort of chap and good company, as I was to find. Always had a tale. Bet he'd spun a few to some poor deceived lasses too. Could never work out where his accent was from, sounded like a bumpkin, but knew a lot of words you'd never get from the usual hodge. Mind, I can quote a bit of the Bible and poetry too – so, why shouldn't he have picked up a bit of learning somewhere. He was a fine broad-shouldered fellow, with the looks of the sort who would carry a barrel on one shoulder and a sack under the other arm. Strange thing was that his hands were not hardened as you'd have thought. You know how labour takes a toll on a man's hands. His weren't exactly smooth, but they had not seen too much hard work as far as I could see. His fingers looked too slim, almost like a ladies. All that said, the thing that struck you about him was his eyes. One moment they were searching your face, next they were smiling, then they would gaze away across the fields as if he were a blasted nature poet. Yes, I thought, the ladies of London town had better watch this one.

"He told me that he'd been learning bookkeeping – his mother and father – in that order – had sent him into the office of a friend, he said because he'd pulled too many sly tricks on too many unsuspecting maids. I told him that they should have had him pressed into the King's Navy, to which he replied that they probably would, had they lived by the sea. Great thing about the Midlands, in my view. Still, I told him, it hadn't stopped me having to go and serve Farmer George, even though I had been unwilling. He'd watch out round Limehouse, he said, though we weren't going that far. So, I wanted to know why he had come to work in the cold weather when he could have sat at a desk by a fire. He said that he could not stand the 'silly details', as he called them, of the office and, as for the fire, well, it seemed that his Master was no better than that Scrooge my lass reads about aloud at Christmas. A good walk on the towpath was healthier, he said, than sitting in a muffler with your fingers pinched by cold and your nose a-turning blue.

"His parents had told him to fend for himself when he told them he would leave the office, so he had wandered a few days, spent his money and by chance overheard Watkins berating a chap for having a pair of woollen stockings out of a package brought up from London. Said he thought Watkins sounded a fierce man as he lay into this chap with threats of magistrates and whippings, before telling him to sling his hook. Well, the lad had gone straight up to Watkins and told him he was the lad to take the place of this chap. Of course, he said, Watkins was in high dudgeon and dismissed him out of hand. He didn't give up though and reckoned he'd judged Watkins as a man of more words than actions. So he flattered Watkins with the justness of his acts and all that eye-wash and told him how he had baulked at the dull life of the office and was searching for more interest, but, unwilling to be in the employ of some old crook, he had been pleased to hear Mr. Watkin's sincere desire for honesty, sobriety and general virtue and had immediately decided that such a Master was the very image of the Master he wished to serve. Watkin's had gone on for a while about how these things were lacking in the younger man in this age, but had given him work on the spot. Now this was his third trip. So, I thought, he's worked out the Master to the very spit: play on what he says as against what he does and you have Master Watkins eating out of your hand. I was just surprised that he'd done it so quickly. Wondered what he'd made of me in the hour or so after we set off for Chedborough Castle – which would take us the rest of the day – though I never asked for fear of being told.

"The canal being pretty level in that section, we had but few hold–ups on the way to the Chedborough Wharf. Things are mighty quiet in the modern day compared to what it could be like back then. That's the railway for you. Although Coventry was awfully chogged up with boats. All those bound for London headed down the Grand Junction or coming back to Brum or the Potteries or Manchester: all met up round here one way or branched off going the other. But that afternoon it was all moving along steadily enough. We moored up at Chedborough Wharf just as the sun dipped beneath the clouds and fired the Castle alight with the last rays of the day. For a few moments, the windows that made most of the walls reflected the rich glow like polished metal and then, with a last flicker across the ornamental ponds, the Castle disappeared into the dusk.

"The wharf manager, who, it turned out, was also Lord FitzHarley's agent, came across to the boat. At first he approached the boy. Obviously thought he was the captain. But the boy led the horse off to find stabling before he came close. So, he came over to me and asked if I was the captain. I told him so and he apologised if he had offended my dignity, but he said that he still had it in his head that the captain should be leading the horse. Well, they had done in the old days and this old lad looked as if he'd seen Noah navigating the Ark: most respectful fellow. Often find that the servants of the wealthy have more airs than their Masters, but he was most courteous. 'Good Evening,' says he, and when I return the greeting, 'Was wondering if you would arrive today – not expecting you 'til the morning. Burton Joyce, manager of the wharf and agent for His Lordship, or rather Her Ladyship at second-hand. Sixty years with the family, forty with this title, which really means man of all business. You, sir, are?' So I told him and we jawed away. He said that we'd have to wait until late tomorrow, so we might as well take our ease. He'd be pleased to treat us to breakfast in his rooms – he waved an arm towards the line of low buildings – and added he'd offer us a bite now, but he had to go to the Castle to check the manifest. 'Even a young man such as yourself will understand that the Ladies have management of the Establishment and that Her Ladyship has decided that some of the furniture she selected at first should now definitely not be taken, so we have to scrub out the second and third choices for the third time. A fresh start is required, I think, so I have a long evenings' work with the house servants to check and pack and have all ready for the carters to bring it here tomorrow.' Then, he turned to go, but called over his shoulder, 'And bring that lad of yours. Bit shy, I imagine.'

"Well, I knew that shy was the least fitting description. I assumed he'd gone off for stabling. Strange he did not enquire. Maybe he knew it well up here. It did not so much as cross my mind at the time that he did know it very well, nor would I have got within a country mile of his reasons for searching out the stabling so promptly.

"John returned with the brushes and comb and told me how he'd groomed the horse, although the stable lad had offered to do it for a consideration. He said that there was a small sore under the harness, so I told him to be diligent in brushing out any dirt for I'd never had sores on the horses when I was with Nat, and now it was my horse I did not intend to start having them. But I told him not to worry but to let me know if it worsened. Truth be told, I liked him for his honesty, but took it upon myself to look the horse over each morning and night from then on. I told him what Mr. Joyce had told me and he asked if we were to have delays, and in the morning, might he not walk over to a cousin a few miles off and be back in the morning? Well, I saw no reason to refuse him, but I gave him a sharp reminder about being back first thing and being thorough with my horse. And with that he set off along the towing-path. Well, why should not a young man with no responsibility – except for my horse – not follow his fancy? I'd have wagered, though I was never one to do so, 'cept on special occasions, that his cousin was some pretty lass and no relative of his neither. And on both counts I would have gone home better off had I been a more sporting fellow.

"And so the evening passed by and I went to my bed early. What time it was I was awoken, I couldn't tell, nor could I say whether it was the sound of running feet that I heard muffled by dreams or the voice of Mr. Joyce calling to me from the path. There was a second voice, younger, deeper and stronger than his, threatening to break the boat open and search it. Well, as I came awake, you can imagine my thoughts. I got up and shouted out that whoever he might be I'd not fought at Trafalgar – well, I had, though unwillingly – to have my British Liberties invaded by thieves in the night and he'd step on over my carcass. Mr. Joyce was all emollient, 'My apologies Sir for waking you, but Mr.

Graves desires your assistance on a most pressing matter.'

"I stuck my head out and the cold air helped widen my waking. Next to the smiling old man stood six and a half feet of hugeness, dressed as if for a shooting party, with eyes like a demon, a puffy leathery face that looked for all the world like some of that smart upholstery you see if you ever move in polite society or have to cart their belongings around. In one hand, he held a lantern, the light from which did not lessen the grim aspect of his face one little bit, and in the other what appeared to be a Brown Bess. An off-putting sight, you'll agree, for an honest boatman who has just woken.

"He let off a volley of words, but kept his gun at his side. 'Let me on, this instant. I know that you'll have been about this night. The same as ever: gypsy you were and though you may have taken to the water you have not changed your thieving nature one bit. We'll have our proof and then we'll take you to His Lordship, who happens to be a Magistrate. Before you know it, you'll be off on a longer trip than you'd wish for.' Joyce was waving his hands about, 'No, no, Mr. Graves you must not speak so or make such accusations without good cause. This man has come from Mr. Watkins to carry His Lordships furniture to London.' 'Furniture, he may take, but he will not have the game from the Estate. You mix too often with these people, Mr. Joyce.'

"So, I decided I would have my say. I was wary of his size and his gun, so I forewent telling him of his resemblance to a stale Melton Pie – big, crusty and half-full of jelly. Instead I took the moral line: always best with fellows of his kind – takes them a back and lets them have their way. 'I should say that I will throw you in the cut if you lay another calumny against my name, yet I think you are the game-keeper for His Lordship – all nice and respectful to my betters, see – and no doubt you have reason for your foolishness. Tell me how I may help you and I will, more so as Mr. Joyce is with you.' The old man smiled, but the eminence rumbled on like an aggravated volcano. 'I'll see aboard your barge and I'll have my proof. Poaching, thieving breed come to rob honest gentlemen of their property. Let me step on.' So, I did, though I told him that I did so in all honesty, that he should find nothing and that I hoped that his words of apology would come as briskly as his accusations – and that it was a boat. Mr. Joyce thanked me and apologised for putting me to so much trouble. 'Mr. Graves has been much troubled by poachers in the last few weeks and he has become convinced that it is all done by boatmen like you and your boy whom we have surely woken. Where is your boy, by the way?'

"At that very moment the gamekeeper pulled himself out of the hold and back on to the path. A last violent rock and the boat was nearly ripped off the moorings as he bounded back onto dry land. Boats weren't made for men of his stature. At first, he had seemed a little chastened, much as I had hoped. I was smiling graciously at him as I registered his initial discomfort. At Mr. Joyce's words he lost all aspect of remorse and blasted out, 'Yes. Bravo Mr. Joyce, you have hit upon it. Where is the boy, your accomplice?' I told him, but the lack of place and name, which would have confirmed the truth of what I said, I was unable to give.

"Graves was furious, but could do nothing against me. 'He won't come back here now.' Graves meant the boy. 'I'll hunt him down.' With that he went into the darkness. I told Joyce what I thought of Graves. He made apology and said that His Lordship was a fine employer and an amiable man too. But he liked things to be right and Graves had not taken a single poacher, though there seemed to be more about than ever. 'The boy has been with Watkins longer than I. Watkins may bluster a good deal, but he allows no dishonesty that he knows of.' Joyce agreed, having often done business with George Watkins and being unaware of his arrangements regarding the brandy he needed for his nerves. 'We'll see what the morning brings, Goodnight to you.' I saw him disappear back to his bed and I returned to mine, ready for sleep. Still, if there were delays tomorrow, then I'd doze until I was called upon to check the cargo as it was loaded.

"It seemed as if I had slept for barely a minute or two. It turned out to be four o'clock when Facey lit a candle stub and brushed himself down, after I had grabbed him by the neck and thrown him to the floor, having taken him for a thief.

"He pushed his hair back from his forehead. 'Pretty good for an old boy. Didn't know you still had the strength,' he smiled. 'Less of the old boy, my lad. Where've you been and what you doing here at this hour? Creeping round like a thief? I've had to answer for you once already this night, so there's at least one other who wanted to murder you.' I'll give him his due, just to show he wasn't all calmness and confidence a glimmer of concern showed itself in the candlelight. 'You and...?' 'Man called Graves: gamekeeper to Lord FitzHarley, big, very big, with a gun.' 'Graves? Graves?' For a moment I thought he was going to tell me he knew him well. Surely he hadn't been chasing Graves' daughter, if he had one. 'No', Facey says, 'Never heard of him, but that makes three, though Graves has no complaint against me. I'll swear to it. Trespass I may have committed tonight, but no game have I poached.' A smile slowly spread across his face – an infectious one, and I smiled, too.

"It turned out that I had been right. The young lady concerned – one with peachy cheeks, sapphire eyes and rose-red lips amidst long golden locks, with as neat a little hull as ever a boatman took voyage upon – was not his cousin. Her father, who was not his kindly old uncle, was after his blood as well. He told me how he'd tried to drop out of a hole in the hayloft whilst his wench had delayed the angry parent with vain stories of hearing intruders, sleepwalking and smelling smoke. Trouble was that as he had dropped he struck his leg on an upright post and had had to hobble all the way home, her father having slipped on the ladder from the hayloft and ended up amongst some sacks with his rump top-end and his legs kicking. 'My good luck, chance smiling on the courageous,' he beamed like a veteran wencher, 'and fortune favouring the brave.' Nicely put thought I. I told him that lady luck would have had to do more than smile if he had come across Graves – or came across him, best keep his head down tomorrow if Graves were seen looming about the place. But he didn't want to talk about Graves.

"Two hours it had taken him to reach the farm and four back. He did not seem to have taken too much harm and there was little likelihood of the offended party coming this far. 'A shame we have to head for another port, I should like to take another try at my quarry.' I told him that we would be leaving the following day, before nightfall.

"That we did was as much due to my determination to avoid incident. I'm for a quiet life. I know I'm too old for anything else now, but I was back then by deliberate choice. I couldn't do with this hide and seek between Graves and Facey. But we only just did it. Joyce would have had us to dinner with him – nice old lad he was, liked some peaceful company over his victuals – and there was nothing but delay throughout the day. All seemed like fuss and more fuss at the time, but looking back, some of the things I saw should have set me thinking. Too trusting, I am by a long chalk.

"The sun was well up the when I showed my face and went off to breakfast with Joyce. I knew where to go by the allurement drifting on the clean air. Just as it should be. I thought of those wage-slaves who'd have been at their mill or mine for three hours already: coal dust in their throats or machines whirring away and demanding them to work. I knew where I was best off. There were the open fields across the calm water of the cut. There were boats moving along and horses plodding in submissive rhythmical silence, marking the path but a little. Even the fly that was coming by made little disturbance. The waterways may have been made by man, but I think of them as part of God's creation, whereas the factory comes from man alone. It benefits man and his material needs, but not his spirit. I was one of those lucky souls who laboured hard, but laboured in the finest monument to the creator. Even Chedborough Castle was an ornament. It was one of those piles that had been built up bit by bit. You could see some old Norman sticking his castle on the little mound, then, in more peaceful times a manor being added, then an extra wing stuck on it by a Tudor and so on. Looks a right higgledy-piggledy place, bit like some try to build these days. The previous night there had been warmth from the reflected sun, now there were crisp battlements, dark against the wooded hillside and the morning sun searched the shadows out of the nooks of the long front and touched the weathervanes and leaded roof-tops. And the smell of bacon. The outdoor life in one nutshell.

"Joyce greeted me and apologised for Graves' conduct and unwarranted accusations. The sunlight and the morning were too good to spoil, so I told him that Graves probably had reason for his anger, but should mind how he scattered allegations about honest men. Joyce knew that a captain's reputation for honesty was half his business, and by way of making up for it asked if I'd like to accompany him to the Castle to see the cargo, take a look at the place, and if Graves were about to be reconciled, for he insisted no man was at his best at that hour of the night. Fetch the boy, he said, have breakfast, then off to the Castle. Where was the boy?

"I decided not to gild the truth, nor be too exact with the facts. 'Sleeping. Returned from relatives this morning. Best leave him to heft for himself and to keep an eye-out on the boat.' Joyce nodded with an as-you-wish. 'He brought nothing back with him but a sore leg from banging into something in the dark,' I added. 'Take a turn round the boat, Mr. Joyce, if you wish. It may not be a Castle but everything on it is honestly come by.' 'I will do nothing of the kind, though I thank you. Your word will do for me. Now, let us have some tea before we set out.' I asked about the cargo: 'I'd hoped to get to view the cargo down here rather than to go up to the Castle to see it. How much delay?' He sighed and finished his tea, stood briskly and took his coat off a hook on the back of the door. Off we went.

"As the Castle drew nearer there was no sign of life at all. There is a serenity about a great house that is so far from the reality of scurrying housemaids, swift footmen nipping about and a whole brigade of servants skivvying away. We went to a rear courtyard, which was full of four carts and sixteen hefty horses. Rushing round, slipping on the cobbles, were a mass of servants loading and unloading – sometimes the same stuff. A man, stood atop, a small flight of steps, was calling out orders. He looked towards us, said a word to a man standing at his elbow, descended the steps and limped vigorously across the courtyard with all around him swerving, halting and skipping, to be left in his wake. 'Lord FitzHarley,' whispered Joyce.

"He was clearly a military man. 'Damn me, Joyce, may have missed Wellington's joust with Boney, but doing battle with Her Ladyship's wishes might prove to be the warmer action. Still feel that piece of shot in my foot – action in France, not Her Ladyship you'll understand' he added for my benefit. 'One or two changes, Joyce. Foolish footmen took the yellow upholstered chairs and loaded them yesterday. All else on top. Should have been the red and pink stripes. Won't be long now. Who have we here, Joyce?' He shook my hand and told me to take care of everything, for 'Her Ladyship was as much a stickler for furnishings as he was for straight ranks and firing drill.' Then he told me how he had seen Graves that morning and asked my pardon, saying that Graves was not a bad fellow, for an artilleryman. I told him that I had been at Trafalgar, which set him wondering why I was navigating a boat when I could have been an officer on a man of war. I told him of the wound to my rump, missing out the vomiting in the Solent. He looked at his foot, then at my face and smiled as one old soldier to another. 'Trouble with Graves is that he has taken against anyone associated with boats. Appears that he caught his daughter in the bushes with a youth; pair of blue trousers at half-mast. Your boy hasn't fair hair and a birthmark on his buttock by any chance?' I said that he was dark-haired. 'Of course,' he replied, 'but when Graves takes the notion of justice to be as he does, a small detail of that kind could be ignored in his quest to bring his quarry to book.'

"The carts moved off and with a short stop to unload the uppermost items of one so that it would pass beneath the arch, they trundled slowly down the long track to the wharf. 'Come along you two,' said Lord FitzHarley, 'jump aboard the trap and we'll ride down together.' As we went he reminded me of the need for all to arrive safe and so that Her Ladyship would find it so when she arrived. His daughter would leave for London the following day with her Governess, but Her ladyship would not be there until a day after Watkins said we would arrive. I explained that we had hoped to have been away that morning, but the delay might be made up. 'If it can be I will be in your debt. I may well come down myself and if I find all in order on time, you will not find me ungenerous.' At that moment a girl who had been walking towards us from the wharf stopped and curtsied as we passed, but she did not raise her head, which remained covered by her bonnet. Clearly a maid at the Castle, Lord FitzHarley wondered aloud what business she had been on. No one had that day off. I wondered, too. Surely, that wasn't Facey's notion of keeping his head down?

"I have to say that any ill-thoughts I may have had towards Facey's intelligence were swept aside by the expertise with which he supervised the loading of the cargo. What with him, nipping back and forth in and out of the hold and calling instructions from the bow before appearing in a flash on the cabin roof to correct and cajole before disappearing as fast as he had come, and Joyce all calm experience on the path, I had little to do other than check the manifest. Most I could read, but there were some exotic bits and bobs that only the rich have names for, but either Joyce or His Lordship helped me out. Lord FitzHarley I liked. He was one of those bluff, military men of that era, who commanded respect and affection in equal measure. You knew he was in charge and he never made it too obvious. Democracy? That was never his mark and patronising by such as him wore thin, but he'd not have stuck at a single bottle of porter for the sake of my soul. Even asked me what I thought of London, which took me aback.

"He said it was a fine City and a man was never short of occupation there, with more opportunities for a young fellow than anywhere else he had seen. 'Not my mark, Sir, but anyone could do worse than try their hand if they want a fortune. I'm more of a countryman: fresh air and greenery is more to my taste. Yet a trip to London with a cargo and a day or night in the metropolis is enticing and I'd never turn it down.' He agreed, he preferred the hunt, but politics and military business often took him to London and he always enjoyed his Club and the theatre. What did I make of the people, he asked? He thought them enterprising in all things, did I agree? 'In all things, Sir, half lawful, a quarter unlawful and a quarter neither quite one thing nor the other. A little wariness is required until one can be sure of who and what one is transacting business with.' 'You are generous, in my view, but then I have to mix at Horseguards and Parliament. You will do for me. Keep an eye out, remember?' He tapped his coat pocket and hopped into his trap and drove away along the track back to his castle.

"Though there were but three hours to go to dusk, I told Facey I'd get the horse and sort out the harness, while the last chests were loaded on. He had organised it and he looked pleased to be allowed to finish it off. When I came back the covers had been pulled over and lashed down, but there was no sign of Facey. I called him and he shouted back from the hold that he would be with me soon as he was just checking the stacking and tying on some of the cargo. The blue sky had clouded over bringing a drizzle and a long gloomy dusk. Facey suggested that we wait 'til morning. He surveyed the clouds, though he didn't seem to notice the larger raindrops that were now falling. His eyes swept a great arc, falling at last on the Castle, which could barely be made out and was only visible because of lighted windows. 'Get on with it. We'd all like to have tea and toast by the fire and a dinner served by lackeys, but your lot is to walk to London behind a horse in the rain. You could have stayed in your office, you could wait for your friend Graves to come a-visiting this night, but instead you are going to sit cramped up in damp clothes and be ready for a damned early start in the morning.' The first hoof moved and the long journey started as it would go on, mile after mile and hour after hour, until we reached Paddington. The Regent's wasn't open in those days, so it had to be Paddington.

"Fortunately, it was a quiet and quick voyage. Early starts and late stops kept the daily mileage high without killing the horse. Seemed to bear up well to my eye. The long hours also curtailed any nocturnal activities young Facey had in mind, if he had more wenches lined-up along the way. I aided him by refusing to moor up anywhere he suggested was a likely spot, making him work the horse hard and having him check the cargo every evening. Mind you, I shall not over egg my pudding. He was fine company and never baulked at work or such discipline as I chose to keep.

"Henry Tompkins, to whom we were to entrust our cargo for shipping on, was not to be found on the evening when we arrived. I asked Facey if he wanted to walk to the Leopard and find him, but he said he had never been to London before and might lose his way in the dark. I told him that he'd found his way round a hayloft and half-way across Warwickshire in the dark and finding the Leopard would surely be easy to a man of such talents. Yet, he was right, of course. This was business and that had been his pleasure. Thus, it fell to me to go. I left him with a warning about keeping a sharp eye out for any pilfering fellows. As we took stock of our mooring and prepared the horse to take it up for stabling, I told him that Lord FitzHarley might be "generous" as we had made up time, so that special care was needed to keep everything safe. Once again, I was wrong all round.

"I should have known that something was amiss when I got to the Leopard and, on enquiring after Henry Tompkins, was quickly attended on by that very gentleman. Nothing odd, you say, for a man of business to be business-like. No, but I remembered what Watkins said about striking a bargain with Mr. Tompkins. First thing he does is offer stabling for my horse at a most obliging fee and calls to a lad who he instructs to take me and the horse to the stables and then to bring me to his booth to make arrangements. It has to be said that the stables were neat and tidy with all accommodation a horse could want. Feeling I had made a bargain I promised the lad a tip if he groomed the horse. He promised to do it well and took me off across the dark courtyard to make arrangements with Henry Tompkins.

"Very amiable he was – and, I thought, very unbusiness-like, given the sharp orders he gave on my arrival. 'You'll have a glass with me while we wait, will you not? I've sent for some and I should not wish to drink alone.' I told him that I had an important cargo – which he said he knew – and that I wanted to get back, my lad being unfamiliar with London. So, I pressed him to set to business, but he asked after my voyage and after the stables and after Mr. Watkins. Try as I might, he would not come round to making arrangements for the following morning. Eventually he ran out of people and places to ask of and we had nearly finished agreeing times and so on when the door burst open and the booth filled to bursting with five or six men, all looking ready for business. I recognised the face of the man, who eventually pushed his way to the front.

"'Blackguard, thief, vagabond, damn you. You shall go before the magistrates and then the assize and then you'll be at the end of a rope if I have my way. There is no escape.' The bluff and jolly Lord Fitzharley had lost his jollity. 'Well done, Tompkins. I apologise if you were put to any trouble by our little scheme. Now we have our thief we shall go straight to Mr. Cartwright.' He turned to me. 'Mr. Cartwright, my good fellow, is my cousin. He is also the magistrate who will be starting you and your boy on your journey to either the gallows or the colonies.' I was taken by both arms and His Lordships men dragged me off. While I protested vigorously, there was little to do but go along and take my opportunity to clear my name of whatever it was that I was accused of, for I was quite at a loss to understand His Lordships change towards me.

"The house of his cousin, the magistrate – who had already been primed, by the sound of it – was no more than a few hundred yards. Bundling me up the steps and through the front door, I found myself in a brightly-lit entrance hall. A bewigged servant standing in the centre pointed at a door on the right and our little party passed through it into a dingy little room, lit only by a couple of dim lamps. It took me some time to adjust my sight, but the magistrate was clearly ready and waiting. 'So, this is the man who has purloined the necklace, the rings and the other items Her Ladyship described. Beyond value, I believe. I know this sort. Steal in the countryside and hope to fence it in London. Overstepped the mark this time. They usually limit themselves to cloth and odds and ends. You know, cousin, I once heard a case...' He was brought back to the matter in hand by Lord FitzHarley asking him to send me to the next assize without further ado.

"'Indeed, I shall do as you wish, cousin. In any case I have a hand of cards waiting for me. I take it that you have nothing to say – and don't bother asking for mercy. You will be taken to Newgate to await trial at the next assizes. Thank you, gentlemen. The authority will follow.' Well, you can imagine how I was lost for words. The might of the law had awed me, though I knew I should speak. They all looked aghast when I blurted out that I knew nothing of what they were talking about. His Lordship looked apoplectic, the Constable had an attack of the vapours, but the magistrate just looked put out at having to wait for his game. He raised his eyes from the paper on which he was writing and sighed. The flickering light showed in his eyes rather more sympathy than I had expected to see. 'Law depends upon the formalities, I am afraid. Now, fellow, do not delay me long. You are guilty, are you not?' I was opening my mouth to speak, when there was a knock at the door.

"Two men entered. 'Ah, Vickers, Sandwell. Where is your prey?' asked the magistrate. 'Flown', one answered. The magistrate rubbed his nose between finger and thumb, looked side-ways at his cousin and pushed the paper on which he had been writing to one-side. 'Are you certain?' 'We waited, Sir, that is the reason for our slow return. There was no sign of the man on the boat or in the vicinity of it.' The magistrate gave his cousin another look, though this time there was more steel in his eyes. He turned his eyes to me. 'Well, we had better have your story.'

"I told him how I had been seized and must have been so convincing in my mystification, which was, after all, nothing more than the truth, that he explained to me what it was that a few moments ago he had been happy to send me to the Clink. With aid from Lord FitzHarley the following emerged. Firstly, Lady FitzHarley had sent her daughter off to London, but had taken charge of her jewellery herself and gone through it with her daughter, much to the daughter's disgust. The night before Her Ladyship was due to set off, she was concealing the box, for fear of highway robbery, only to discover that the box was empty of all the most valuable pieces. A hue and cry followed and all the house staff questioned. It emerged that the daughter's maid had gone absent – the one we had seen on the track as it turned out. She was easily pursued and caught, but refused to say anything other than she knew nothing and she would never tell what she did not know. To His Lordship and Her Ladyship this had meant one thing: she had taken it to the boat and we had brought it to London to sell it as best we could. Graves had added his bit. I could imagine him dourly telling His Lordship how Facey had been away from the boat the night before and what better excuse could I have than being in His Lordship's trap and all the rest of it. Of course, it made no sense and I pointed this out. His Lordship didn't even look sheepish. 'Let us go to the boat and examine it. Perhaps your accomplice has treated you as dishonourably as one would expect from a fellow thief.' I had taken my fill of this. I kept a civil tongue, you can be sure of that. 'My

Lord, willingly, let us go and you shall see that I am innocent of any of this. A babe could not be more ignorant of these goings-on. As for Facey, I cannot answer for him.' Mr. Cartwright shrugged his shoulders wearily and called for his coat, hat and stick. A carriage was summoned and for the second time in my life, I had a jaunt with the nobs. It was not a pleasure. His Lordship looked sullen – worried most like about what her Ladyship would say. I'll wager he spent the next few days on business at his club. Mr. Cartwright questioned me, but I could tell him little other than I knew nothing, that it was my first trip with Facey, that Watkins would vouch for me and that he had to believe what I said. Did I know any of the maids at the castle? No. That was about it.

"The boat was there and on close inspection, which took over an hour, all the goods were found to be present and could be accounted for. Tompkins was fetched and told to get on with unloading it. A pinch-faced fellow who turned out to be Lord FitzHarley's London steward, went through the manifest and every box, trunk, bag, case and as dawn began to light the sky announced that it was all present. Mr. Cartwright was not pleased. He had told his cousin several times that if we had stolen fine jewellery we were unlikely to have made away with a candlestick. His Lordship, on hearing this, demanded that all the upholstery be examined most thoroughly for marks that the stitching had been unpicked. As the two argued and pinch-face droned away through the list and Tompkins grumbled at his men, I was ignored. I sat there, in the knowledge that everything was there, awaiting Facey's return. I'd give him merry hell for leaving his charge unattended. I looked at the corner where he had sat and stowed his stuff. Only then did I notice that his bag was not there. I looked at the arguing cousins, at the watchmen searching away and the miserable steward reading his lists in the dim light. I felt content for the first time and laid back to rest, keeping one eye open for any shenanigans.

"At dawn the carts trundled away. The arguing cousins stopped bickering and I was finally able to tell them: 'His stuff has gone.' 'So, there we have our guilty man. We must immediately...' FitzHarley said. 'If...' his cousin butted in, '...we have one at all. Be watchful, but the thief will be in some dark court where there is no law.' FitzHarley argued the point, but had to give way to the magistrate's experience of the city. They might still find Facey and they might recover the jewellery, but it would be through watchfulness and Mr. Cartwright's ability to gather information.

"I still can't be sure if His Lordship was disappointed, as if he had chased but not made a kill, or frightened of facing Her Ladyship. He had energy though, didn't he just. He was for scouring the city that moment and was about to rush away when Mr. Cartwright brought me to his attention. 'I am yet to be convinced, but I'll press no charges. Rest assured you will never be far from my sight.' Mr. Cartwright did not argue with FitzHarley, but pointedly thanked me for my forbearance and the manner of my cooperation. He smiled and trailed off in the wake of his cousin.

"I dropped into the cabin and pulled out the bed and fell asleep. As I awoke, with the sun shining into the cabin through the open door, I thought to myself about how to proceed. Natural, I was for getting off home as soon as I could. I didn't want Watkins hearing of all this second hand. Yet the more I thought on it there was just one way to clear my name fully – to put it above any suspicion – and that was the hardest choice. I knew I had done nothing, but could not prove it because it seemed that I was an associate of Facey and he may have thieved. On the other hand, if I searched him out and were successful in finding him, might it not look as if I were after my share of the loot? Maybe, but it struck me that if I found him and brought him to Mr. Cartwright, Facey could prove his innocence or otherwise, and I would come out well whichever way things went. If he were never found, then I could never clear my name and, as Watkins said, that would be very bad for commerce. Truth was, though, I hadn't any more idea of where to start than a kitten. A word with FitzHarley would have been most useful, but was unlikely, and to ask any of his skivvies would have been asking for trouble. So, I just decided to take a walk. To cogitate upon a course of action, if you like. Always done my best thinking when having a wander.

"It was whilst out walking that I had the first piece of good fortune I had had since getting to London. I'd been walking for a long old while and found myself in sight of St. Paul's. I thought of what old Watkins had said and decided that I should take in a bit of cultural life myself. I'm no particular sort of a Christian, but you should remember that back then few ordinary country people ever got to see all those famous places. Now, I'd been in London many times before, but Nat was a man for seeking entertainment rather than improving his mind. Naturally, I'd always gone along with him and even when I became my own master I wasn't against refreshing myself in the Blue Posts or the Castle or the London Bridge Tap or a handful of others. Yet that time I chose to go to St. Paul's.

"Now, for that first bit of luck. As I trudged up Ludgate Hill, I saw a carriage coming towards me. There were lots of wagons and vehicles about, of course, but this was a nob's cart and no mistaking it: footmen at the back and livery all over. And it was one I recognised, for it was none other than the FitzHarley arms that were displayed all over it and them. Well, you can see how I decided that the best thing to do at that particular time was to jump into some little pightle. After all, as far as I knew he still thought I was guilty of thieving and with his lackeys and a horsewhip to hand too, you'll agree my reluctance to be seen was no more than common sense and no cowardly act. I congratulated myself as the carriage passed by with me sheltering behind the bricks of the arch that formed the entrance to the yard of the York Arms. So, I stepped back out onto the street and nearly pitched Lord FitzHarley on his arse. That has done it in a dish now, I said to myself, as he roared out some oath. It wasn't a threat to leave me to the mercies of his lads, who had jumped down from the carriage that had pulled up but a few yards past the archway. They jumped to the conclusion that their master was being robbed, but he soon got to his feet and they hung fire. I turned away and made to walk off, having muttered an apology, but he'd had a clear view and yelled after me. And what he yelled surprised me.

"He let loose the sort of jolly bellow that must have welcomed his hunting friends on a frosty morning. 'What luck! Captain, come and share a bottle!' I looked at him and he said, 'My treat, come along now!' I stood stock still in amazement at what had come over him. While I took it in he clasped me by the shoulder and pushed me into the yard and up some steps into a parlour and was calling for brandy, 'or would I prefer ale? And chops or a steak pudding?' In short he treated me as Robinson Crusoe would have treated Man Friday if there had been a good tavern nearby and he'd had money in his pocket.

"'I fear I have surprised you, Captain. And I must say that I greet you with the greatest joy and the highest regard. I sent a man down to Paddington to seek you out, but hide nor hair could he find.' That was the nearest I got to an apology for having come within half an inch of sending me on a trip to the Antipodes. At that time, I was perfectly happy to settle for no apology and half share in a bottle of brandy. I told him how I thought I had been badly treated, but that I would accept his offer. That was best: to him, after all was said and done, I was a boatman who should have been proud to be patronised by one such as he.

"He did condescend to explain the alteration that had suddenly come so unexpected on his manner towards me. 'Damn expensive those diamonds and pearls and whatnot. Never like being out of pocket. As for the daughter, I have never seen her in so many tears and as a doting parent I cannot suffer that. Do you have daughters? Then you'll know.' Not bloody likely, thought I. 'As for Her Ladyship: had I not heard her tirades on modern morality before, though this one was notably violent, I would have hidden beneath the table. Thank God she is now arranging the domestic affairs and the furniture in each room to the very inch. What does one have servants for? I shall tell you, Captain. To save fellows like me from the Ruler of the House when she has a bee in her bonnet. Then there is Cousin Cartwright, of whom it must be said, is too clever by half and always has been. For once, I saw the chance to make him skip to my tune, only to have the victory snatched from my grasp. Pleased there is no animosity between us. As a noble tar whose valour saved our island from the Frogs, you will know how tempers blow hot and cold. Pleased to settle issues over a bottle,' he paused.

"He began again, as I was about to speak. 'Then, this morning, my sweet Amelia – my daughter, you know – came to me and, wiping her eyes – which were sore and red with the ocean of tears she had shed – put her hand on my shoulder and said that though the loss of her jewels were a blow to her tender heart such as she had never known, she would not have me pursue a man who was so utterly innocent of any crime as you. Of course, she had no more reason for being convinced of this than I had, but she spoke so purely and with deep emotion, that the sacrifice of justice was too high a price for her happiness. Do you read novels? My daughter does. Consumes romantic notions by the shelf full. So, I was on the verge of dismissing this as the type of claptrap engendered by these books, when I realised that she was probably right, and so, damn him, was Cartwright. Can you read at all?' I told him that I could read a little, enough for business and had a memory for plays and things of that kind. 'Good,' he says, 'I should leave it there. Few things seem to enfeeble the mind more rapidly than reading books.' The bottle was empty and how he had drunk most of it while talking constantly I could not fathom.

"As he rose to leave he said, 'Mind you, a word with that lad of yours would be most interesting. Have you seen him? No? Probably gone for good, more is the pity. Well, if you do I shall not be ungenerous. Must go, I have to see Cartwright again for my sins. There's some beggar chap seems to have taken up residence opposite my townhouse.' With that, he threw some coins – too few to pay for the repast - onto the table and marched out of the parlour door. Good riddance thought I.

"In the late light of the autumn evening that illuminates the city with such calm that it becomes peacefully beauteous despite the hum of movement and coming and going on the street, I thought little of what FitzHarley had told me. I walked towards the great Cathedral, bottom half in chilly shadow and smoky air and half warmed in the rays of the westering sun. Amid the bustle of the City, serenity stood in the work of man. I can see that wonderful sight still. I did intend to enter the building and have a look, but as I came by, I had my second piece of luck. In all the multitude of milling men and women there was one man caught my eye. I stared at him, because though he was bearded, a fair old forest of hair and all; though he were grey; despite the fact he limped and leant heavily on a stick; in spite of all these, I knew the eyes. Facey. It was him. It may sound foolish, but I was sure it was he as he was the very spit of him, though he looked little enough like him. I gawped like a fool and knocked into an old woman who cursed me for pitching her flowers out of her basket and called out robbery. Well, that saved me, for just as he turned to look in my direction I tripped over in the collision. I turned to see him walking slowly on, back down the way I had come. I followed. The old woman yelled, so I threw her a couple of Watkins' shillings.

"Now, my first thought had been to go and scrag the Devil and get out of him what had gone on and his part in this whole business. Yet, for the first time that day I thought hard and chose to follow at a distance. There was a chance it was not him, so best be cautious. Best beard the leopard in his den. If he had taken the jewellery, maybe he'd lead me to it and I could do a good turn for the aristocracy. That never does any harm, even if I cared not a whit to see FitzHarley again.

"Now, it seemed to me that the biggest problem would be if he decided to cut down side alleys and through back lanes. There he would see me more easily and I might mistake the way as he turned a corner. Fortune smiled on me yet again. He made his way by the main thoroughfares where I was hidden in the crowd, but could keep him in my view. Eventually we left Holborn and entered an area I knew nothing of. Houses – well town mansions is nearer the mark. Fewer people, but trees to hide behind and little plots of green amongst the buildings. Still on we went, until, as night fell and the windows of the houses lit up the street, he halted by some iron railings by a green, opposite a house that was lit up as if candles cost nothing. There, he sat down in the shadow of a tree trunk, visible to me, but, I thought, not to anyone in the house.

"He was watching intently, never taking his eyes off what he could see of that house. A few folk passed by, wealthy fellows, who either threatened to kick him or tossed him a penny with equal lack of charity. He didn't even take notice of me coming upon him. He just croaked, 'Penny for an old soldier, invalid of the Peninsula, Sir?' Give him his due, thought I, for when I kicked in his gammy leg he didn't even raise his head, just said, 'Took a musket ball there, Sir. Lines of Torres Vedras, Sir, with the Great Duke hisself, Your Honour.' Mind you he looked up sharpish when he heard my voice. He would have sprung up and run or struck out, but I had him by the arms directly and hauled him onto the green. All was quiet about, being the time the wealthy would prepare for the night ahead.

"First he denied that he was Facey, but soon came round to admitting his true identity. He would not let on the first thing about his being there dressed up as a beggar, though he did make apology – most politely, too – if his running off had distressed me. Distressed! I have never thought of myself as anything other than a peaceful, gentle fellow who asks no more than to go about his business and have done, but I twisted his arm so far up his back at "Distressed" that I was surprised only that it did not snap in two. He screamed out loud. I asked him if he knew how close I'd come to the assizes because of him. He denied knowing what I was talking of, so I heaved his other arm half-out of the socket. He screamed again and this proved too much for the owners of the house opposite. A moment passed before the door was flung open. A rush of men poured from the door. At their head was a figure I knew well with a voice I'd have avoided at all costs. The house was FitzHarley's.

"It took me no more than a moment to put two and two together and to realise that I had best drag Facey out and present him to His Lordship. Thus, I could show that he hadn't come across two criminals arguing over their loot. No, he would see his old friend, the honest Captain, doing as His Lordship had asked: bringing him John Facey.

"And, God bless him that was just what he did see. Didn't he just stand and stare, though. He told his servants to relieve me of the prisoner and grasped me heartily by the shoulders and shoved me towards the flooding light of the open door. Not bad for a chap who'd been bent on sending me to the gallows only the day before. He sent a footman to get Mr. Cartwright's advice and then called for Lady FitzHarley and Miss FitzHarley to see the show. The ladies need not have been sent for, as they were already descending the stairs to see what was happening. Her ladyship looked angry at the disturbance. Miss was distinctly perturbed, being on the verge of tears and, on reaching the foot of the stairs, promptly went into a swoon. Her mother ordered brandy and cooed over her, while His Lordship looked at me and said, 'Reading. Always swooning. Damn all novel writers.' He indicated a doorway on the right and the whole party entered what was obviously the Library. His Lordship must have seen my puzzled look. 'Serious works. Prestige. Read one on hunting and two on war.' With that explanation of the books, he sat down behind an immense desk and immediately assumed an air of sombre authority. There was silence and all were still.

"That is with the exception of Facey; he looked nervous, but was gazing about him. Surely, he was not thinking of trying to escape? The silence was broken when the door opened and in came Miss FitzHarley followed by Her Ladyship. Facey stared at her and in his eyes spoke of pleasure at her recovery, fear for what might happen to her and noble selflessness. 'I am guilty,' he said blandly. Then he repeated it three times, ever more loudly and with increased conviction. His Lordship was struck dumb, less because he disagreed, but more because the pleasure of interrogation had been denied him. However, his discomfort was not ended. For, next, his daughter rushed towards Facey, pleading, 'No, no, John my darling, this is too much to do, even for Love. You must not say you are guilty of anything less noble than that deepest, eternal love that will overcome all things.' Her mother tried to stop here there and then, but she knew how to play the parent game. She turned to her father and approached with head bowed. She knelt. She waited for him to tell her to leave the room and such foolishness did her no credit. Then she raised her head slowly and her blue eyes stared into his. Though not as comely, to my mind at any rate, as some of the tavern wenches along the cut, no doubt her delicate beauty suited the aristocracy: but, as a man of my acquaintance over Brierley Hill way said, 'She could never heave a hundredweight on coal on 'er back and tip a quart of ale down her throat all at once.' We had different measures of women's usefulness back then.

"Poor old FitzHarley who had matched the Frenchie's in Spain, was unable to stand his ground against his daughter's assault, though he looked far from pleased with the retreat he beat so briskly. He first dismissed the servants, telling two to stand outside the door and a second to fetch Cartwright – he'd not given up all hope – then bid me leave. But again, the lass struck up and begged him to let me stay so she could make apology for all the hardship and distress I must have suffered. 'Dear father, even such a rude mechanical is worthy of our respect and may play a noble part, in spite of their base instincts, deserving of our condescension'. I bit my tongue. His Lordship winced, but was a kitten in her hands. And so I was there as she told her tale.

"The facts she gave were as follows. Facey was not Facey, but Trevelyan Barnard, son of Sir Piran and Lady Angharad Barnard of Penragdo Hall, Cornwall. Secondly, he was her true love. I should say here that throughout all these revelations Lady FitzHarley snorted disgust and His Lordship puffed amazement, combining to make a fair go of a steam engine heading up a bank. The true love bit lead to an unusually violent explosion of steam from Her Ladyship and a volley of oaths from his Lordship that would have floored a rank of lady novelists. Facey or Trevelyan was glowing with manly pride at the bravery of his little Miss. Next, she said how they had met at a theatre, an announcement that caused the parents to look daggers at one another for lax supervision. I expected her to say how Facey or Trevelyan was an actor who had joined a company to escape being sent into the Church, as a younger son. But no, he was going to inherit. He had five thousand pounds a year and more.

"FitzHarley wasn't impressed by the figure, but butted in to ask the young man why he had not approached him as was the normal style? Five thousand was not to be sneezed at, though it was less than he would have hoped. Yet he was, he said, a man who would not stand in the way of his daughter unless she was utterly foolish and besotted – which she clearly was in this case. Had Trevelyan a career in the army, perhaps?

"Trevelyan said not a word. He had no opportunity to answer. Daughter was off again. 'Oh, father, would you have me a widow?' Before he could say he would not see her married to this rogue to begin with, though a widow was not such a bad thing with prospective wealthy husbands about, she went on. 'No dear father, my precious hero did all this for romance. Yes father, I begged him to carry me off so that we could flee and marry. For love of me he agreed that we would elope. A grand romantic gesture to usher in our perfect love that would last until our dying days and then be transmuted...' She drifted into misty sighs in an effort to faint once more.

"FitzHarley was not impressed. He said so and commenced to swear vengeance on all novel writers, whatever their sex. Lady FitzHarley hushed him and told her daughter that this was preposterous nonsense and she should give up all hope of any liaison with 'this boy, this thief, this immoral molester of innocent femininity.' The daughter was on the verge of tears. Facey denied the last accusation and the daughter explained the theft.

"Turned out that she had given her jewellery to a maid to give to Trevelyan who, as Facey, was posing as a boatman. A romantic notion she claimed, one that proved true love. Mother, she explained, would never have let her get at her jewellery, so they had smuggled it to London, where Trevelyan and she were to meet. However, mother had spiked their guns when she had arrived early following the discovery of the theft, soon followed by His Lordship. So, Trevelyan had been forced to hang about outside the house in the hope of seeing his beloved or meeting with her maid. That was why he was there that day. She had overheard her father damning me to blazes, but could not see an innocent man suffer, so had convinced him that I could not have played a part in any of it. Yet, she regretted that this had meant I had been able to find Trevelyan and bring him to book.

"The FitzHarley parents were stumped. They loved their daughter dearly. It was easy to see that they were searching for some form of words that would have flailed her without actually causing her death by fright. She and they were saved this when, absolutely on cue, Mr. Cartwright was announced. Fitzharley damned his presence and then remembered that he had sent for him.

"All was explained. 'We can still have him for theft, can we not?' 'No,' said Cartwright, 'She gave them to him and they were hers to give. No theft was committed, though I would counsel him to fetch them from the safe place he has concealed them and return them tomorrow.' 'But, dash it, man, he wanted to run off with my daughter. What about the Marriage Act?' 'Cousin, I understand your desire for vengeance, none wishes to appear foolish, but he did not run away with your daughter, least of all did he marry her. No, I can see no case, though perhaps we could ignore all this and have him whipped in the stocks for begging. No? Well that is the best we can do. Now, I will return to my card table. Trevelyan – if that is your name - I suggest you beg forgiveness and return the items tomorrow.' With that he left, triumphant over his rich cousin once again.

"It seemed best to get away from there, so I left with Trevelyan, having promised to make sure he went home, wherever that was. I asked him what the truth was? Had it all been as the girl had told? 'Well now, you know that night at Chedborough Castle when I went off to tarry awhile with the farmer's daughter? Well, that was true. Do you need a boy for the homeward trip?' 'No.' We walked a fair way back past St. Paul's and into the silent City. He didn't seem to want to say much, though I badgered him pretty well all the way to his lodging.

"Plain, but clean, it was, so I took him up on his offer of a place to kip. Next morning, he dressed up smartly and we went to a bank, where he had kept a box. He took it to FitzHarley and waved farewell to his love who stood tearfully at an upstairs window, like a fairy-tale beauty imprisoned by ogres. 'Sure, you don't need a boy for the trip, Captain,' he says. 'Alright, but it'll be your last trip with me. Agreed?' Truth was I had had enough excitement and I could not help but feel that young whatever his name might be, would always attract it. And he was as good as his word to me, which I believe was more than could be said for his word to Miss FitzHarley. She married the Duke of Rutland's son. Saw it in the paper. Died in childbirth. Never heard nor saw anything of Facey again.

"And that, my girl, is romance for you." The young lady sitting at his bedside smiled. The oil lamp flickered in the draught from the window where the sash fitted but loosely. She passed him a glass of water, which he sipped slowly.

"Great-Grandpapa, is that all true? It is so romantic and so sad. Had she eloped successfully with Trevelyan, they may have been poor but happy for ever and she would have seen her children grow."

"Who can say, my dear? Who can say?"

The young lady said he should rest now and he submitted willingly as his energy was gone and his head was heavy. "And what do you read of as you sit by my bedside, my own Lady With The Lamp?"

His eldest great-granddaughter began a synopsis of the sensational romance that lay on the table, but, as Lord FitzHarley would have advised, he had slipped into a fortunate sleep before she even began.

"O Taste and See!"

Silent August evening sun yellowed the hollyhocks along the cottage wall, leaching out the pink-flecks and the dry purples as the day slowly drew to its close. The sun had scorched the earth all day and was now sapping the last of the petals colour. Behind a low wall, neat rows of vegetables reached deep in the dusty soil. The gliding boats and the heat-muffled plod of horses slowly moving the goods of Empire at a pace that ploughmen had trod for many centuries disturbed the soft, still air not one bit, the countryside was sleepwalking into evening. Deep in sleep, or so it would have appeared to anyone who had poked their head round the little gate from the towing path, in the shade of a heavy-laden apple tree, a venerable man rested his eyes. His beard, no longer as full as it had been when first he was old, extended nearly to his belly. Face concealed by a straw hat that had slipped over his eyes and nose, contentment filled his snoring, as easy at evening as the tired sun which lit the wall. If today were his last then what better way to spend his final hours than snoring in a cottage garden, by the waterways on which he had spent the long-ago years he now softly recalled. The rumble of snoring from that distant land was the only sound he made. For he still dreamed contentedly, though what it was he saw he could never remember.

He could remember that first day he had come to this cottage, Monday 12th October 1795, he could remember his father's delight and his mother's joy: new employment, new house, life to live. Yet, his afternoon dreams were as the mist that had but a few hours past hung droplets of water on the boughs above. To one boatman, who passed by every fortnight or so, he was "a true wonder of the waterways". Maybe, he was on his first voyage to Birmingham, with Nathaniel Jones on the "Pegasus", with that load of crates belonging to some family fleeing from Napoleon's conquest of somewhere or other: Brummagen gent and his family – been out there setting up mills or some such thing. He remembered being ten years old and using the little bit he had learned at Sunday School to make out the names on the boats. Yet chronology sometimes eluded him and his memories were disordered patches on a dazzling counterpane.

Had his hat been on his head and he not been wandering in the days of his youth, he may have chosen to see, through the garden gate, a chestnut mare, carrying a dignified, upright figure, soberly dressed in decorous black, symbolic of office rather than summer common sense. Dust puffed up by the hooves settled on the long straight track that ran the mile or so from the village to the cottage by the canal, as the horse approached at a languid hot evening plod. Had the old man seen this gangling figure approaching he would have leapt from his chair and rushed into the old hayloft. Had he been able to rush anywhere, he would have done, but the two sticks by his side, marked his incapacity. In any case, he was once again amongst the wondrous, sparking workshops of Birmingham, looking again on the hammering din of engines and men beating in the heat of the Workshop of the World.

On dismounting and hitching the reins of the mare to a wooden rail, the dignified gentleman knocked quietly on the open door of the cottage. At first there was no response but the sound of beans being chopped on a wooden board. The visitor extended his neck around the doorpost and looked with penetrating eyes – eyes that could have discerned Un-Godliness on a distant planet – into the dark of the interior. As his eyes adjusted, the chopping stopped. A neat, plump woman of some fifty or sixty years appeared in the cool shade of the stone-flagged kitchen onto which the door opened. This was Mary Jagland, third child of the slumbering ancient she kept house for, and her husband's work paid for. Thus, of course, she was in charge. Her hair was tied in a bun and though it was clear from her hands that she was not a genteel woman, she had achieved decent respectability. A thorough Victorian was she. Her husband was skilled and well thought of and could look forward in his old age to the beneficence of the Squire for whom he worked. Her children had bettered themselves, whether it was through apprenticeships, to tradesmen in Coventry, or as banker's clerks in Market Harborough, or as indoor above-stairs serving girls, who had attracted the attention of a dairy-farmer near Banbury, in one case, and of an estate manager – a Dissenter, which she felt was not good, but at least a hard-working man – near Daventry, in the other. She supported the rector and the squire in efforts to improve the morals of the village poor through the sticks of religious tracts, allied to fear of the Good

Lord and the Workhouse, whilst a place in Heaven was dangled as a distant carrot before their eyes.

She was always pleased to see Mr. Doddrington, whom she regarded with respect and who possessed one of only two wills to which she had ever really submitted, and that was only because had she ever challenged him, the very structure of her world would have shaken.

In Mr. Doddrington, the rector whose head protruded round the door without revealing the rest of him, as only his head could, she had found a figure within the establishment to whom she could happily agree and ally her desire for self-improvement and decency. They were twin spirits, and with their coterie of the committed, they fought with fiery desire for the betterment of all, except the rapidly growing Baptist Meeting. As one they acted for the moral welfare of the common man and his family in much the same way as Mr. Segger, the Estate Manager, aimed to better the Squire's income whilst making the men work harder for the good of their character. Even Mr. Doddrington had failed to make an impact on custom at the village inn.

Eyes adjusted to the darkness, the rector greeted his ally in his own way: hearty, condescending and full of approval for the worthiness of a neat cottage and an industrious husband and wife.

"A package should have been delivered here yesterday, Mrs. Jagland."

Since the railway had come to cross the canal some thirty years ago, what had once been a busy wharf had become an occasional drop-off, busy only at the bidding of the Estate, to provide for the needs of its farms. Soon it would be harvest and there would be hubbub and coming and going. For now, the boat that had handed over the package that morning had been the first for a month that had done more than moor for a night or stop and inquire after the old boy, who sat summer-long on view to his admirers under his apple tree. Some had caught him awake and they were generally the ones who had eventually decided to moor for the night, having had their progress so delayed. Mrs. Jagland found them provoking, but short of taking a longer route, there was little they could have done to remedy this.

"This morning, Mr. Doddrington," she said, almost apologetically. "I see they are from the Society. Good News to support our Labours."

"Indeed so, though, Truly, we must Trust in the Lord, for without Him our Labours will not meet with success." The rector and the respectable woman both spoke with capital letters when discussing their Mission.

"The Lord has provided us with these Arms for the Battle, may we have the Fortitude to see the Conflict through and gain his Victory." Mrs. Jagland was clearly on the verge of something grand. The rector could hardly discourage her, though he had hoped to have his thirst quenched by tea.

"You revive my spirit," he managed. Then came the offer of tea.

"I'll fetch the tea tackle," said the reviver and scuttled back into the kitchen.

As she busied herself the rector spoke pessimistically of the new tracts. "The trouble is that these people whom we strive to bring to God, seem to have such little care for the Salvation of their Souls or their prosperity upon this Earth. Last month, I passed a tract entitled "He Raiseth the Poor from Out of the Street and Lifteth the Needy from the Dunghill," to Samuel Walker. An intelligent man, for one of his order, and he took it from me and promised to read it. It explains how through Temperance, Labour and Opening his Heart to the Lord, the poor man may rise to esteem himself amongst his fellow men and understand his place. Well, a week ago I saw him and asked after his studies. You will understand how heartened I was when he said he had read it and taken it to heart. Then he dashed my hopes as speedily as he had uplifted them. I shudder to tell you that he told me that he had lost sixpence in the dung heap at the back of his cottage and had hoped to read something of the Lord raising his coin."

"He would spend it at the Moon and Stars."

"Indeed. But that was far from the end of it. He said that if the Good Shepherd would allow him to run his sheep on what but fifty years past was the Common, he would not be needy in the first place."

"Progress passes him by, Mr. Doddrington, but surely not so, as to down hearten a Man of God?"

"Well, I shall finish my tale, then you may judge if I am downcast with no good cause." The shocked rector continued his dirge. "He told me how he appreciated my kindness so, that he had passed on the pamphlet to his grandson, that scallywag of a Youth, Henry Blackwell. At first I was suspicious, for he continued that his grandson was collecting these good works for his protection. Yet I was pleased, for did not the father welcome the Prodigal? I remembered what a poor reader Henry had been at school and how the master had to use the cane much more than one would hope. I prayed that the boy had seen the light. Walker told me that he had given it to Henry in return for fetching him a quart of beer from the public house, whilst he was cutting wood for his Lordship. Yet I did not worry for the fact that News was spread amongst the

Recalcitrant filled my bosom more than any pot of beer could satisfy the sinner."

"You should not have placed such hope in that boy. He'll throw all your care back in your face."

"And so he did. On Saturday, I saw Henry and other young men playing at cricket. Now I, Good Lady, am no Puritan. No, cricket encourages manliness and discipline. So, I strode across the green to where they had set the wicket and were all sitting down between innings. All stared at me, though I cannot think why they should greet me with silence. 'Take up thy bat and walk?' said I. A joke. To break the iciness of their reception you understand. 'Try your arm, Parson', pipes up Will Stratton. 'Thank you, but my exertions are of the Spirit. I saw Henry amongst you and thought I should express my Joy that he has turned to the Word to shed Light upon his Way.' At this point Henry blushed as red as any apple and the others either stared at him or at me, sniggering in a most repulsive fashion. I warned them not to mock, but exhorted them to imitate. At this point a most remarkable abomination occurred. I am not sure I should go further, such was the vulgarity of their gestures. Some patted their shins." The poor man was shaking.

"Mr. Doddrington, do please sit. Though a woman, I may prove more of a Man of this World than a spiritual gentleman such as yourself, having such a father as I do and knowing the canal boat people. I fear not to hear whatever you have to tell. Surely, their shins were no abomination?" Seeing him still indecisive as to whether he should continue with his tale, she said that he was right, likely as not. Though she laboured in the name of the Lord, she was but a frail woman.

"No, no, Good Lady, you are more than that," said the Good Man. "I will tell all. The Youths, all stood and gestured to the front of their...that is...the part of the anatomy that...their trousers below the abdomen...the gesture was a patting motion."

Seeing that the rector was struggling to be accurate without offending her modesty, Mrs. Jagland encouraged him to move on with, "And what do you suppose they meant by that?"

"I was strict with them and reminded them of my position and office. I told them that I assumed they had been drinking as there could be no other explanation for their wickedness. They took note. I then saw Henry sneaking away whilst I admonished the others. So, I summoned him back, "Mind not their mockery, you who seek protection from the Word." He did as he was told, I am pleased to say. Yet he walked backwards and with knees knocking together and seemed to be struggling with pain in his belly. So, I went to him and turned him bodily to face me. I saw his belt loosened and his hand in his trousers. I ordered him to show me his hands. He begged me not to make him, but I was insistent. I was incredulous when he drew from his trousers the very pamphlets I had given his grandfather. Torn, twisted and stuffed into an old glove, moulded to a shape appropriate for those parts, but those very ones, no doubt. Looking down I noticed more. His trousers, around his ankles for his loosened belt, had concealed several more pamphlets tied around his shins with pieces of string."

Mrs. Jagland waxed wroth with indignation and interest: what, she asked, more?

"I asked him what he meant by this. Yet he ran away."

"Wickedness."

"Wickedness. Indeed."

"Though a youth may learn better."

"Truly. Perhaps we should approach his Lordship with a view to providing proper organisation for sporting activities? Suffer the little children or the vulgar youths. Is your father easier?"

The second man to whom Mrs. Jagland submitted, but only under protest and when compelled to do so by some tricky artifice, was her father. Her Christian obligations gave her no choice – and technically he owned the cottage.

"Easy is not the word for him. I have tried hard to help him reform, yet he is recalcitrant," she sighed as if her father were a wilful child, though he was not.

"Well, I must see him, I suppose. He never welcomes the Word of God, it seems, yet if Daniel could face the Lions, I cannot fail in my pastoral duty by ignoring the spiritual welfare of such a man. I am sure he has goodness in him."

The old boatman opened his eyes into the narrowest slits and saw two familiar faces looking down on him.

"Damn you Beelzeebub, you shall have my corpse but never my soul." The old man challenged the forces of evil, then opened his eyes fully. After a momentary stare, as if to catch his wits, he spoke. "Parson Doddrington, daughter, I was all in a dream, a-fighting the demon drink and all other diabolical manifestations."

"Bless you!" Things were looking better for the Parson.

"Don't you mock, Father. I know your games," she explained, "I have stopped his beer allowance, vicar. I will not permit it in the house."

"You're a Guardian of the Workh'us, Parson? The old men there has a pint a day for medicine, I heard."

"I was out-voted, Mrs. Jagland." The greater need was to explain to the daughter: he felt that he would wilt under her disappointed stare and so excused himself. "Some of us protested in writing to the Commissioners in London, but they insisted that they should have it." To the old man, "Abstinence is the only sure way to Heaven."

"And I aren't a-going there now, am I my boy? Not yet, any road."

"It is never too late, Father. Maybe a taste of the Poor Law would do you good: if the beer provided by the Union suits your taste."

"You'd have me there, I know. If there weren't considerations. And I know from John Jones - skipper of the Invincible," a word of explanation to the Parson, "that you've been talking with that old witch Martha Herring, boney old baggage she is, that the Guardians over at Towcester told her to pay seven and six to keep her mother in the Workh'us or they'd send her back home."

"Your daughter meant that you have time to repent."

"I remember the time George Harks and meself had a whole firkin o' beer shared between us. Still got back on the boats and was off to London the next morning. It was that gin as did for that poor wench."

"What poor girl?" Mrs. Jagland wondered why it was that Mr. Doddrington's curiosity always got the best of him.

Her father winked at her. "How about a pot of that refreshing but uninebriating brew, daughter? Take a seat Parson."

"We had all been refreshing ourselves. In those days, you hired men to leg you through the tunnels down Braunston and Blisworth. Took an age. We're going back to the time of Waterloo, or just after. Important men on the canal then. Stuff from Brummagen we had on board – for the army. Anyway, we had a bit of refreshment and a song and a bit more and another song. You know how things go around? And there was this wench, a-sitting in the corner, all quiet and alone. Nothing to remark about her, except that she was dressed in white, splashed with mud from where she had been walking, but a white dress, long belt wound around her waist, cloak folded on the floor by her feet – all white."

The man of the cloth looked concerned.

"I'll not offend you with that sort o' tale. For all we ever knew she were a poor honest lass a finding her way home, taking on spirits against the cold. Bitter it was, though icy clear and moonlit bright. Well, she headed off and none paid much attention. Soon after our money was all spent and we went our way. Ah, tea. Thank you, daughter, that'll help the tale along, no doubt. Now, as we walked down by the top lock, George catches sight of a bit of white stuff in the pound. In the moonlight we see that it is the billowing dress of that girl as had been in the corner. So, George, he reaches out, but she's too far off. So, he kneels down and stretches out. His fingers touched the hood of her cloak, so he reached further. At that very moment, just as he firmed his grip on the hem, a gust of wind caught her and dragged her away. Brave old George was never one to let a lady go once he'd got a bit of a hold on her, so rather than ease his grasp, he lurches forward. In he went gasping at the cold.

"With me on the lock-side and two in the water, there was only one way a man should act to any credit. Well, George was never a swimmer and his hefty old coat was dragging him down. So, I pulls off my coat and me boots and leaps in. I was splashing like anything as I helped George heave himself onto the side, still holding that poor girl.

"Well, you can imagine that folk from the tavern had come along to see what all the noise was about. The girl was freezing and had a gash down the back of her head. So, they stripped her and wrapped her warm and sent her off to Northampton Infirmary in a cart. George and me? Heroes of the hour – that was us. That cold water had sobered us up too. Well, they wanted to treat us for our brave deed and we could hardly disappoint our host: not genteel."

"Well, well, a noble deed, sir."

"Yes father, but why did the unconscious woman in the bulky skirt and cloak float on the water whereas your friend, Mr. Harks, did not?"

"See how my own seed has grown to doubt my word? Well, no doubt she is a self-improved woman with a lot of book-learning. Those dresses women had back then kept her afloat I once thought: but no, that won't do for my daughter. I see. In truth, she is right, for it was more remarkable than even that – though I prefer the first explanation for I would not want folk to lose trust in my word. When she slipped into the water, as surely she did, as the gash on her head proved, she snagged her long belt that had been wound round her, around bit of raised stone. Out it span, but must have been knotted well, for it held her firm in the end."

"And it was the water that sobered you up father."

"It was the beer that filled us with heart to do the brave deed. Would a man leap into a pound on a belly full of water alone? And as the old song went, I did not feel the cold, 'for I stuff my skin so full within of jolly good ale and old.'"

"An ancient ditty, but was it not drink that lead the poor girl astray?" The rector felt satisfied.

"She fell in for she was drunk, doubtless. But that was gin. Gut-rotting filth, never touch it, take my word upon it. Nothing great was ever done on gin. Gin Alley, Beer Street – I saw them once. Beer is the stuff to fill the belly of the Englishman, and with respect to present company, it never did me any harm for more than a day or two."

"And it is two weeks since you had any. A man of your age should think less of his belly. Though that consideration is now, thankfully, placed in the Hands of the Lord. You have had your last taste of ale father. And don't be so argumentative with Mr. Doddrington, who has come to see you and seek your Salvation."

"Thanks kindly, have yer brought a flagon Parson?"

"You see his obstinacy Mr. Doddrington. It breaks a daughter's heart to see his rejection of all that is good."

"I am sure your father is a man of..."

"He is a vulgar Old Devil."

"He came to seek the Salvation of that packet anyways. I may not see so well to look out the letters, but only one sort of stuff comes in those. I do wish I still had my eyesight so well and that I had learned my letters with more attention when I was young."

"Have you tried spectacles?" The rector sought out an opportunity to pacify the situation. In truth, though the old man was so recalcitrant as to dismiss the Church of England, he was only slightly less abusive to the Baptist Minister, Mr. Ashton. The old man, he had been told, had two years earlier determined on baptising the pastor in the canal, only being thwarted by the lack of a two additional inches to his stick. Mr. Doddrington had felt a sinful twinge of jealousy, as he would have not had the spirit to undertake such an assault on a fellow man, even a Baptist.

Spectacles would be dangerous tools for an old man trapped in his garden by his beloved waterways – especially with pamphlets such as, "The Trumpet Call to the Nation" and "Wickedness in the City" around. When he had heard his daughter announce the arrival of these gems, he had cast his mind back to when he had been a young skipper with a pocketful of money in London. "Wickedness in the City". Might be worth the effort, but not as good as the real thing. How did these people know about it anyway? From the conversations he heard, their idea of wickedness was a dirty shirt on Sunday. His ideas were less advanced.

"A kind thought sir," the old man toadied, "but your troubles would be wasted. I am sure I have lost my letters. Though, it would no doubt do me good to read the Scriptures again."

"So, you did read the Word! How gratifying to hear. And is it your desire to return to the Lord?" Too soon, too soon.

"Well, it weren't so much Scripture I read as the dockets for the cargo and the names of the boats. I tried a book once, but it took all my puff to do a page or two."

"You should have persevered."

"A fine thing, meaning no disrespect, for a scholar like yourself and even a woman like my daughter, who are but part employed in daily labours, but for a working man!" He paused and noticed the look on his daughter's face – a putting–up-with-you-would-occupy-a-saint-all-day-long kind of expression – that he dismissed an assault on the idleness of people who had time to read. "Once, though, I did meet a writer and I used to like to hear the news and the readings."

Mr. Doddrington liked to hear the old man talk of the past. He was interested in how things had been. He was certain of the doctrine of the Church and his desire to build Zion in Britain was heartfelt. Indeed, he looked upon the Church of England at the start of the century, before Victoria was Queen, and frowned on the lack of enthusiasm amongst the clergy. How glad he was, how he rejoiced that the Evangelicals had won the day and that the Church had become more dynamic and active. Yet he could not help feeling that the slumbering Church of the last century had done less to alienate the ordinary man. How sad that they paid so little regard for the efforts of others on behalf of their souls.

"Was it Dickens, or perhaps Thackeray?"

"No, no. It was down on the Basingstoke. Now it was rare to be down that way and I knew the line only a little. So, I ends up one evening and no chance of refreshment in sight. So, I moored up and set the horse to feed, rubbed him down and brushed out the dirt – cleanliness, Parson: horse can't be dirty. Summer it was, early June. Long days. Anyhow, I'd just pulled the stopper on a little when-in-need flagon o' cider that I kept hidden away and had set myself to watch the sun set and breathe in the sweet scent of a summer eve, when I spies a figure riding a horse down the towing path. Well-dressed man: gentleman. Strange to see in them days at that time o' the day: drinking they was and eating their ten course dinners or wenching. You see this was back in the days of King George, afore her Majesty, Victoria, had set the moral tone from the top. You'd have thought them days awful wicked: Georgie set the moral tone from the bottom, you'd say."

"Quiet," the rector agreed. Mrs. Jagland had gone back to her kitchen to wait for her husband.

"Now Parson, this gentleman comes alongside and asks me how far it is to the such and such farm. Now, you'll understand that I was always a bit suspicious down there on the Basingstoke – being so close on the way to France. Well, I told him he'd picked the wrong man. He tutted, but then asked me about trade and we got talking so friendly-like that I offered him some cider, which he took. Now, I thought, this is no claret or port gent. He pulled a big lump of cheese out of his pocket and sat down aside me. I went to discover more emergency refreshment and things went along. Most pleasant fellow he was and not the least bit ashamed to share in that little home. No, he told me how he would rather spend his time in the company of the honest labourer, the independent man, the yeoman farmer: he who tried to make his living through his own efforts and did not try to starve the poor. Peter Porcupine."

"Peter Porcupine?"

"Yes. For all your learning you've not heard of him. No, Peter Porcupine he once was. When he'd been in America."

"I hope that he had not been a Revolutionary?"

"Far from it, he'd come back to England because he was against it. Trouble was, he found England in such a state that he became a bit of one. Porcupine wasn't his real name. Nor was Peter. I doubt you'd have heard of the Weekly Political Register either. I used to hear that read aloud. Good sense, I thought. This fellow then takes another swig of cider, though he was against drunkenness. So was I, but he thought it a waste for the labouring man all the time, whilst I had a sort of one day after opposition. Now, he asked, whether this was not finer than any dinner with tax-eaters up in Parliament? He said he had recently had a great disappointment when the electors of Coventry had been misguided enough to take the usual bribes of the placemen and ignored his earnest wish to be their Member. He looked on the verge of oratory, at which, I am told he was a dab hand, but breathed the sweet air of the evening and was becalmed and took another long pull at the flagon."

"You met with a man who had stood for Parliament? I don't mean…"

"Met? Fraternised, I'd say. So, he tells me all about the things he'd done and where he'd been. Can't say I'd have wished to join him: army, prison…no, he was no criminal, so hold back your disapproval – if he had a been he might have got in for Coventry. He got to Parliament in the end. For Oldham, wherever that is: somewhere up the other side of the Potteries I believe. Strange thing was, when he got in there, he had been on trial for sedition just the year before. So, most remarkable he got in without being a proper crook."

"Ah-hah, I have it." The rector butted in. "He was a radical! Doubtless like that heathen Bradlaugh. He has been in prison too, yet was still seen fit to take his seat."

"No. Not like him at all. No. Cobbett weren't like him at all. Not as far as I know. See the bit of his conversation that you should hear is his words on beer."

"No. I will not take sides against you daughter. She is right to dissuade you from imbibing strong drinks and spirit liquors."

"But she has not dissuaded me, she's just stopped even the smallest drop. I haven't reached my age, whatever it is, by being dissuaded in anything I like. He told me that he believed that beer taken in moderation, was nourishing for both old and young. Then he took another pull of cider. He gave me an example. He said, take a pig. Every family should have its pig he said. Give it tea-leaves to eat. Waste away it will and the poor man gets no bacon. Take another pig and feed it the mash from the home brew – didn't like brewer's beer, mind he was a strange sort of chap – and the man's pig will reward him with good fat meat. Now what reflection is that upon the health of a man fed on tea?"

"Just so," the rector thought poor men should keep pigs too. "Yet, even the atheist would say that a man is not a pig."

"No, but they both need their feed, and the rich would do well to remember that. He pours more cider down his throttle – even I was starting to be a bit disapproving. For a man who was against drunkenness he did well on my cider. Mind, even the most sober man may work up a thirst on a long day's travel.

"Besides, beer he said, was good for the soul. I heard that in the old days when the Church used to dole out beers. I remember my granfer saying how his granfer told him how they used to dance in the Churchyard with the Parson handing out bread and cheese, and the Churchwardens tapping the barrel. You modern day Churchmen need less enthusiasm for the Lord and more attention to the old ways. But that was not his point, he said that a man who drank tea could not work a day in the field and worse: Old England would lose her hardy men who had set Old Boney on his heels and stuffed him back into prison. Tea – weakness: beer – strength. As for the women, whores!"

Pausing for the hoped for response, the old man quickly stifled the rector's exclamation.

"That word may offend, though it hardly used to in my day. If it offends I am truly sorry for it. But that was what he said. His words were, I remember clear as day, for they struck home, 'a preparation for the brothel'. All that old clack women make when sitting round waiting for the kettle to whistle. Idleness he said. Rich women may prattle about womanly things, but the wife and daughter of a poor man need to brew and wash and cook and feed the hens."

"As I do for you, you ungrateful old fiend", his daughter had returned, Mr. Jagland's food gently simmering in the pot. "Brew indeed. My word, there'll be no more brewing in this house."

"Your mother brewed a fine drop of ale. They all stopped to have a drop. My mother gave me beer as soon as I was helping father. Proud I was when I went off to work with beer in my bottle. Bird scaring – earning my keep – not going off to school 'til I was twelve."

"A shame father, for you may have learned more manners and more sense."

"I know scripture – 'In pain shalt thou bring forth children'. That's some. Your poor old ma. But it don't end when their babbies!"

"Hollow vessel." She looked around for Mr. Doddrington, but her support was not to be seen.

He had said "Good-evening, I must hurry along." He had said it quietly so neither had heard. At that moment, Mr. Jagland came into the garden, hot and hungry from the gardens of the big house. Tender greetings followed. He explained that he had seen Mr. Doddrington trotting away from the house. He then went to his supper, his wife at his side.

The heavenly glory of the quiet golden sunset was wafted over the wheat fields by a warm breeze. On the slopes of the little hills, the green woods rustled gently in the breeze as the still blue of the sky showed the first streaks of colour that bring on the end of another summer day.

A faint whistle, from behind the high wall that hid the garden from the towing path, hardly broke the peaceful scene. A whistle that some might not have heard or would have made others suspicious. The old man rose slowly, for he heard it and was not suspicious. Picking up his sticks, he walked steadily to the gate at the end of the garden and turned towards the canal. There was a young lad holding out a quart jug of ale.

"Mr. Higgs told me to bring it down."

"God Bless you and he my lad."

"The word went out that you were hard pressed and that you wanted something to keep your spirits up.

Jim Finch told him, he'd dropped you a little present yesterevening."

"A health to the navigators. Where you moored? Come and have a bit of talk."

"Go to go. Mr. Higgs said that your lass is an old witch who'd hang my hide from a flagpole as a warning to others. 'Don't let her catch you', were his last words before I came."

The old man paused. He had to admit it. There was some truth in it. Like to know where she'd get the flagpole from he thought. "Get along then, I'll keep me ears open. Pass it along." A good lad, he thought, running back to his master – and where next? He held the quart in one hand and leaning on one stick – it would not do to give away too many secrets to the enemy – made his way into the garden. He pulled his coat about his shoulders and quaffed a mouthful of the wholesome liquid. Staring into the malty ale, he reflected on how right Mr. Cobbett had been all those years ago. There was depth in the brew that provided much a man could need. Cobbett may have been short on the quantities, but, thought the old man, he was along the right lines. And its current rarity gave it a tang; an illicit sip filled with promise that only the like of Romeo had knowledge of. He smacked his lips and raised the jug again. He brought it close to his mouth, hesitating so as to prolong the anticipation nearly to ecstasy. He glimpsed sideways and caught sight of a stony-faced daughter piercing his reverie with the sort of disapproval that no daughter should direct at a venerable parent.

Attack, attack! "O taste and see how gracious the Lord is! Scripture!" he declaimed, keeping the jug out of reach.

His daughter paused and looked at the sticks and the open gate at the end of the garden. She stormed through it, but returned empty handed.

"I know where that came from."

"The Lord will provide." He was enjoying his moment.

She wondered if she had been beaten in this battle. Surveying the ground she noticed a package. She picked it up. Mr. Doddrington must have forgotten it when he had disappeared so suddenly. She was correct. In his haste to avoid acting as arbiter between the old man whom he knew he should have disapproved of, but quite admired in a rather worrying way, and the helpmeet of his campaign, whom he liked but was frankly, scared of her censure, he had taken a diplomatic exit.

"Indeed he will." She picked up the package, which had been opened by its recipient to check the contents, and lifted out the top pamphlet. As the old man supped his third sip and the light faded too slowly, she began: "Hearken, Incorrigible Sinner to the Words of Thy Saviour", by Mrs. Abigail Fotheringham-Battle, of the Mission Society for the Spiritual Healing of Navigators. Part One: "Though, in this World..."

And the darkness came to a warm summer night. A fly boat made good speed passed and silence fell at the end of the day the Lord had given.

Great-Great-Grandmama and the Wooden Leg

This was not the first story I heard in my mother's house. Nor could I say which one was, such was her propensity to tell a tale at the raising of a hat, let alone its drop. Most of her tales were moral, or at least, intended to be educative. Moreover, her narrative abilities were clearly inherited from her father, who, in the years when I came to know and appreciate the fact, told tales just as well. The stories had morals without being obviously moral. The old man stood firm in his belief that he had only avoided supping with the Devil by taking a good hard look at the bill of fare. This assertion he made often and loudly when my mother was within earshot. I am sure that I learned much from both.

From my father I learned of different things. He was, fortunately for the household, a quiet man. I was sure that he must have had excitement in his youth, yet he rarely spoke of himself. He was a fine example of the mid-Victorian rural artisan: though he worked at the Great House, neither he, nor his Lordship, regarded him as an outdoor servant. They both knew his place. From that place he cared for and fed my mother, my elder brother, my two sisters and myself – along with my grandfather. Though I reject his Victorian forelock-tugging subservience, I do owe him much for he taught me about plants, trees and flowers. He taught me as we worked in the garden, or as he showed me his gardeners – by which he meant His Lordship's gardeners – latest project, in the gardens or glasshouses of the Great House. When we walked, his talk was always of tree, crop and hedgerow, or berry and nut. Mine was a summer long childhood walking in lanes hanging with branches bowed with plump blackberries and lingering with the sweet refrain of juice-stained fingers licked by blackened tongue.

From this interest in nature, grew an interest in the proper names of the plants which my father named in common parlance, my grandfather providing numerous alternative names when more vulgar alternatives were to be had, for example the red hot poker was known to him, he said, only by another name. My father used a few Latin words for the more exotic plants, but I wanted to delve deeper. Mr. Doddrington, the Parish Priest, arranged for me to borrow books: once I was loaned one by Her Ladyship, who was always happy to improve the minds of the local youths.

Soon I became curious to know more of Latin and so I set about learning with discipline and thoroughness. Which, through my own hard work and the favour shown me by, what my parents would have called "our betters", I eventually attended University and became the successful lawyer that I am today. Now in politics, and hoping to succeed at the next election, I might seem ungrateful to my benefactors in holding socialist principles contrary to their beliefs and inimical to their perception of their descendants' interests. If this is so then it is only because I believe that the opportunities I took should be available to all children regardless of the kindness or meanness of those who see themselves as their betters. This, though, is not the place for polemic.

It was when I was in my early thirties that I began to ponder on where my intelligence came from. Surely, it was not down solely to study: there must have been some inherited aptitude. Thus, one evening in spring, whilst visiting my father in that lovely old cottage by the canal, I broached the subject of my ancestry.

My father looked at me. He was thinking about what might be of interest. I said that I would like to know as much as there was to be told. I felt that this was necessary as my father would never have assumed that, with the exception of gardening, anyone could have been in the least interested in a single detail about himself. However, my mother saved him and began to tell me about my father's father and mother, some great-aunts and uncles whom I had seen but rarely, if at all. Then she moved onto my father's grand-parents. Sturdily independent artisans and labourers, frequenters of the Church in preference to the ale house – though not to its total exclusion. Disciples of Samuel Smiles and the Lord in equal measures, though never admittedly, and always pleased to admire their social superiors though not to mimic them.

A brief pause came, so I asked her why she had not said anything about her own ancestors. To which she replied, "All very respectable folk, but they must wait. There is bacon in the larder and potatoes in the oven. I know you will be happy with that." She looked at my father, who assented by raising the corners of his mouth ever so slightly. "I shall be two hours, I should think. The Committee for the Conversion of those in Heathen Lands." She added the latter for my benefit.

A voice piped up from the chair in the corner, where my grandfather sat. "Don't see why you can't leave those Brummies alone."

My mother ignored him and pulled her coat around herself. "There'll be no need to come for me Sammy." My father had looked as if he felt he should not allow her to walk home in the dark. She walked out of the door and my father, to avoid the ominous prospect of conversation, sprang to his feet — he was fit for a man in his early sixties, though this was not as uncommon amongst those who laboured as some political figures, ignorant of the reality of rural life at that time, would like to make out — and took hold of the skillet and knife and set about the bacon with remarkable dexterity for a man married to a fine cook, jealous of her parlour-kitchen.

I must admit to enjoying that feeling of sitting at the big oak table with the victuals filling the room with mouth-watering airs. Now I have a cook and other servants to take care of all my needs, the kitchen is a place I visit infrequently, and then to be met by embarrassed silence from the maid and interrogation from a cook intent upon getting me back to my place as speedily as may be done.

"Respectable folk, she said." My grandfather spoke. "Shouldn't wonder if she might make exceptions!" He meant that she generally felt him to be the sort of ancestor whom she would shut in the cupboard or banish to the garden given the chance.

"Still, I'll tell you about my old granfer and granny, if you like."

Unnecessarily, I said that I would, though he had already commenced before I had assented. And, as usual, I was thankful for his long memory and life. As he spoke I suddenly became aware of being taken back to a world before the late Queen, indeed, to a time when George was on the throne and the United States of America was a revolutionary notion held by few and Bonnie Prince Charlie was alive.

"Most of all I shall tell you of what your inheritance owes to a wooden leg."

I believe that storytellers use this hang-out-an-oddity method to gain the interest of their audience. I doubted whether a wooden leg would be quite as important as this introduction suggested.

"Your grandfather had a wooden leg? Remarkable. How had he lost his limb?" I wanted to cut to the quick.

"Never he had."

"Surely not your poor grandmother? A man in battle might, but not a woman, surely?"

"Nor had she. Though as for battle!"

"So, there is martial glory in our ancestors?"

"If you let me tell you then you shall know, though martial glory wouldn't be what many would call it. Brave, perhaps; martial, not like my injury in the service of Farmer George, no, not martial. Funnier, I reckon, than shot in the rump, but painful enough no doubt."

"Well who had the wooden leg and why is it of such importance to our family?"

The old man sighed. "All of a rush you men of law, 'cept when the clocks running in the court."

I ignored this and sat and listened. Trying to rush my grandfather when he was embarking on a tale was a largely pointless exercise. In any case, as I was to stay the night anyway, there was nothing to be gained. My mother would be home before he finished and, if he had his way, he would finish as she entered the room, with a resounding reprise of the element that was most likely to agitate her.

He began.

"Now, The History of My granfer and granny, much as that old Macauley told the history of our nation. Though I have never studied the past I shall stand by the truth my lad."

"Firstly, you'd better understand as how my granfer was a carter, just as my old dad was. Now granfer went working when he was a young man and barely left home, over in what they call the Black Country. There was all sorts of little ironworkers there: locksmiths, nail-makers, all kinds of this-smith and that-smith – colliers and all. All doing bits of what-not, and this and that, and doing their bit of farming on the side likely as not. This was when there was still common fields and the rich folk had only gone so far as to rob the folk of most of the best farmland. Any road, he went over to Brierley Hill or some such place to cart coal over to the Severn, there being no navigations as could be used at that time. He used to lead long old rows of pack beasts all tied one behind the other. Once, even had a notion to go into selling the muck, but he never had time to stop and bag it all up. You had to keep those pack beasts on the move: mind, shouldn't have wanted to follow behind.

"He went back and forth and back and forth as often as he could, and the beasts' good would allow. So, natural he took lodgings with a local man. He told me how first few days he could barely pick up a word this chap, or any of the other folk spoke to him. Outlandish way of talking they had. Still as good folk as any are, I'd say since I had the boat out that way when I was working. And he agreed, fine old folk, who'll see you right for beer and bacon. Don't suppose you've drunk beer from that part of the world. No, thought I was right. Black and thick and the most wholesome I know of. And as for the bacon. They love their pork over there. All keep pigs, well most who can feed one did. Wonder what the place is like now? Spoiled I shouldn't wonder. All that industry buried beneath workhouses and factories and town halls."

How right he was. A perceptive man of the old independent labouring class. As I have come to realise, the industry of the individual artisan or labourer when working free from the stifling influence of the factory is a very different thing from the enforced labour of the wage slave. I said so. My grandfather looked puzzled, but said that it sounded "just the ticket".

"Now, he lodged with this chap and his missus. And a fine old couple to set tongues a-wagging they were. She was a beauty of some twenty summers and, by the looks of her, no winters at all. Yet she was a labouring lass. She worked for the colliers. She hauled coal for it to be loaded onto the beasts. Put it in these great baskets that hung down either side of the beast and pulled it over for loading. First day after he'd taken lodgings he saw her at the pit. Not a bottomless deep hole like they have now, but a pit even so. There she stood, basket o'coal over her shoulder and waving at him with the other hand! And could she drink her beer too. That night, there she was with the other pit lasses, all a-flirting and teasing the lads. Buxom lot they were, but she stood out with golden locks and tight waist."

I butted in. "How debased they sound. She was a married woman, in an ale-house. And I wish you would not speak of women so. I, for one, am pleased that the reformers have done a little to raise the moral standard of the oppressed weaker sex."

"Oppressed is it, you say? Those were different days lad. Besides, I wouldn't have you think ill of my grandma."

"Your grandma? I thought she was married to this chap that your grandfather lodged with?"

"So I did."

"Ah! Do I detect a mining accident and a tragic bereavement followed by an attachment to the lodger? Quite scandalous, but understandable." When away from the law, I was, at one time, prone to flights of fancy. The old man said so, though not in so many words, if the derisive bellow that shook his frame can be described as a word at all.

"Ha! I have you again. No, you don't. Nor did she wait for a tragic bereavement to form an attachment with the lodger." He paused, studying my face, as I sat with an obviously shocked expression. He was waiting for me to comment.

"Thought you'd have something to say. Seems that you're more your father's son than your mother's. No harm, neither. Wonder what my little daughter will say? I expect one of us might tell her. Perhaps it would come best from you."

I thought that in this, as in a surprising number of things, he was right. It was true, that though he and my mother were forever aggravating each other with their words or seeking opportunities to antagonise the other, they cared for each other in a way that open affection only hints at: the truth was that they were very similar people moulded by different lives in different ages. He smiled, seeing that I understood that this tale was to be sympathetically relayed to my mother without unsuitable detail. I thought it was a mark of great respect to her feelings that he had sheltered her from events in her family history that would have shocked her, though not shaken her, to the core.

"Don't be too ready to blame that pretty lass. Though she laboured as hard as she drank, she had the heart of a woman. Though her poverty had driven her to a marriage that she regretted, she still had her life to live." I anticipated a descent into sentimentality and told him that this was unlike him.

"Sentimental don't mean it was not true enough. Mind, you'll know better than to say sentimental when you know more of the chap that she'd married: the man in whose house my granfer got his feet under the table. He was a most extraordinary old boy. He was an old boy too, when set aside her, maybe twice her age. And as she was a beauty, he was as pug-ugly as they come. Much of that could not be laid to his charge, it seems, but as chalk and cheese they were. To begin with, he had smallpox scars all over half his face and down his neck. I say half his face, but once they must have covered it full. But, deep blue and red rakes had been hacked through scab and skin alike. One half of his face had been riven in some pit explosion. Took out an eye too. The socket he covered with a patch made of leather, but wasn't above frightening folk by baring it when he'd drunk heavily. Which was pretty much most days. Strange thing was he was a colossus of a collier. All the men feared or respected him, for his strength and his freedom with treating his butties. And all this with a wooden leg to stump around on."

"He sounds like a remarkable man, though not one for a lady to associate with. How did such an unlikely couple marry?"

"You speak truly. They were the strangest pair ever to be harnessed to be sure. But if you think about it, she was a beauty and he was the best man in the workings when it came to pay. Looks aren't everything. Seems that he had treated her to drinks when she was a bonny sixteen and had bought her a dress and promised to buy her another if she would come and live with him. Well, what better offer was a girl like her to get, even if he were an ugly old bruiser who had the freedom of all the beer-houses? So, they married. I know you're going to say that she sold herself. Well, thank your parents for having enough to keep you from going against niceties. Life was different then."

I had been about to be disgusted. I kept quiet. Maybe he was right.

"Yet it was a marrying for benefit of both and not likely to last once that benefit wasn't to be had. Seems that marriage to this old boy had worn thin after a couple of years. He took to beating her when he came home drunk, though nothing too severe, then falling asleep 'til morning took him back to the pit. He rioted with his butties and she with her friends. He didn't even show her the sort of attention a husband should. Beyond his capability, I should say. He spent all his money on beer and took hers too. No more dresses. There were many young men around about there who cast thoughts and eyes her way, for they could see how the tide had turned. Yet none dared go further, so in awe of him were they all. If one had dared she may have gone with them."

I was appalled by the moral laxity of these people and thanked God that I had grown up in an age of undoubted improvement. What I did not understand was that grandfather was about to lower the tone of the tale even deeper into depravity.

"So, up pops your ancestor, my granfer; about her age and nobby as a cock. Finds himself lodged with this lass and her husband. Now, you can understand how he betrayed the hand of hospitality I'm sure. Temptation there was beyond resisting. So, one night Moses – that was the old boys name, or such like – comes home for he's spent all his money at some ale-house or other - and finds the two of them: her with dress up, him with breeches down, all ready to set to. Now what do you think he did?"

I made no answer. The scene was so far beyond my experience.

"They thought he'd fly into a rage and set about them with his belt. But no, see, he'd not reached a state of drunkenness yet. He knew the lie of the land. Even so, you'd have thought he'd be put out of sorts. But all he does is demand my granfer's rent a week afore it was due and went back to his drinking!"

I found this beyond belief. How could this man, I asked, see the marriage vows he made before the Lord so profaned and react in such a way? I answered my own question. Clearly, I said, the man was no more than a drunken sot. I was about to say that my ancestors were little better than rutting beasts, but I halted, aware that there was certain to be another twist. I merely said that I was horrified that my ancestor had shown such little respect for morality and less, for I realised that this was at a time before moral improvement, for the sanctity of marriage. Had the sacred vows meant nothing to him? Women were weak, surely he should have shown restraint?

"Should not say that to your mother! Hey, Sam Jagland, weak women." My father raised his eyebrows in agreement about the likely reaction, as he set food upon the table: spitting bacon, hot potatoes and butter. Plain fare, but good and wholesome. I still prefer it to most of the courses at the fine tables I now eat at. Pickles and chutneys too.

As we ate, grandfather continued his tale, still managing to be first to a second serving.

"Vows? Who said anything about them?"

"But they were married were they not?"

"Of sorts."

"Surely, even in that era, marriage was marriage."

"Not there it wasn't. Half the people who lived together had never been married in a Church. Still thought they were married properly. Just as happy and lasting too. At least they could get out of it easily, but most never wanted to – not more than normal anyhow."

All this sounded very nice and convenient and a good deal too lax. I did not speak, but grandfather read my thoughts. "Well, it was no worse, as far as I can see, for ordinary folk anyway. The nobs would never do with it: scared of what'd happen to their inheritances. But these folk had no money other than that they were going to spend. Besides, it wasn't always nice and comfy."

"Now Moses didn't come home for a few days, and my granfer had to spend a night or two away. He'd done his regular trip and there was some kind of problem with the loading of the boats, so he ended up kipping on the floor of an inn down by the river. Now, that very night, the old pug-ugly comes home. He been paid and was bellowing like an old bull. Finding his rival was not there he set about his wife – if you'll let me use that term. Well he flailed at her, but in his cups he was no nimble dancer and she dodged him for a while. She hoped he'd collapse in a drunken heap, but it was she who tripped and he forced himself upon her. He did as he pleased and blacked both her eyes, laid her cheek open and left her ribs all a mass of black and blue. He left her on the floor and took himself off to bed.

"Now, here's the spirit. When she came around and lifted herself to look in the old scratched mirror, she saw what he had done. At first she cried out loud, her ribs being jabbed with pain as she sobbed. But then she took matters in hand, as you'd hope your kith and kin would. Didn't she just. Well, she goes across to the bed and in the little light of dawn that showed into the room saw the snoring great brute that had once treated her to drinks and a dress. She wanted to spit on him. Instead she looked around for something to thrash him with. Then he started to wake. He stirred a little and yawned, stretching his brawny arms out wide. She would miss her chance of revenge if he woke fully. So, quick as a flash she sees the one blunt instrument to belabour him with. She pulls off his wooden leg and commences her work to such effect that before he opens his eyes, they are closed up! Not only is he blinded, but in an attempt to get the better of her he rolled off the bed and tried to stand. Course, he falls in a heap and she carries on as he lies there helpless."

I was shocked to hear of such brutality from a woman – more particularly a pretty ancestor – though clearly little more can be expected with regard to the violence she had suffered and the monster who had dealt the blows.

"She paid him his due, by all accounts. Thrashed his body, but more, much more, she smashed his soul. He was all a-begging and pleading that he'd never meant no harm and how he'd change his ways if only she'd forgive and forget. But she weren't giving in, though she hardly believed she done what she had. Fair shaking with rage she was, for hours she shook with disbelief that she'd thrashed that old Devil. No, she weren't going back.

"Course, Old Moses or whatever he was called knew that too. When all had calmed down and he lay on the floor with his cuts and bruises and she lay on the bed with the blood drying on her cheeks smeared by her tears, they must have made things up and talked civilly, for when granfer comes through the door, there they were united in a course of action.

"Mind you, my granfer was not having it to begin with. No, he was for fetching the Constable and having Moses summoned by the Magistrate. When the lass told him that it wasn't only Old Moses who'd done assault, he was for thrashing the old boy and heaving him headfirst down his own pit. His blood was up and she brought his ardour down by saying that she and her husband had agreed on what needed to be done and if he'd listen they'd tell him, though he must say not a single word of it to any other."

"But surely Moses wasn't her husband? You said he brought her a dress and treated her to drink?

Well there had been no wedding. Why did she and your grandfather not walk away and marry?" I thought I had him there.

"How little you learned men know of the pride of an ordinary man and woman. You know even less of how folk who couldn't afford the law used to get by. Listen. Treating and buying had been their marriage. To them, like to all ordinary folk, a bargain sealed with a drink was the law. Binding, were it a cow or a pig or a wife they were getting. People had seen it happen. The act had been witnessed in some tavern or other so it was well known to all that she was Moses' missus."

"Yes," I said, "but that is not marriage! All they needed to do was to go and marry properly." I saw his point, but felt that ignorance of the law and, indeed, morality could not have been that great even amongst the lowest orders of society. Not in England, at any rate.

"Tripe. What need had they of law? And as for morals, they'd no greater need than we have, no lesser either. Moses would not let her go to her new man, though he said he was happy enough since she was going anyway, without some way of showing that he was letting her go. She was likewise all for it. People would call her a common slut if Moses didn't pass her on all respectable-like. Couldn't have my granny labelled a whore could we now?" At this I must have looked as though there were no question that she was little better than a woman of the street. What expression made my opinion clear I know not, but the old man latched onto it and anger shone in his old eyes, the usual puckish glint fleeing before the flame of justified outrage.

"Don't you dare think that. Strolling about Banbury market wishing the farmers well and waiting for them with their bills and rents to come to your office where you take their money and never see the dark of the back alleys. Oh, they are there, even in Banbury. Take a look around and you'll find girls enough to call slut and whore and baggage. All of them will have their life, but not so you'd notice. Privilege you've had and forgotten where you come from by the hard work of others."

On reflection, it is hard to feel that he was not right. I had worked hard to get where I was, but I had never had to speculate on when or on what I might dine that day. So, I said no more and he went back to his tale.

"Even the dregs like them had their bit of pride and wanted everybody to see that they were doing what was right and just according to their ways. Drunkenness and beating and all kinds of sin may have been their habits, but even they wanted their little world to see it done proper. As for the law, it took much from them if they ever fell in its clutches, and gave them nothing: best keep away from what they'd never have money to buy. I know you lot will never understand how things were, or are for some. Trouble is today the rich shine their light into the black of the coal pit but never go down the shaft: they see the boatman and his family, but only ever go aboard to condemn what they see."

There was a pause. I was angered by his words, but grand-filial duty curbed any response. On reflection, his words were wise, though the rich have never gone down into the pit or into the tiny cabin of the boatman if it were possible to avoid doing so. And, of course, generally it was.

"Anyhow. A couple of weeks later when all the bruises had faded and the scars could be masked, Old Moses and his lass was seen walking up the street: him in front and her behind: in his hand a rope and about her neck a halter. Lead her up the way, kicking up mud as they went, just as if he were Old Giles bringing Daisy the Cow to market. Neither of them was smiling, dead serious they were. Don't think bad of them: this was the way of their world and the best they could manage.

"Now, they come into a tavern yard and no sooner had they arrived than my granfer comes out with some butties and a cry goes round about. The yard filled up in the blink of an eye, with all sorts of folk coming to see the show. And that's what they got. Old Moses climbs up on a cart and calls out for beer. The lass stood atop a tun. Beer was brought for both and off goes Old Moses after this fashion. He says how things can't be helped and how there need be no hard feelings as no harm has been done. Then he called for more beer and said how he'd treated this lass to a dress and sealed the bargain with drinks and so they'd lived as man and wife for some years. (Cries of 'Well said Old Moey' and 'Good for you, boy') but that things had come to pass and that he was putting her up for auction."

I exclaimed.

"Yes, selling her to the highest bidder, he said. Don't you worry, it weren't as bad as your modern morals would have it. So, Moses starts his pitch: 'She's a fine lass, like a coal barge, bluff in the bow and round in the stern.' Vulgarity knew no bounds in those days, but I'll not spare the truth lest you get the wrong idea. All the fellows laughed at that and called out to see. The lass smiles back at the crowd and gives them, 'Shame on his tiller for he never could navigate the journey to the end.' The women cheered and Moses smiled and got on with it. He called out for more beer to ease his throat. More beer was brought and both drank deep. 'Her's a hard working lass and can heave a hundred of coal on her back, sell it and tip the profit down her neck in no more time than Old Tom's dog can scrag a rat. She do go well in harness but being a spirited jade takes a firm hand.' The crowd cheered. The lass yells out, 'Firm hand? Firm anything, I'd be lucky. Any of you young men care to ride?' Again there was general uproar. So, Moses pulls off his leg and bangs it on the tun to bring them to attention. Now he says, who'll bid? 'Five pennies,' shouted one, 'a shilling' another. 'Come on', says Moses, 'there's more value in her smock than that.' He called out for more beer. This arrived. He then offered to throw the halter into the bargain and was ready to speechify again, when an old woman called out, 'Alright old 'un, have done now.' He looked at his lass and saw a line of tears running down her face. He turned to my granfer and looked him in the eye. 'What d'ye say, Sir?' 'Seven and six and a gallon of ale to drink to the bargain.' The money changed hands and six pennies were returned for luck. The crowd left the yard and my granfer took my granny and Old Moses into the tavern to drink their health's and seal their bargain."

I was astounded. I had heard of this sort of sale before, but was astonished that it could have occurred in my family, even if long ago, and was deeply aware of how shocking this would be to my mother. I was wounded; she would be mortified. I said that he was right to have spared mother the details and that I would tell her if I thought it fit, but would, in any case avoid the sordid elements of the tale as far as was possible. There would, I thought be little enough left of it.

However, I did feel it necessary to ask the old man how he knew this. He said that he had had it all from the man himself: his grandfather. I asked why he had not told the story before, surely it was just the sort of yarn he liked to spin. Wouldn't want to offend he said, which was not true, though he would not have wanted to drive his daughter to absolute distraction. Besides, he said, it would never have done to give "Sammy", my father, ideas. Father smiled and put the kettle on the range.

I have often wondered why he made no comment. I once thought that it could only be explained by his reluctance to comment on almost anything apart from the quality of dinner and the beauty of plants. Now, in more mature years, I cannot help but conclude that he actually enjoyed the prospect of my mother's discomfort. I make no claim that he was a malicious or heartless man; his enjoyment would not have allowed her to be distressed about something that was truly important. After all, there was every prospect that she would never hear the whole story and that, even if she did, it would be dismissed as the fanciful nonsense carefully gauged for maximum effect that my grandfather was one to indulge in.

In the sharp early morning light that woke me I was able to broach the topic. Do not think I did so gratuitously. Truth was my guide. Whilst the old man had convinced me at the time, the whole notion of one of my ancestors buying another had niggled at my mind even as I slept. It was clearly absurd, yet it was perfectly within the realms of reason given the unimproved state of the lower orders in the era when it supposedly had occurred. So, at the first opportunity I spoke to my mother. She was preparing food for the day and offered me ham and eggs for breakfast: Banbury was not such a long way, but it was a tedious country journey by train which halted for milk churns and somnambulated to a succession of junctions where one had to wait for other trains that were always late. As usual she served a breakfast fit for a man set on a busy day.

My father was out, having set off for work two hours before. I asked where the old man was. Apparently, he had gone to sit on the towpath no doubt, said mother, in the hope of learning and spreading scandal in equal proportion. This suited my purpose. So, thanking her for breakfast I pitched in and outlined the previous evening's discussion. I told her of the strange marriage contracted between the peculiarly hideous Moses and the handsome lass, of the interloping lodger and of the extraordinary resolution of the problem. Of course, as I had promised the old man and as I would have in any case given my natural sensitivity, skirted around the worst aspects of the history. I told her nothing of the violence or illicit sexual activity or of the squalid detail of the sale itself.

In truth, I did not know what reaction to expect as I recited the sad story. However, one of that would fall into one of two possible categories was most likely. I expected the reaction to be broadly dismissive of the whole business supported by an assault on my grandfather's character or to be an angry refutation based upon the obvious good character of all her ancestors. What understanding, if any, she had of evolution I do not know, but she certainly felt that children who had succeeded as hers had done could only be descended from people of moral stature.

To my surprise, she listened in silence to what I said, that is, except for the occasional acknowledgement that I was speaking. This made me reluctant to conclude given that the eruption was likely to be more violent because so long deferred. Fortunately, her apparent acceptance of what I said enabled me to complete the story without resort to sordid details. At the conclusion of my monologue there was no explosion and no sob of anger or distress. There was, to my amazement a calm silence that caused me to speculate on whether my words had driven mother into some trance-like state as she continued to peel potatoes and put them into a large pot apparently through pure instinct.

"What do you make of that?" I felt the need to prompt a response. Yet none came. Perhaps she was angry with me. "I was shocked, mortally so," I added quickly. Yet my mother maintained her purposeful preparation and did not so much as mutter a word or let go a sigh to indicate resigned acceptance of a family scandal. "I hope you are not too affected by this news?" I thought it best to ask, kindest, too, of course: I admit no want of filial care.

Her reply astonished me. "Have you prospects of rising further in the law my son?" This nonplussed me. Then I realised that she was obviously making conversation to hide her emotions. I should have expected that; my mother derided self-pity in herself as much as others and it was clearly pointless to vent anger on the messenger. Humour her, I thought: all for the best.

"One always hopes, but I have been cultivating connections with Professor Lloyd-Williams of Oxford University. He hopes to be Master of one of the colleges." (I shall not say which, for he was unsuccessful.) "When he takes up his post he has suggested that the legal matters will be removed from the current lawyers and placed in the hands of a new, more forward looking partnership. I have every hope that this will be good business for our chambers. It will also connect me to influential men in the judiciary."

"Well-done, my boy. You'll rise to Queen's Counsel yet, I should hope. Imagine that. The son of a gardener acting in the highest courts in the land in the cases of greatest weight." She did not sound proud. Indeed, there was a flat note in her tone that seemed to deprecate my achievements even whilst praising them. She could be cruelly and obviously sarcastic, but this was not that: I knew her sarcasm well.

She continued, "All the newspapers recording your words and them to be read in breakfast rooms of the rich and the tap room of the worker and in all the parlours of the land."

I replied that it would be gratifying to think so, but that such notions were wildly speculative at present. I told her that at present advancement might be hoped for, but I had already come a long way from my humble origins.

"Humble indeed." She did not mind being of humble origin: it was her place and she wanted to belong to it. It was something to be proud of. She neither wished to be rich, and therefore dissolute, nor from the lowest orders, and therefore either criminal, feckless or devoid of the power of self-improvement, possibly all three, and certainly dirty.

I took the opportunity to return to the first topic of conversation. "Self-improvement, mother, one of the great virtues of our age: I a lawyer with a grandfather who was a boatman, who was himself the grandson of a man who bought his wife in a sale."

"We have come up in the world, have we not, my boy?" I assented with a nod. She went on, "Step by step, each generation doing its little bit. The spirits of the age."

"Very true. We have risen alongside the great achievements of science and engineering; expansion and imperial glory; reform and government: all aspects of life. Literature and intellect." Maybe my grandfather's grandfather and grandmamma were of the lowest order, but without them we would not have progressed. That was the key. I need worry no more about a long past scandal. If that had been the way of their time, it was no longer the way of ours: we had aided our nation in its advance and we were all the better for it. I was reconciled to my genealogical discovery.

My mother repeated one word. "Intellect."

"And you amongst them: those men who have improved their intellect?" She continued, after a short pause.

"Well," I said, "I suppose I would number amongst the more humble of them, but yes, I suppose I am."

"And a great advance it must be to have such book-learning and brain-work for a lawyer to be taken in by an old man who never even went to school and who had his intellect addled ever since Trafalgar: if you believe that tale of his as well as this new one."

"Mother, there is nothing inconsistent or fabulous about the tale he told me. Indeed, there were numerous details that I have spared you that would vouch the veracity of what he said, if only circumstantially. Moreover, I see no motive in his being less than truthful. After all, if you have cause to be ashamed of your ancestors, he has more so, being in closer proximity to them."

"'Tis not my ancestors shame me but my own clever son, who gets hooked in like a trout fish by my old father angling for a bit of fun at all our costs." She would not accept that her denial was due to her desire to avoid association with such events, however long ago they may have been. I told her so.

"Now," she said, "is that so? Perhaps you have not heard how his grandfather was a spy for the Jacobites, a highwayman and inventor of a machine for spinning wool yarn powered by dogs in a treadmill, or how he escaped from transportation by jumping off the hulk and swimming underwater all the way from Stepney to London Bridge only to spend his life evading justice? Or that he was the offspring of some Lady and a penniless tinker? He had an eventful life to be sure. Though his greatest miracle was surely the grand-siring of such a bumptious old villain as my father."

I felt foolish.

My grandfather called out as he entered the room, having been out in the yard, eavesdropping by the door, "Thank you daughter. He did have a most eventful time of it my dear, but he couldn't have done them all, I wouldn't think. Maybe he told me a few little tales. Wonderful imagination. Wish he'd passed it on."

Mr. Jones in London

I once asked my great-grandfather about his first trip to London. He told me that he first went there in 1804 and was pressed into serving the King at sea, and then proceeded to tell me all about a much later visit he had made to the Great Wen. "No tale to tell o' the first trip, my boy. All went straight and easy for once and Nat was taken by a cold in the head afore we got as far as Brentford, so he could do no harm amongst the ladies and the beer houses. No, first time there I saw nothing but the wharf and heard little but Nat snoring, 'til the press gang came. But later..."

I had asked him to halt at this point. He had often told us all that he had served his country heroically at Trafalgar, even though he had been a pressed man, he had done his duty as requested by the Hero himself. Indeed, the old man claimed to have met Nelson and to have exchanged words with him. I doubted this. No one, family member or visitor, had been able to drag the tiniest piece of corroborating evidence to support his claims. It was not as if he were a reticent man. He loved telling tales, I use the word advisedly, to anyone who would listen, and was, it must be admitted, an admirable storyteller on a long winter night.

Yet we all knew there were limits with regard to the extent to which his tales were safe to be relied upon as evidence of events. He was not strong on chronology. Nor was he wedded to the truth. I am reluctant to accuse any of my elders of deliberate deception, so will put his lapses down to a desire to entertain and to provoke the listener, especially if my grandmother was in earshot. If he did not tell untruths, he had, at least, a streak of creativity; if he was not inventive, then he had indeed had a colourful life. I am not sure if in his later years he knew the difference, though my grandmother maintained that he calculated the effect of every word he said and cared not whether it was true, untrue or of mixed origin. We knew there were boundaries to his veracity, but we knew not where they lay.

This was one reason why I desired to tease out a tale of London and draw him into a Trafalgar story or two. I hoped that I could tell my children, when they came along, that their ancestor had fought in the great sea battle of the war against Napoleon. As I am sure you would agree, a father must encourage the virtue of veracity in his offspring. Thus, I had to test the old man's memory.

That I failed is not surprising. Nor was I too disappointed at that moment. After all, though he was old, he showed all the signs of extending his already considerable longevity into a tenth decade. So, bored as I was with life as a clerk in a trunnion foundry in Thrapston, I welcomed an adventurous diversion, even if it might be only half true, more or less. In any case, I had come to visit for a few days and enjoyed my grandmother's cooking even more than the tour of the castle gardens my grandfather had given me that day. Tomorrow, I would attempt to tackle Trafalgar.

"No, nothing to tell of my first trip there. If you'll hold your tongue though I can tell you of London. Trafalgar? Well, I served my King, but that weren't London.

"Rum old place, Cockney. Cock-eggs that comes from. Folk always about their business, even when they have none. Nat had a love for getting the cargo stowed and setting off up town. I never had. Better off at home than in that place; better off in Brum even. No, London was never my joy, though when you're there and you've money in your purse, well, a man's bound to have a bit of joviality. Any road, I had to keep an eye out for the old captain lest he spray the silver about too merrily. Remarkably generous chap, Nat. Distressing to old Watkins it was, on account of it being his boat and his money."

He appeared to be drifting into a reverie of past acquaintances. "I believe that thieves and murderers were around every corner," I said, hoping to get away from a monologue recalling his tow path acquaintances. "No police, rookeries side by side with the wealthiest folk in the country. Yes, crime and evil must have stalked the streets."

He looked at me, open-mouthed. "What you wambling on at lad? Course, there was bad goings-on then. Are now like as not, though fortune's done her bit to keep me away for many a year. Lords and commoners, financiers and jobbers, all there. And the whores, of course." He had raised his voice and glanced around to see if my mother had been within earshot. She had not. "Pick pockets, confidence men, tricksters, the swell mob; right thieves' kitchen it were. Bow Street Runners. Heard o' they? Hard men; thief takers, better than had gone before.

"But I, and I stand by it, was always innocent. All I cared for was to hand over the cargo, eat and drink and head for home as soon as maybe. But Nat was captain, so he told me we'd have a rare old time. Rare for me it was; run of the mill for him by all accounts.

"Well, as we went on our way, he told me to take care in the big city, telling me that, as a country lad, I'd be easy meat for the swells. He told me to keep myself right by his side where he could take care of me. 'Keep yer money hidden, stay sober and never have nothing to do with the ladies you meet at the Blue Posts down Holborn, or elsewhere, but specially there.' Golden rules he called them. Sober, I thought? We'd see. I said to myself that maybe he laid off the drink if London was such a den of vice and wickedness. Well, I was only a lad.

"So, there we were, a few hours later, all the cargo gone off by the carriers and me walking up the town for a bit of merry-making and a bite to sustain us in some fancy chop house. What struck me was how money sat right up close by poverty. Course, Nat had a pocket full of notes and coin, so we was fine for all we wanted. And, chops downed, what Nat wanted was a drink. I said to him that he'd said to stay sober, but all he replied was that London beer was piss with no danger of causing intoxication in a robust chap like him. He said we'd make our way to the Castle, but as it was a way off, we'd just stop in the Black Horse or Prad and something as he called it, or something of that sort. So, in we went. Well, captain, I said, you've a more remarkable thirst than ever if that beer be piss. He'd swallowed the lot in two mouthfuls and was calling for more. As he did this, a timid little chap comes over and says, 'By your speech I know you're up from my neck of the woods.' Turned out he was too, from the next town to where Nat had been born. Mind you, he was a quiet fellow, seemed to be in the wrong place. Market town man in the thronging metropolis, that was him.

"Then he spoke up once more. 'Would you help a fellow countryman?' I thought he wanted money, but was wrong. Turned out that he was a stranger in town, only there because he had to call on some lawyer chap about a bit of inheritance from an old uncle. All he wanted to do was to have some friendly voices around, 'specially as Nat knew his way round the city. Then he pulled from his coat pocket a purse fit to burst. Coin mainly, but a few notes poking edges out too. Nat shoves his hand back towards his coat and scolds him about flashing so much money. The chap looked amazed and thanked Nat, saying it was only his intention to show that he was able to offer us food and drink, and a place to rest our heads, should we help him. Said his name was Samuel Farmingham.

"So, Nat looks him up and down and without so much as a glance in my direction clasps him by the hand like his some long lost friend of boyhood and slaps him on the shoulder, declaring, 'Us men of Lichfield and Tamworth must put aside our differences when here in the Great City, must hold firm together. Take my word, I'll render you what help I may, with all my heart I say so!' Magic words food and drink, less so the food. So off we goes. The chap says he has been recommended to the Old Black Horse, not this one, but the Old Black Horse, and that it could not be far, he thinks. So I tagged on behind as usual. Well, I feared missing my share of the victuals.

"As we go, Nat berates him, very gentle-like – we'll don't do to be rude to the cook afore dinner – telling him to keep his purse and all it had in it out of sight. The poor old boy was most apologetic. Nat told him to follow his example. I sighed, but no one took notice of me.

"So, we goes on our way, turning down a little alley full of some mighty unfriendly looking folk. I didn't like it one bit. The chap said he was told it was a short cut. Yes, I thought, to get your throat cut. Mind we were no sooner into it than we were back out on the high street, which one I couldn't say, but broad and bright and so different to what lay behind it no further than where you're sitting from me it seemed. There were all sorts of shops and folks of all kinds coming and going. Carters pulling goods to the inns, servants chasing errands for their betters, swells and sportsmen going their ways: all hustle and bustle and life. Bloody horrible. And there was the sign of the Old Black Horse. In we went, into Nat's world, though the place was a bit short on tarts. You do know what they are, my lad?

"It looked like an orderly enough place as any tavern was in those days. Our new friend calls for ale and chops and we sit ourselves down in a corner, near a youngish chap looking down at his boots, but leaning back in a high back chair, while blowing slow puffs of smoke from a plain clay pipe. He was alive, but not so you'd notice unless you was bothered. I knew how he felt, but as Nat was calling for more beer, I knew I'd best stop idling. Strange to say, it had the same effect on this snoozing chap.

"His head jerked up so quick that his billy-cock nearly went for a burton. He was younger than Nat, and the other fellow, but older than me. Hooked nose and a tumble of fair hair, with bright blue eyes. Striking looking chap, not handsome. And then, he pipes up. 'Now, if I am not mistaken gentlemen, you hail from around Lichfield. Pray, forgive me, but in this place, it is good to hear a familiar tongue. I am Darcy Bludd, gentlemen, and am happy to make your acquaintance.' I could see Nat thinking how he was going to get stung for another pot of ale, but he called for it and shook the fellows hand, telling him how right he was and how gentlemen from the same country should always do one another a good turn when abroad in the land of Cockney. Farmingham didn't look so happy about it, but took his hand. Bludd turned to me and I took his hand without enthusiasm. No, truly, I did. He may have been an honest enough man, and I had no reason to think otherwise, but I was a bit of a suspicious one when I was young. But he hailed me as friend and asked me how I liked the city.

"As I talked with him and the words went round when the beer and the chops came steaming to the table attended by a likely looking lass with dark eyes. Nat noticed them, but she looked longest at me. Anyhow, I didn't let myself be too distracted as she went off to her work. Shame, thought I. Better off in the village inn than the busy tavern, my lad. Don't suppose you know otherwise. No, I remembered that I'd need to keep my eyes on Nat, now he was calling more loudly for more beer. He was telling the striking chap, Bludd that is, about the folly of old Farmingham. Bludd agreed. 'Yes,' he said, 'Keep your property away from the view of the scoundrels who attend your every move in this town. Fortune smiled on you when you fell in with men of your own ilk: honest and fair spoken.' 'Hear, hear,' chimes in Nat. Poor old Farmingham, didn't look like the sort of chap who wanted to be lectured. But on they both went.

"All the time I was wondering how chance worked wondrously; all these chaps from the same country had met in the greatest city in the whole country. Put them in Banbury Market and they could have gone all day without hearing their home tongue. Strange, I thought, how things go around. Yet, it was strange too. Later on, when I put it to Nat that Farmingham had gone along to his Old Black Horse pretty well for a chap who was a stranger, Nat told me that he must have had directions in his head from whoever told him to go there for his chops.

"Bludd was saying, 'No, no, Sir,' to Farmingham, 'You must be tutored by me, dear fellow.' Then he gestured us all to draw round close, as if he were about to show us some great secret. And, he was, I suppose. 'Look here, my friends,' he drew out his pocket watch and then stretched his gentleman's fingers into the pocket from where it had come. Out came a small wad of notes. He opened one and briefly showed us the writing on it: a bank note. Quickly he refolded it and, along with the others stuffed it dexterously back from whence it had come. He quickly replaced the watch. 'There Sirs, there. The safest vault for your paper money, when you are out and about.' Farmingham looked amazed at the idea, which was, I suppose, clever enough. Nat looked amazed at the money.

"So, Farmingham draws out his timepiece and reaches for his purse and spills the lot on the floor in full sight of the assembled tavern society. Nat and I scrambled about on the floor with Farmingham picking up coin of all types, while Bludd took hold of his paper. Well, Bludd tut-tutted and told him to let him come to his aid, which he did nigh on before Farmingham had so much as sat up. Bludd quickly stuffed the notes into Farmingham's pocket and shoved the watch after them with no delicacy. He apologized, with a profusion of gentle chaffing about the ham-fisted countryman and his abominable clumsiness. Farmingham thanked him and they went on swearing eternal friendship and wishing all good fortune to one another and ordering spirits to cement the happy chance of their making acquaintance.

"So, it all went round until Bludd ups and leaves, throwing coin on the table to pay for all our sustenance as he stands to go. Nat looked delighted and Farmingham was all effusive thanks and happiness that he did not have to expose his fortune to the greedy eyes he was now convinced were encircling him.

"With Bludd going off, Nat decided we should move on too. 'Come along, Sam,' he said, 'Time for some more entertainment and jovial company'. He calls the maid who takes the payment and off we go out onto the street.

"We must have been in that tavern some time, much more than I thought and I was about ready for some sleep, but Nat had decided we should all try our luck, as he put it, at the Castle. Now, the Castle was an odd place. There were, may still be if I were able to get about and tell, places of repute and places of ill-repute and the society to be found there was much as one would expect. The Castle, though, even then, was a place where folk of all stations in life were to be found, though most of the women I came across there all came from the same set. It was said that Prince George himself was to be found there at times, though it always seemed moderately respectable to me. Truth was that it was frequented by men who loved the ring and there was always money changing hands on so and so against Tom Thigammy or Bill Whatsit and Big Joe or whoever. Lots of women, too, but most were less concerned with purity of the ring than the swells and what they were laying out.

"Happy to say, I was comfortable there. We ate and drank, and the conversation about wagers was most enlightening. Managed to keep Nat's or rather Mr. Watkin's cash out of the book-makers possession too. So all went well. Farmingham kept quiet, but he would not leave to go, though he was yawning like a good 'un.

"As we were on the verge of leaving, a couple of women came across to us and asked us if we might be seeking lodgings. Farmingham says we have lodgings nearby. Nat and I looked at him. What he meant was that he had and we were, he was sure, likely to find shelter at the same house. A house, he pointed out, of the greatest respectability. One of the women turned on him and told him that there was more than one respectable house thereabouts and that she could see that the other two gentlemen were not of the same impudent mould that he was. This made Nat hoot with laughter and bade the 'ladies' follow us out of the Castle and lead onto the house.

"We parted with Farmingham, who, once more asked us, then begged us to come the few hundred yards to his lodgings. Lizzie, the younger of the two women, told Farmingham that it was a lice-ridden hovel for all its fine furniture and that they could offer much more homely comfort at a much more reasonable fee. Nat asks what these comforts might be and Lizzie giggled, and her elder, who turned out to be named, Jennie, said that they were nothing more than warm and soft but well enough for all their humbleness.

"Well, Nat blasts out a guffaw that could have been heard in Hampton Court and slaps Lizzie on the rump, declaring that she is a jewel and that friend Farmingham was a bumpkin. Jennie leers a smile at me and asks if I agree with the Captain. The Captain, suppose he was. I should have told her that Farmingham was neither here nor there and that she and her slutty bitch of a sister were pox-ridden whores. Didn't o' course. Didn't know they were sisters at the time.

"Well, I didn't want to have as much as a spit to do with either of them, but I knew that Watkins wouldn't be happy if Nat was robbed. Cudgelled, maybe right enough – and the dear old chap deserved no less – but when his money was in Nat's pocket, Watkins came over all paternal. So, I followed on to keep an eye-out for 'the Captain' in case he sailed in stormy waters.

"Lizzie and Jen had been saying how their berths were all softness and comfort. Truth was they were through a little doorway and into hall, where a screw-faced old bat sat by an empty grate. She jumps up like jack in the box and welcomes her girls and tells us what fine chaps we are and how happy she is her lasses have brought home such fine gentlemen and that she has nothing in the house but her medicinal gin which she can't spare at less than a sixpenny piece, but we'd be welcome to help ourselves to all the comforts of the house. Looking round it seemed to me that six pence would have paid for gin and all the other comforts twice over, but Nat had already settled down and had Lizzie and glass in his grasp.

"I know I should have dragged him out, but he was a big chap and I was the boy and he was the Captain. Still did my best to keep Jen away. I'd fought against the French and got a blast of ball in my buttocks for all my bravery. I weren't going to catch the pox from this old fireship without a fight. The old woman hands Jen another glass and tells her that I need a bit of courage for I was but a young man. Well, I wasn't that young and I had some courage, but fight as I would I was outwitted by Nat.

"After a bit of saucy chatter, he and Lizzie stand up and she announces that they are withdrawing – strange way of putting it – to a chamber to converse more privately. She slings one of his arms over her shoulder and grips him round the waist with hers. Like this they crab across to a dismal stair case that leads up into a dark landing. I wasn't too bothered about his morals or his health. The Good Lord had probably given up for that matter. What worried me was what might happen to the coin in Nat's purse now he was not only drunken but in the grips of what passed for a passion.

"You'll see that I had but one course. I up and grabbed Jen and said adieu to the wrinkly old matron and dragged her into the stairway and up into the realm of darkness. Didn't take much dragging after she got over the shock. Still, I had only the best intentions.

"The latch on a door to our right was dropped and there was a great thump as, I guessed, Nat and his Lizzie found the bed. He told me later I was wrong, he'd fallen over a stool and was knocked unconscious. Just shows how strange the noise is in some of these London houses. That Lizzie made enough of a racket for two. I wonder what she was up to on her own?

"So, Jen getting less fearsome by the minute pushes the next door open and we glide in, dropping the latch behind us. She led me over to a bed by the wall. Now, I went and lay there as it was right by the wall that divided us from the room where Nat and Lizzie had gone. Perfect, I'd be able to keep an ear out for his well-being. For an unconscious man he certainly set about work sharp enough. Of course, to disguise my intentions I had to let Jen act in a distracting way.

"Well, we are all flesh, so don't you look so moral. I wake up to find Jen curled up beside me and to hear Nat snoring like an old steam engine. Walls must have been a sight stronger than they seemed, against that broadside.

"As I lay there wondering if I'd caught something nasty, being in proximity to that old tart, nothing more nor less than that, and wondering if the roof would stay on, I heard three sets of footsteps coming up the stairs. Well, I jumps up and adjusts me shirt and such like. Thought this might be the old hag from down below come to rob Nat and bringing a bit of help in case Lizzie had not done her work well enough. Jen didn't stir, as I went on tippy-toe to the door. No, I had no idea what to do. Two hefty rascals against an honest lad like me? Never held with that good over evil stuff when it comes to a brawl. No, I just went over out of instinct.

"Then, my heart stopped pounding as soon as I heard the big thump on the next door. They were knocking. Well, they obviously meant no harm, did they? In any case it seemed only fair to wait for Nat to wake up and wobble over to the door. I heard him open it and so, opened mine. Jen sidled up beside me, but I hushed her up and directed her back inside with me elbow.

"There, on the landing was the old biddy and a couple of fellows, one a thick-set chap about the size and shape of a big barrel and the other a sturdy bruiser of some six feet up and across. Nat was leaning on the door post blinking and muttering.

"'You Nat Jones?' The tall one started off. 'Captain Jones?' The little one said nothing.

"Nat was never one for riddles, so I answered that he was.

"'Strange looking sort of Captain,' said the tall chap. 'Odd garb for a Captain, more like the ship's monkey.' His companion remained silent.

"Nat was still puzzled by the first question.

"'Captain of the Pegasus, currently moored down the Lea,' I said.

"'Oh, I see, not a proper sea Captain.' The tall chap didn't seem impressed. 'Not even a Newcastle Collier: not even a Geordie skipper.'

"Nor was I impressed. 'Honest profession, what's yours?'

"Both looked and without speaking a word made me regret questioning their honesty. 'I'm the boat boy,' I said.

"'Odd boy,' said the tall one.

"'Old boy,' added the barrel. Both laughed great belly-ripplers at their wit. Nat woke up.

"'Where am I and what's all this row about?' Nat spoke. Well, woke up was over-egging it.

"'You been robbed?' The tall one asked.

"At first Nat seemed to think that they were making some gentlemanly inquiry as if he had been they wouldn't do it again. Nat put up his fists and barked to me to do the same. The two just hooted.

"Well, I thought, if you Cockneys reckon you can stand a mill with us fellows then you just look out. But they just ignored us anyway and pushed into Nat's room.

"'Got much coin about you, skipper?' The tall chap asked. 'Notes?'

"'I'll not...' began Nat.

"'No, you wont,' said the stout little bull terrier of a chap. Both roared with laughter.

"'Just take a look and we'll turn our heads.' The tall one spun round on his heels and was mimicked by his little companion.

"Nat searched through his waistcoat and coat and looked on the floor and under the rickety old bed. He looked up at me, white with horror and said all a-tremble. 'No, not one. But I should have.' Then he must have woken up good and proper, because he hares round the room roaring threats until the little chap stands in his way and the big chap turns and smiles.

"'Well fortune has favoured you. You've been robbed and you don't even know it. By the way, skipper, she took your timepiece along with the rest.'

"Nat was puzzled again. 'Lizzie? You mean that little bitch?'

"'Lizzie?' That what she called herself this time. The tall man looked grave.

"'Her name is Sarah Perkiss and we have her...'

"'Not you and all...' Nat interrupted the sort man.

"'We have more sense than you bumpkin boatmen up from your pit hovels. T'aint us that has been relieved of our worldly goods, is it?' The tall man made Nat look a bit sheepish.

"'But when your up in town, gentlemen...' Nat clearly wanted to explain, '...as a bachelor fellow...'

"He looked at me for support, but I slapped my hand over my mouth and he went quiet.

"'Don't take it so hard, Captain,' the tall one looked kinder, 'She had others than you and not doubt got away with their money...and their watches.' Nat felt his pockets and gawped even more stupidly. 'Come to the magistrate and you'll find what you have lost and let us all pray to the Good Lord and the pox doctor that she's not left anything behind.'

"Nat was all eagerness for me to go, but the two constables, as they turned out to be, insisted that Nat go. Needless to say, I went along to protect him. On the way the constables explained, indeed they asked forgiveness, but they said they had never before come across an arrest where the thief was taken before the robbed man knew of the crime. They went on; tall chap, Bryant by name, had been walking down a nearby street when he sees Lizzie or Sarah come tumbling out of a tavern door. Recognising her, due to her renown in the area as a prostitute and a nuisance to the peace, and, added little barrel, Dobbitt by name, many a-time complained of for taking what was not hers – though never caught – amongst other things, he goes across. Well, Bryant said he thought he'd be taking her before the magistrate for breaking the peace yet another time. Yet when he got there he was amazed. He told how she drank, but he had never seen her so roaring intoxicated before. Turns out she'd fallen out of the door, not been thrown out as was usual. He said she looked at him, struggled and spat. He told her he was taking her before the magistrate and she blurts out, 'Twas Suse what robbed the Captain.' She then realised what she'd said and clawed to get free. At that moment Dobbitt had come around the corner and between them they'd tamed her, taken her before the magistrate where spitting and cursing she'd coughed up the whole story and what was left of the money.

"'She'll be off to the hulks or to bedlam, one of the two. So long as you say it is her we'll have her committed for a felony. Seven years transportation, with luck.' He'd just finished as we reached the magistrates house.

"'Good morning gentlemen.' The magistrate, a Mr. Hulley, seemed most amiable. He asked about where we came from and what we did and where we had been the day and night before. Well, Nat answered.

"The magistrate thanked us for our answers. He then looked serious. 'They do breed acute fellows in Staffordshire, do they not?' Hulley, too. I wondered if all Londoners were as witty.

"'Nat is from Staffordshire,' I said. 'I'm from Warwickshire.

"'Ah, my deepest apologies for my mistake, Mr. Carter, how proud that county must be of its sons that loyally bed whores so they may watch over the Staffordshire men. Listen to me gentlemen and take note. You have been fools. You have equally been most fortunate. Whilst your morals may be matched by men of the same station in any country, it is the task of the law to protect all, even idiots. Take greater care of your Master's interests in future. Now, Jones, we'll bring the lady in and you must identify her.'

"Nat did and we never saw nor heard of her more.

"As she was taken out, all ragged, torn and knowing, I looked at her. She could have made a fine lass: bit of country air, good scrub, yes, she'd have been a pretty lass. There she was with the pale skin of the city; sunshine and a roll in the meadows was what would have saved her from rotting, as she most like did.

"My thoughts were broken in on by a noise outside and some lackey coming in and announcing that there was a Mr. Farmingham who was most insistent on seeing Mr. Hulley immediately.

"Mr. Hulley was about to dismiss us, when he was interrupted by Farmingham bursting into the room with a great deal of puffing and fuss, shouting, 'Hold Sir, I beg you hold, Sir!'

"'Sir,' he addressed Hulley, 'I saw these men come in here not half an hour ago and immediately went to search out a magistrate, to find, Sir, that this was itself the home of a that shield of the poor victim of wrongdoing. I, Sir, am amongst that number and these men were, I swear, with me when I was robbed. You do not know the relief I felt when I saw you had taken these thieves, these felons, for that is what they are.'

"Hulley looked open-mouthed at Farmingham. 'And who are you Sir?'

"'Farmingham, Sir, Samuel Farmingham, from Lichfield, Sir. I have business in London, Sir and these men have robbed me.'

"'You lying old bastard,' says Nat. 'Gratitude for taking you under my wing? I'll skin you...'

"'Protect me, Mr. Hulley, from this...'

"Hulley scowled and told him to control himself. 'These men are here because they have been robbed and the thief has been caught. Now, Mr. Jones, be quiet. Farmer or whatever you said your name was, be careful what you accuse these men of. Now, tell me your story.'

"Farmingham did, stopping only when Nat interrupted with threats, which Hulley stamped on. I waited all quiet an innocent. Best policy. Done no wrong, of course, but a hold your peace is my watchword when there's magistrates about. Farmingham told all that had happened but added in that we had lulled him into trusting us by claiming to come from his home country of Staffordshire and then having drawn him in, robbed him blind by pretending to teach him how to keep his paper safe. Switched it by sleight of hand, we had, he said.

"I looked at Nat's thick fists and fingers like plump sausages, I thought of how nimble he must have been with four quarts of ale inside him. No defence in law, I suppose.

"Hulley was looking most perplexed. 'Another paragon of that unfortunate county? Well, Jones, Carter?'

"Off went Nat, until Hulley told him to be quiet as he wasn't having that sort of abuse in his house. He turned to me and nodded for me to speak. So, I told him, how we'd met Farmingham, helped him out and all the rest. How we'd met Bludd and how Nat had no sleight of hand worth the name after a bit of refreshment. And how we were both as innocent as babes.

"Hulley sighed. 'Innocent, indeed. Explain how Farmingham got these flash notes? Explain who stuffed them in his pocket? Mr. Farmingham may be a fool, but the law is there to protect fools.'

"Farmingham was on the verge of protesting, but thought better of it.

"'Bludd,' says Nat.

"'Mr. Bludd,' burst Farmingham, 'Mr. Bludd I have already met with since and he was of the greatest assistance, while you were, it seems cavorting with whores. Mr. Bludd...'

"'Cavorting with whores? You old...' Nat was boiling.

"'Farmingham,' said Hulley, 'What bank were your notes drawn on? Hand me your notes, Mr. Jones.'

"Nat thought twice, but held passed them over.

"'No Mr. Farmingham, these are not those you speak of. I suggest you find your Mr. Bludd.'

"'But, may I beg you, Sir...'

"'You may not. I suggest you all go back home to wherever it was you all came from and perplex the magistrates of that county.'

"So we did.

"A couple of months later we were back up in the city. Watkins had told Nat that he'd never skipper another of his boats if there was any more business like last time, so Nat was on best behaviour. Like a Methodist preacher he was. Bit worrying really. Strange thing was that he decided we'd go and see some improving places so as to expand our provincial minds and be more like men of the world. So off we went into the heart of the city and then down to the river. In those days the riverbank was all wharves and yards and hodge-podge of wandering folk and boatmen shouting the odds. Not improved like it was later, dirty and full of the stench of the river.

"Well, we stands by a wharf and looks up and down the river at all these great vessels and all those tiny boats, scattering all over the water and skitting between the full-riggers. Wonderful sight, 'specially from the bank. All those folk who look at the ships and see adventure? You know the sort of bright-eyed lad who finds his fortune on the briney. Bugger the lot of them. Quiet life, that's the thing. Adventure and a life on the ocean. Brings my guts up just contemplating it. Here's the place to be, as far as you can be from the sea and sailors and captains and the press.

"Still, fine sight to see.

"'You been to sea, aint you?' says Nat.

"I said nothing. 'Wonderful life I should think. Wish I'd had the chance. Opportunity, that's the thing for a young chap. Surprises me that you didn't stick to it my lad. Still, you aren't the type to leap at a chance are you? A good chap for a canal you are. All familiar and no excitement.'

"I ignored him.

"'I would...' Nat tailed off. Then he punched me on the arm said 'Bludd'.

"I turned and Nat roars 'Bludd'.

"It was too. Nat was turning redder by the second. I could see he was about to boil, so I told him to shut up and we'd follow Bludd and quiz him. Too late.

"'Bludd! Bludd!' Nat's voice didn't so much echo as fly around from ship to ship. Bludd looked over his shoulder, saw Nat running towards him like a madman, and broke into a run. I soon caught Nat up, but neither of us could make much of Bludd. He was going like the clappers and we followed as best we could, but made nothing of his lead.

"All we could do was follow, which was made easier by the broad streets. He was in sight. But as we ran harder and harder and made a bit of ground up, Bludd went to ground amongst a line of low shacks that could have been boathouses or workshops or pigsties, but were probably home to some poor devils. Nat and I reached the alley and there was the maze. No sign of Bludd and no sign of life. Just the sort of place to feel a knife at your throat. We both hesitated and then gave up. Nat told me to go and look while he blocked the way in. I told him that he could go and flush out Bludd while I went for a magistrate. We'd halted and neither was going further.

"A great sound of cracking wood came from the dark, somewhere down the alley. We rushed towards it, turning a couple of corners. There, by the edge of the water was Bludd. He was pulling a leg from the place where he'd gone through the rotten wood of a bit of jetty. He looked up and saw us. He limped to the edge. Nat stepped forward and Bludd jumped into the river.

"Nat looks at me and says, 'Get out in a boat and haul him in.'

"'Not I'.

"'Come on boy, you been to sea before'.

"'All unwilling. You get out there'.

"'I'm skipper, you do as I tell you'.

"So, we let Bludd get away with a soaking at least and a dose of gut-rot or worse at best, not that we were bothered. Back on the boat, we decided that Bludd would either be dead from stinking foulness of Old Father Thames or from the miasma, from which we hoped the country air would save us, or he'd drown or choke on his own vomit. Good riddance said Nat. The preacher bit didn't last once we were heading home.

"'Still can't fathom why you didn't go and apprehend him'. said Nat.

"'No matter, now'.

"'But a young fellow like you, full of enterprise...'

"'But not full of that gut-rotting concoction...'

"'What would Nelson have said?'

"'Nelson can whistle...'

"'But his spirit is lost amongst you young folk...'

"'Where were you...'

"'Yes, sad to say, the young men of today, even those who served with him have let the memory of the Hero depart from their spirits...'

"And on he went, all the way to Brentford."

Mr. Happy Does Nothing

"Fiddlesticks", says I. "Tripe and Onions, my boy. How little you know of the way of the world for all your book-learning."

"But, mother, I must insist that it will bring shame upon me and destroy my name and with that I will lose the respect I have from my flock and so with it will go my living and any prospect of gaining another. I shall be shamed."

"So, you shall and it will all be brought about by your weakness in dealing with that flighty wife of yours."

"So, what should I do to prevent such a calamity? I do not believe it is too late to act in some way. Please, mother, act as my advisor."

Mrs. Jagland and her son, sat before the fire in the house by the wharf. The flames kept out the otherwise pervasive dampness of a September afternoon. It was a rare visit by son to mother, though she knew something of the predicament of the Rector of Littleborough, from the letters he dispatched on a weekly basis from the study of the overlarge parsonage he occupied with his wife. It was to her that he owed his living. Her father, the local squire had given it to him so as to keep the Church in the family. His only son could not be expected to go into the Church when a military career beckoned, so his youngest daughter could marry the young man he had met on the train and to whom she seemed to have no great objection. The young man was one of promise: a scholarship boy who had made the most of his education and actually learned in a scholarly fashion whilst at Oxford. Of course, in the squire's opinion, such attention to learning befitted someone who would have to earn their living and was quite contrary to both his and his eldest son's experiences of University. In any case, with eldest son married off and into the army, eldest daughter wedded to a wealthy city banker, it was clearly the duty of the youngest daughter to secure the family control of the village Church. And for all his manful Godliness, this young fellow had the wherewithal to become a Bishop – the squire was sure of it. All that was required was to keep him from getting too involved in religious matters and to cultivate a few old friends in the Diocese.

"I told you, at the outset, that she was too pretty a face to be happy in a country Vicarage. Not one for visiting the sick and aged as her duty should be, I'll be bound. And now she has run off with a painter. If only you had listened to me two years ago."

"Artist. I would not say that she has run off, either. Not exactly. In any case she has visited the poor and the elderly and mothers with little babes and taken soup and bread. She is a good Christian woman, mother, and I will not admit that she is acting willingly. Seduced, as is the weakness of her sex, by the smooth words and the primrose path: her guide on the road to ruination, that painting fellow I welcomed into my home...our home." He seemed to be clutching at straws, as far as his mother was concerned. She told him so.

"You talk as if he'd dragged her into the haystack," said his grandfather.

"We will manage without your vulgarities, you wicked old man." He'll be stirring things up, thought Mrs. Jagland, who knew her father well. "Thomas is in need of guidance, so we can do without knowing how these things were done in your youth."

"Best if he had," continued the old man, who knew his daughter well enough to ignore her after lunchtime. "Painting, is it? That's bad my lad."

"Grandfather, it is not the painting to which I object: it is the familiarity, the apparent ease of kindred spirits that meet with a conjunction of being that I have never felt between myself and my Darling."

"There's your answer, Tommy. You drag her into the stooks and I'll warrant that..." The old man was cut off by a look of the kind no daughter should give an aged father.

"Fine talk to a man of God and your own kin." Mrs. Jagland looked from her father to her son. "Now let us consider what is best done. And you, father, fall asleep as is your usual habit at this hour or when serious thought is called for."

"Or learn yourself how to paint." Another glare and then old man closed his eyes obediently, though they all knew his ears would stay open.

A month before Thomas had written to her explaining how a Mr. Rodolfi, who was on a walking tour, during which he was painting pastoral landscapes, was staying with them and would remain there for a week. This was a pleasure, in his view, as Mr. Rodolfi, though given to artistic fancies, was a cultured man who discussed so many subjects with ease – a rarity in the rural Midlands. Moreover, he had given the errant wife lessons in watercolours. During the course of the stay, the Rector had been summoned urgently to attend upon the bishop and had been away for two days. He had suggested that Mr. Rodolfi accompany him and see something of the city. On the one hand he enjoyed the artists company and felt that it would be pleasant to discuss the works of art in the Cathedral with him – all the more so as it seemed that two days of tedious meetings on ecclesiastical matters lay ahead of him. In addition, it would, he felt, be improper for a strange man to stay in the vicarage, even given the presence of the housekeeper and maid. However, at the very suggestion his pretty young wife had pouted and declared that it was a poor husband who trusted not his own wife and that it was quite wrong of him to take away from her the entertaining young fellow who had already done so much for the subtlety of her brushwork. But, no, perhaps it was she who should come with him to ensure the safety of the ladies of the city. Needless to say, Thomas gave way under the force of argument, embarrassment and downcast eyes.

So, he had gone and Rodolfi had stayed. On his return he found his wife at her easel, with Mr. Rodolfi pointing out refinements to her technique.

They were sitting under a tree in the vicarage garden. The low branches in the full leaf of summer kept the afternoon sun at bay as the Master and Pupil sat together. They had their backs to the door from which the Vicar emerged into that bit of paradise that is a country garden. Pleased to be home, full of goodwill, he was about to hail his wife and Mr. Rodolfi with "Good Afternoon", when he was suddenly halted in mid-halloo.

The scene was perfect. From his wife's white gown and bonnet, to Rodolfi's too artistically rakish straw hat, it was the summer afternoon in a country vicarage garden that God would have created for the Sabbath. Mr. Rodolfi, who was sitting to the left of his pupil, moved closer to her by shuffling along the bench. He moved but a couple of inches, but none the less the two inches that make the difference between sitting under a tree and sitting together under a tree. Thomas was once more about to call out with a rather less hearty greeting, when once more he was reduced to silence. Rodolfi's right arm reached slowly around the narrow shoulders of the petite form and gently touched the arm of the pupil. Thomas checked himself, reflecting that this was surely just an attempt to correct some clumsiness or to encourage more delicate work. How long the hand stayed on the lower arm for he did not know, but he soon became aware that be it never so short, it was a darned sight too long.

It was not one of the meek who will inherit the earth that crossed the grass with lengthening strides, but something more akin to one of those Old Testament fellows who went about smiting the enemies of the Lord. His 'Good Afternoon' that had begun full of affability and happiness to be home but a few moments before, was released like a war cry.

"Well, I must say, Sir...and my Dear...," he spluttered as he rounded the easel.

"Hello, My Darling, how lovely that you are home for tea."

"Tea? What was..."

"You seem flustered, my Dear."

"This gentleman had his arm about..."

"Francis was kindly showing me how to...Oh, My Dear. You are jealous?"

"What have you to say? Mr. Rodolfi?"

"Oh, Tommy My Love, Mr. Rodolfi – Francis – is teaching me his technique." Turning her head to the Master, "Take no notice, Francis. He has a bad head because the Bishop has spent two days boring him silly about Methodists."

"Baptists," corrected Thomas.

Thomas was already feeling foolish, despite the fact that he was sure he was right. There had been something in it, he was certain. Yet Rodolfi sat there looking innocently mystified, whilst the pretty lips that teased and reprimanded all at once and those lovely eyes made him sure that he would have to defy his better judgement.

Tea arrived to drive away the frisson. The sunny afternoon drew on. Thomas saw the paintings his wife had done and listened to Rodolfi praising her talents and wishing he could stay longer to teach her more and to do more sketching and, maybe, work on a few local scenes. Inevitably, he was invited to remain at the vicarage as long as he wished.

"That is too kind Mr. Jagland. I am most obliged to you and to your lady wife. I have much to do elsewhere, however, but maybe there is something to be said for concentrating one's attention on the beauties of one piece of countryside rather than spreading one's efforts too thinly. I accept. Now I must write some letters, so I will leave you for a while."

"I have to go and see the sexton before dinner, would you like a stroll up to the Church, Mr. Rodolfi?" That would at least take his fears with him.

"I fear my letters will take all my time, though I should like to visit the Church with you one day. Country Churches possess such simplicity. And not a few surprises! Who knows what beauties one has kept secret in this parish." And, with that, Mr. Rodolfi, sauntered across the grass and entered the cool of the old house.

Two pairs of eyes followed him and then turned to look into the other.

"How was the Bishop, my Dear?"

"Worried. Dull. Look, Katherine, what was that fellow up to? He had an arm around you."

"I told you. Was the Bishop very worried about those nasty Methodists?"

"Baptists. Well, it is a fine thing for a husband to return to his home to find his wife cavorting under a tree with a man in a straw hat."

"Francis is an artist, a straw hat is part of his uniform."

"The hat is immaterial. The closeness on the other hand..."

"Was that of a Master coaxing improvement from his pupil."

"Well, I think it should not happen again. In full view of the passing villagers too. They could see. There, where the hedge is low. What will they think?"

"I can hardly be expected to learn landscapes indoors. Besides they would have to stand on tip-toe."

"That is not the point, my Dear. I...we have a position to maintain. How can I combat the rise of Dissent if the lowest elements in the village discover a closeness between a married woman and a stranger in a straw hat."

"I was unaware that the Methodists encouraged either."

"Baptists. Katherine, you twist my words so that my real concern is ignored. Think what this could do for my reputation. What will your father say? How can I progress in the Church – as he wishes – if you are even suspected of intimacy with another?"

"I expect father will be more surprised that the worried husband invited the interloper to stay as long as he wanted."

"I didn't...I enjoyed his conversation, but most of all he obviously brightens your hours."

"And like a flare he will burn bright and disappear, Tommy, while you will be my eternal flame..."

"Really? My Dear, I did not mean to..."

"I forgive you Darling. But do not doubt me. And, for our love I promise to sit away from the view of villagers, just in case Mr. Rodolfi forgets himself again."

She offered him her cheek and he kissed it tenderly, the calmness of the exterior masking his emotions which were still simmering, though they had gone off the rolling boil.

"Now, off you go to see God."

He looked puzzled.

"Godfrey. The sexton. You have to see him before dinner."

"Yes. That's right. I was puzzled for a moment. You said God."

"Darling, those Methodists must be stopped before you lose all humour. Now off you go. I'll be safe from Mr. Rodolfi and you'll be back for dinner."

They kissed discretely and parted. His footsteps could be heard on the road. The hard ground of summer gave a harder footfall than the mud and puddles of winter. A few steps had sounded and then they stopped. A slight grunt was heard behind the hedge, at the point where it was lowest. Naturally, this drew Katherine's attention. And there she saw her husband's brown hair briefly appear above the hedge top and disappear just as rapidly.

A shuffle of feet, another grunt, the hair reappeared. She was about to call out to her husband. She felt annoyed that he was so concerned about whether a passer-by might have seen her over the hedge, and she wished that her Tommy would be so foolish more often.

She did not call out. A new sound was added. The creak of cart wheels heavily laden came around the sharp bend of the road that ran round three sides of the vicarage. A rustic voice called out, "Hello Mr. Jagland, need a hand, whatever 'tis you're about?"

The voice was that of one her father's carters, though she could not recall the name. A smile crept across her lips as she thought of her poor husband's embarrassment and heard him reply that he was attempting to see if the bank and hedge combined were enough to give privacy to the garden.

"Mrs. Jagland seems contented enough sitting there at her painting. Mind there are few hedges that I can't see over," said the carter helpfully.

"Quite so. Thank you."

"Mind Sir, I cannot see that gentleman who has been making such good use of your trees for a sunshade. Mind, you being away from home, you won't want to be hearing about him."

The vicar thanked the carter again, but with less embarrassment and more testiness.

In some villages the Church and vicarage are next-door-neighbours. That had been the case in Littleborough, but the old vicarage had been burned down two centuries ago. The new one, and it was still thought of as new, with all seventeenth century conveniences and more modern additions stood almost as far from the church as it could be without being detached from the village. The walk up the gently sloping track that was the main street allowed the vicar to survey his flock each time he went to the church.

The Church and Main Street might have been almost anywhere in the mixed-farming growing counties. His walk would take him past the respectable Inn, the less respectable public house and the dingy little beer shop where only the poorest labourers refreshed themselves. The shop that was butcher and grocer, the cobblers, the bakery; there would be numerous women working at their lace, bonnets protecting them against the sun; the men would be at work and the children would be at the school. He liked to pass the time of day with them, even those who did not attend as often as they should. He was a kind man and genuinely liked most of his parishioners, but today he wished there was an underground tunnel to take him to his meeting with the sexton.

Thank fortune, or rather The Lord, that it was harvest time, he thought as he passed the few people who were in the street; old women mostly, bonnets like haloes, gossiping over their lace pillows. But, he wondered, what was the subject of their gossip? They did not look at him with any less respect than was usual, nor did their gossip cease: good signs. Yet he was sure that stories must be being told. How could it be otherwise? A stranger, a foreigner, an outlandish fellow, with an easel; a bohemian in a straw hat; the Reverend Jagland not at home; his pretty wife under threat.

"They will call me a hypocrite, of that I am sure mother."

"Foolish, maybe, my boy, but hypocrite never." Mother's words were hardly comforting.

"I am not sure which I would prefer to be regarded. And now I must prepare for my visit to the bishop next week. He was displeased with me on my last visit due to the growth in numbers amongst the Methodists as well as Baptists in the parish – so many that they now intend to build a Chapel. I will write to him and my father-in-law resigning my living I think. I shall retire to scholarship and maybe a little teaching."

The sad young man finished his tea and said that he would stroll along the towpath for a while and maybe something would come to him; some scheme that would solve this knotty problem. For he no more wished to lose his wife than he did his living, though his reputation was so important. The sun had appeared and was burning away the mizzle that had left tiny droplets of water on the leaves of all the plants. These now shone like so many tiny gemstones. He noticed them and wished that his emotions and mind would undergo such a rapid change. They did not.

As he strolled, haltingly and ill-at-ease, the world rushed past him. Twice fly-boatmen cursed him for standing bemused as they sped along. Subconsciously avoiding the horses and the boys that followed them, unaware of the colours, some dull and faded, others bright as a new sixpenny piece, he wandered without aim and without any solution to the difficulties he faced. At least none of these boat people knew his business. Indeed, he had read that most of them were so morally lax in their attitudes and, worse, in their unrestrained behaviour, that they would only have mocked him because of his social position and not because of any sense of immorality.

For a few moments he stood and watched the boats work their way under a bridge, passing on towards London or approaching on their way to the industrial heartlands. To be able to move away, to disappear, to pass out of sight under a bridge or round a tree-fringed bend and to be thought of no more by those who stood looking on. There was no hint of envy in his thinking this: he merely wondered if there was an equivalent means of escape for vicars run aground. Of course, the boats still carried the weight of cargo wherever they went and they would return or journey on. Yet it was a poor captain who could not steer a safe passage and a foolish lad who did not guide his horse, he reflected.

Were these poor folk with no decent home in which to bring up their children and accord themselves the comforts that even the poorest labourer afforded himself to be pitied for that? He had always assumed so. Now he wondered if it was not men such as he who, forced to reside in one place in a position of responsibility, who were to be regarded with most sympathy. What did these boatmen have to do but labour he wondered? If they laboured and thought nothing and behaved as they wished, what did they lose? He had read that drunkenness, ignorance, sexual immorality and dirtiness were rife on these boats. Yet what did these people lose by it?

As he looked he saw men at the tiller, boys behind the plodding horses, children running along the bank gathering berries, women with babes in arms steering as their men folk ate: a parade of people occupied with their work. Even away from the hedge, he could see fields of the ordinary Hodges gathering in the harvest. Well-ordered lines of men rhythmically swinging their scythes, stepping over what they had cut down as they advanced as a rank of infantry on exercise. Behind, women and children gathering up the fallen stalks as boys waited with stones and dogs for the rabbits to break cover. Wagons in the rear: such precision, each with his or her task.

Clearly, he had his work to do. He pondered if "wife of the vicar" was enough labour to occupy his wife. He thought not, though real work would be more than he could allow her. Yet, surrounded by these apparently ignorant people each doing their bit, it became clear to him that whatever God intended for him he must immediately remove Mr. Ridolfi from his home. He realised that he had been weak in agreeing to the sweet words of his dear wife. He should have saved her! He, a man of God, had failed to protect his beloved. What could one expect from a woman no more or less tainted by the sin of Eve? Nothing. Yet, his sin was greater for he had failed to act responsibly, not just for his own career and happiness but for the woman for whom he should have borne the greatest duty of care. He would return home now and deal with the canker that had infested his Garden of Eden, damn his straw hat. Ridolfi and his easel would be flung out onto the street, paint pots close behind. He would confess his foolishness and, in his next sermon, he would exhort all good men in the village to defend the morals of their families. He hoped that his dearest would also see this as a romantic act of gallantry.

Having reached this decisive moment he realised that all was stymied because he had to be with the bishop first thing the next morning and that, despite the speed of the trains of the day, the timetable would not enable him to return home, act and get to his destination at the appointed time. Why was the Bishop such an early riser? Always at his desk by seven thirty Mr. Jagland had been told. To keep his eight-thirty appointment in the Cathedral City he would have to be there that evening. There was nothing to do but try to maintain resolve until the opportunity came to show his wife that he, though a spiritual man was quite capable of ejecting a man in a straw hat from the vicarage and hurling his trunk after him, should it come to that.

His stride quickened and he soon came into sight of the cottage by the cut, with the pale stone of the walled garden. The sun had brought his grandfather out onto the canal side, where he loved to be. He was leaning on his sticks as he chewed the fat with an old acquaintance that happened to be passing by. Business was not so vigorous as to prevent social calls. Grandson did not envy his grandfather's age, nor did he consider him a reprehensible as his mother did – though he often wondered about the salvation of the old man's soul. No, what he envied was the way his grandfather seemed content and easy with people. Many liked him. Even Mr. Ashton and Mr. Doddrington, rivals for the said soul and victims of the old fellow's idiosyncratic behaviour, if attempting to knock one into the cut because he was a Baptist and continually bating the Anglican clergyman, could be described as idiosyncratic, had a well-hidden regard for the amiable old curmudgeon. Yes, thought the grandson, his ancestor could, and did, say whatever he liked and get away with it where others would receive a slap in the face or more formal dismissal. There he could see him, probably chawing with the son of a man whom he worked with, all for old time's sake. There was the son of the boatman standing by listening intently to the old stories, as a burly woman went back and forth from pump to boat with a bucket. How happy the whole scene seemed: how far from the turmoil of his recent life.

This reflection just goes to show how far we can misapprehend the things we see at a distance. The woman was berating man and boy in language that the good clergyman was, fortunately, to remote to hear. By the time he arrived at the little group of figures, the burly woman has disappeared into the cabin and could be heard clattering pots and chopping vigorously. Even this had not moved her man. The little boy still stood staring at the old storyteller, but what he heard was not an old story.

Had not the old man beckoned to his grandson by waving one of his sticks in his direction, he would have passed by in horror. For what he heard was the tale of his own recent woes. At first he did not believe what he was hearing, but he was hearing it. His own grandfather was telling all his grandson's troubles to a family of bargees. Now he knew that his mother should have been believed. Her reports of the old man's disreputable behaviour had always been received with a liberal pinch of salt, but now he heard it with his own ears. He knew he should walk briskly past, but he knew also that if he were to face down his wife and send a healthy young artist packing he could not ignore the affront being committed by a friendly old relative. No, to avoid this confrontation would so shatter his mettle that his nerve might never recover, especially if the Bishop kept him all day seeking God's help.

Thus our hero marched up to the old man, the middle-aged man and the little boy. Ignoring the latter and only half addressing the boatman, he laid into his grandfather as best he could.

"How dare you...how could you recite my private woes to these people? I know that I should respect your grey hairs, grandfather, and I am not a man of violent mood or conduct, but to tell those things that pass between a man and his mother to these bargees is frankly unworthy of you. I distinctly saw this man smile in mockery as I approached. You did, fellow, distinctly. Well, let me tell you that my affairs are not the business of these people. My profession is the most respectable of all callings. These people can know nothing of either morality or reasoned conduct. Such things are not within their capacity. And before you say a word, I have resolved to act and will do so as soon as I return from seeing the Bishop tomorrow. That artistic fellow will feel my righteous wrath. So there is no mockery to be made and nothing for waterside gossip that will pass up and down with these boats."

He turned to go before there could be any response, his intention being to march triumphantly away leaving them in awe-struck dumbness. He should have known better. As he swept round dramatically, he heard his grandfather say, "Blast his foolhardiness, mind, Vesuvio, why should you even think of helping him out now? My grandson, a man of the cloth too. In spite of all that I know you'd have stood by for your old dad's sake."

Help. The one word that really seemed to matter. It rankled. How could this rather shabby looking man and his ragged child and that woman help him? He spun around to face them and advanced angrily. With cutting sarcasm he begged to know if Mr.

Vesuvio knew the Bishop well enough to put in a good word for him and maybe he would do so at the next Diocesan Garden Party.

"It's Happy. Mr. Happy".

The reverend gentleman did not like his grandfather's words. "I am not happy in the least. Not with you nor with the situation I find myself in here or domestically. I am…"

"Not listening," interrupted the old man. "We all know well that you're not happy. I meant he is. Mr. Happy. Mr. Vesuvio Happy."

The vicar looked surprised.

"Well, where's you manners, as your mother would say. Come along now, 'tis a fortunate for you laddio that this fellow whom you have insulted so freely, along with all his kind, is more happy than Vesuvio and, for the sake of the friendship twixt his late lamented dad and myself, as well as his own good nature, is willing to help you out."

His grandfather was right. Rudeness had not been called for. He said so. "But I fail to see how, Mr. Happy can be of any assistance."

"My Dot's a Longbottom," butted in Vesuvio.

The meaning of this was apparently obvious to all, except the one to whom it was addressed. So, Vesuvio repeated it. "Long line of 'em too."

"I am afraid that I do not follow you, Mr. Vesuvio."

"His good lady, the one as you can hear a chopping away is a Longbottom before she married into the Happy's. This lad is their son, Septimus Severus."

"I am pleased to meet your family Mr. Happy. I thank my grandfather for introducing you all, but I really do not see how you can be of assistance in this matter and I would be grateful it if you forgot all you have heard."

"Hold on you young fool and think. When that Bishop wants to know about the goings-on with strange fellows in you vicarage, what will you say? Yes, your worship, I invited him. Yes, he has caught the eye of my flighty little missus and they've been displaying their misconduct to the village. That'll put you top of his list!"

"Of course, I shall tell the truth, but I will add that I am resolved to remove the gentleman in question upon my return home."

"And he'll wonder why you haven't done it already. I can hear you, well I left him there once and Lord knows what happened, so I did it again. Clever man, he'll think, just the ticket for an Archdeacon or whatever they have. No, won't do. What you need to do is to tell him that the man has gone and that you acted with decision and determination. That's the way to show Bishops."

"And what do you know of Bishops? Nothing, to be sure, but there is something in what you say. However, had you listened carefully you would know that I cannot return home before I meet with the Bishop. Thank you for you intervention grandfather, I am sure it was well intentioned." His anger had declined and he felt quite humble that these ordinary folk should be willing to assist simply because he was related to an old man who had once been a friend of a relative.

"I know a sight more about Bishops than you may think. Much more than you know of boats and women too. I'll tell you about the Bishop of Winchester or Chichester or maybe just Chester who wanted to buy my horse one time, a wager it was, racing to Oxford. But not now. And before you go on insulting folk who scrimp their lives in a little boat cabin you should do a proper day's work yourself. And hear that chopping down in the cabin? Content yourself that Dot and Vesuvio are married good and proper and that this here Septimus Severus is the legitimate product."

The Reverend Jagland, like his grandfather, could not hold a grudge for long and knowing that he may well be doing an injustice apologised for intemperate remarks, though all the Parliamentary Reports complained of many moral offences amongst the boat people, they did this in the general sense and such reports clearly did not apply to present company.

Mr. Happy smiled on, wondering how he'd look as a Bishop. There was a brief silence. Vesuvio looked at the old man and they both looked at Thomas. Septimus Severus, realising there was man's talk about to happen made sure he stayed quiet, so he could stay and hear it.

"Littleborough's full of Longbottom's," drawled Mr. Happy.

"I know. I have christened and married several. I even buried one a couple of months ago," agreed Thomas, still not catching on.

"Great-aunt Letty."

"Letty Longbottom. I buried her."

"Great-aunt and a bit of something of her below." Thomas was still unclear about what this was leading up to. "This here gentleman buried Letty, Dot."

The chopping stopped. There was a momentary pause for reflection followed by "Thank him" booming from the boat.

"Liked you, Letty did. She was pleased you buried her."

"Most kind, Mr. Happy. Mrs. Happy's relative was an excellent parishioner. Her cakes were one of the great attractions of our parish show. Beyond compare."

"Rest of them Longbottom's like you too. Not too Churchy for their liking. Even Miserable Rueben has a good word for you. That's something."

"I am gratified. It is a shame that I may not be their parish priest for much longer."

"Just what Mrs. Happy was saying before she went off to get my dinner after the old 'un had yarned on about your troubles. Vesuvio she said them poor old Littleborough Longbottom's; they might get a Churchy one, she says; you need to do something, my Lovey. Well Sir, when my Lady sets me a quest, I never refuse."

"I fail to see how you can be of help, though I thank you for your kind thoughts. Now grandfather, we had better..."

"We, my lad, had better stop here and you had better take some notice. Remember that this gent here has extraordinary power. He being of gipsy stock."

"Grandfather, Mr. Vesuvio I really..."

"The old 'un, doubtless, extravagates my power. But I'll give you a good bit of advice and assure you that should you follow it; all your troubles will be gone by the time you get home and the honourable bishop'll think none the less of you and yours."

"I think that I know my own business. As for lying to a bishop…"

Mr. Happy, looked surprised, but it was the old man who interrupted the Rev. Thomas. "Who spoke of lying to a bishop? Only you, because you don't listen to your elders. Now hold up and hear how Vesuvio and the Longbottom's can come to your aid."

"Oh, very well. But I will shun any illegality or immorality."

"There now," soothed Vesuvio, "there'll be neither of those. To the contrary, morality will be the heart of our solution. It might raise a row, but no one, not a soul, need have their head cracked or their ribs busted in."

Thomas looked as though he hoped what he was hearing was true, but doubted that it could possibly be so. But he listened, for though he knew his own business, he knew only that everything was hopeless.

"Now, Sir," began Mr. Happy, "all you do is as I say. You go see his honourableness and when he starts going on about your missus and your lodger, all you says is that you showed him the kindness of

Christian charity, but now you'd shown him the toe end of your boot. Tell him how he took advantage. No, don't use them particular words. Say how he abused your welcome and that, though nothing had gone on, you realised that his knocking about the place was leading your flock astray. Tell him you booted him out. That at that very moment he will have left your home and gone, never to return."

"Thank you. The Bishop might accept such an explanation. There is a fault with this scheme. He will not have gone from my parsonage. He will still be there. I cannot go home," he was starting to raise his voice, "and make him leave and get to the Bishop in time. I will not lie to the Bishop."

"You'll not be lying to him," roared the old man, raising his voice even more.

"The man will be there. I will be informing the Bishop that he is not. To tell him so would be untrue. Now, much as I respect your age, grandfather, and Mr. Happy's kind advice, I must decline."

"But he won't be there, that artist chap will have gone. Just listen for once. Carry on Vesuvio, though I am at a loss whether you shouldn't just save your wind." The old man glared at his grandson. "You pay attention: too much learning and too little wisdom."

Mr. Happy continued. "All you have to do Sir, is to say it. Tell your tale. All will fall into place. I see it."

The reverend gentleman looked at the boatman. "And how...no, on second thoughts, I do not wish to know what you intend to do."

"Me Sir?"

"You have some action in mind. I do not wish to know. Nor will I have violence."

"You are addled, boy." The old man was beginning to wonder what they had taught his grandson at University. "How can Mr. Happy here, and his wife and child, let alone their boat, get all the way to Littleborough in time to do anything anymore than you can? Take his word. You won't be telling your Bishop untruths, though why he should worry if you do, I can't fathom, and by the time you get home you'll find that all you told him will have come to pass."

Worn down by the hopelessness of anything else, the rector of Littleborough gave in. He thanked the boatman, though he knew not what for and turned to leave.

"Here, have you no reward for all this generosity. I should be generous if I were you. Shoes for the boy and a bonnet for Mrs. Happy. Not to mention that scraggy old nag that pulls his home and business." Thomas turned back and drew out his pocketbook.

"Tis tradition to cross the palm of the gipsy," smiled Mr. Happy. "But, don't think…"

"No, no. I insist." Thomas was embarrassed by being inveigled. He now realised that he would be paying for Mr. Happy's beer that night. No doubt, Septimus Severus, would have a night run down the towpath to smuggle a flagon to the Old Man, who was still under the yoke of abstinence. He had a good mind to tell his mother.

Within the hour, Thomas was away to his nemesis; Mr. Happy was leaning on the stern rail as Septimus Severus followed the horse the last few miles of the day; and the old man was tucking into the floury potatoes, the buttered green beans and the thick slices of bacon, cooked by his daughter, and washed down with nothing more than tea. The old man could do nothing to help his grandson, for whom he had limited sympathy in this case anyway. Too many books, too little life: how could the Church hope to save any ordinary human. He thought. Mr. Happy was heading in the general direction of Littleborough, but when he moored up as close as he could to that village the soft summer darkness was laying its satin spread over the land. It was ten miles to Littleborough and Mrs. Happy had stewed up a pot of meat stew and he had done a full day's work. The train carrying Thomas rumbled at Sunday evening stopper pace through the long dusk of the fields and village halts. At the second of two more market towns he changed trains. The new train was faster, but it was dark when it pulled in to the city station. The clear night sky had a summer moon. Its light caused the Cathedral towers to appear even more dominant than usual. Close by, the early-rising Bishop would be asleep. Thomas made his way to the Bishop's Palace, was greeted by the butler and shown to his room. It was nearly midnight. The bishop had been abed since nine.

The interview was held over breakfast. Of the food, nothing need be said. There was a good deal of friendly questioning about the village, the school, the Mothers Club, the Sunday School and the Boys' Improvement Class: especially the Boys' Improvement Class. Thomas was happy to talk of these things because they were carrying on happily, with some success – even in the Boys' Improvement Class. Yet he knew the question of the day must soon be addressed. Breakfast finished and the Bishop invited Thomas into his Study.

The Bishop was much more the man of the world than Thomas, and had been appointed to his Diocese as much for his ability to play the political game as his scholarship or spiritual qualities. He was, however, a sensitive man who genuinely cared about his flock. The big question was one for the Study, not the breakfast room.

Thomas followed the advice that Mr. Happy had given him. After the Bishop had introduced the topic and gone into some detail about his concerns, Thomas managed to get his blow in. He explained that he had expelled the fellow, though he denied that any impropriety had taken place. There followed a veiled reprimand regarding the situation and advice for the future should any such circumstances threaten the standing of the Rector of Littleborough again. The Bishop explained that he was reassured by the response the rector had made to his questions. Then there was a return to gentler discussion. The interview appeared to be reaching an end. Thomas looked forward to leaving the room and breathing a sigh of relief. And a short prayer begging forgiveness for misleading the Bishop: Oh Lord, I will act immediately when I get home.

"Well, Thomas, we had better be off." The Bishop rounded off the discussion.

"Are you going on a journey, too My Lord?"

"Of course, I am." The Bishop looked perplexed. Thomas was surprised by his expression. They looked at each other, both puzzled.

"Sorry, sorry, Thomas. My apologies. I did not say. I am coming with you."

Thomas did not faint and his heart did not pump like a steam engine. He did not blush or panic. He did not know why he did none of these things. He did blurt out, "But the chap has gone, honest!"

The Bishop smiled, though he caught the whiff of a rat. "So he has. But you have had a hard time of it, so I will return with you to Littleborough." He even attempted a joke: "You have, at least one spare room."

"Yes, of course, we have three or four. Yes, he has gone, but you wouldn't want his room. No. We'll give you the room that overlooks the meadow with the little river."

"Thank you. Idyllic. I do like visiting my parishes Thomas."

"But, why rush? Why not come in a month when we'll have Harvest Festival?"

"I hold Harvest festival here. You would think that you did not want me to come."

"Not in the least, My Lord. No, I was thinking of your convenience. The fellow has gone and you have important things to do."

"Not least of which is to show my support for you by walking along the village high street, past those Methodists who are leading so many astray, and those Baptists whom I suspect of spreading rumours in this case. My presence will show both my confidence in you and concern for what has been said. I shall only stay the one night."

Only one night, thought Thomas. Could he keep Rodolfi out of sight for one night? Would his wife say nothing? No. It was all up with him. He would be found out, unless Rodolfi had just decided to go of his own accord, which was highly unlikely, or Mr. Happy had done more than drink the rector's health in return for his money.

The Bishop speculated on why Thomas seemed so on edge throughout the journey. He said little, but he was beginning to think unpleasant thoughts about what he was going to find in Littleborough, in general, and at the rectory, in particular. Meanwhile, Thomas wondered whether throwing himself on the mercy of the Bishop would not be best: to confess all. He decided against it. He hoped that some opportunity would arise for speaking to his wife and Rodolfi before the Bishop was able to. Yes, he would take the Bishop and his luggage straight to his room and allow him to change into clothes suitable for a summer's day in the country.

Walking, at the Bishop's request, the three miles that separated Littleborough from the nearest railway station, Thomas firmed up his plans.

As they approached the Rectory he said that he would show the Bishop to his room and then order some tea, which they would take in the garden. The Bishop, to his surprise, agreed with this plan of action.

Thomas led the Bishop, at a more than vigorous walk, into the house and up the stairs. There was no sign of either his wife or Rodolfi. Breathing a sigh of relief, he deposited the Bishop in a sun-filled bedroom with a view that brought a smile of warm appreciation from the guest. However, Thomas had no time for accepting compliments. He was off down the stairs, three at a time. Now he wished there was a sign of his wife and of Rodolfi, or at least the housekeeper.

As he landed with a thump in the hallway, his hopes were gratified. "Mercy!" cried the housekeeper. Thomas looked round and saw her. Even better, behind her, open-mouthed stood his wife.

"Ah! Yes. Tea for three, please Mrs. Simpkins. Yes, tea. Hello my Dear! The Bishop has come to stay the night. Upstairs, changing. May I speak with you my Dear? Dinner for three, this evening, Mrs. Simpkins? Sorry to trouble you, but he just decided to come and stay. My Dear, this way, please. Tea in the garden, Mrs. Simpkins. Thank you."

It was only when they stepped from the cool shade of the house into the hot afternoon sun that made

Littleborough shimmer that afternoon, that Thomas noticed that his wife looked pale. Moreover, she had said not one word. He had obviously startled her.

"My Dear, where is Mr. Rodolfi? Is he out painting?" He did not wait for a reply. "He must leave, my Dear, he must. It is imperative for us both that he does not meet the Bishop."

"No, he is not out painting. He has gone."

"Gone where? I must see him immediately. Did he indicate where he was going?"

"No. He has gone. Wales, I think he said. He left before breakfast."

"What, my Dear? Gone for good? Blessing of blessings."

"Yes, he had rather overstayed his welcome. But, I thought you liked his clever conversation?"

"I did. Look, if the Bishop asks, just say that he left a couple of days ago. No need to say more. I'll explain later. Tomorrow. You looked pale when I first saw you my Dear. I am pleased that the colour has returned to your cheeks. Sunshine is a marvellous tonic."

"Maybe I am blushing at being asked by a clergyman to tell untruths to a Bishop."

"You don't mind do you? Really?"

She smiled and said that she did not, but that she would expect an explanation later. An explanation of everything. Thomas looked at her quizzically. "Yes," she said, "I want to know the whole story of last night's events."

As it happened the Bishop was as good as his word. He strolled up to the Church, spoke to a few parishioners, admired their children and blessed the labourers who straggled home from the fields as the sun began to set. He ate, slept, ate again and set off to retrace the three miles to the nearest railway station. The perfect visitation, thought Thomas.

He walked with his superior to the turning of the road and they said their farewells. The Bishop reminded him why he had come, but said that he would think no more of it. Thomas said that he had become a wiser man and thanked the Bishop for his thoughtfulness and concern. Then they parted.

A lovely summer morning: sunshine, a light breeze, home in his parish with no Bishop and no, most of all, no Rodolfi. He marched home: a march of victory, though he knew for certain that it was fortune that had brought him through. Fancy Rodolfi just going off like that. Bless his Darling wife for doing her bit so well. He told her so as he met her on the doorstep. She smiled. Yet in her eyes there was a hint of a tear. He reached out to hug her, but she side-stepped him and walked past into the garden. He followed her, hearing her sniffs turn to sobs, then, by degrees to uncontrolled crying. She sat in the very place where she had sat with Rodolfi.

Thomas was worried. He had never seen his wife cry before. Was it for Rodolfi or for him, or for what? He rushed across the grass and sat by her. He gently wrapped an arm around her. He was gratified that she did not shy away. He whispered words of love and comfort. The cries became sobs. She took his handkerchief from his coat pocket and wiped the last tears away, sat bolt upright and began an inquisition. Thomas explained all that had happened at the interview and how he had lied and that it was only fortune and her discretion that had saved a dangerous situation. "Imagine what your father would have said?" He finished.

"Is that all?" She clearly expected more.

He said it was and that there was nothing else to add, as far as he knew. She looked at his eyes. "You really don't know, do you? I am so glad of that."

So was Thomas. She told him what had befallen her the night before and what had lead Mr. Rodolfi to leave. "There were dozens of them, at least a hundred. Maybe more. All blacked up, with hats and hoods to cover their faces. I was terrified. All of them pressed into the lane around the house. I do not know what I would have done if any had come into the garden. None did, though I was afraid it was a revolution."

Thomas was puzzled. She went on. "It must have been after midnight, though I could not hear the chimes for all the noise. Yes, Darling, they were making a shocking row. Some had tins and others had buckets or pieces of wood. There was even an old hunting horn being blown. On and on they went. I was so scared that I sought out Mr. Rodolfi." Thomas looked concerned. "He had knocked on my door to see that I was safe, but I told him I would dress and then meet him on the landing." Thomas looked less concerned: there was little else Rodolfi could have done, after all.

"Then they all went silent and some others came marching down the lane. In the moonlight I could not see what they were carrying until they were just outside the house. I thought they had some sacks on a beam which they supported on their shoulders. Yet, when they came close to the house, I saw that they were not sacks. Well, they were, but they had been dressed up. One had a bonnet like mine and wore a dress, the other had a straw hat, the very image of Mr. Rodolfi's. It was awful, my Dear. I wished that you were there. Mr. Rodolfi put a comforting hand on my shoulder, but I pushed it away, you know."

"He seemed so calm, despite this terrible noise and the crowd of angry villagers. Then one of them, I could not see who, took out a piece of rope and made it into a loop. Just like a noose. It was a noose. And they put it over the straw hat and around the neck of the figure of Mr. Rodolfi. I turned to look, but he was gone. I heard him in his room. The key turned in the lock and I heard clothes being stuffed into a trunk and paints and easel with them. When I looked out of the window again, the people had gone. The last few were just visible heading up the lane. Everything was quiet and I thought to myself, what a beautiful moon. But I was scared without you."

"Dearest, what can I say? We must ask the constable: where was he? Why did you not send for him?" Thomas was indignant at such behaviour by the villagers. Respected him, Mr. Happy had said, which just went to show the worth of his advice. And his grandfather's words.

"I could hardly send poor Simpkins for the constable with such a ferocious crowd milling about in the lane." That was true enough, thought Thomas.

"Well, I shall question him most closely." Thomas thought again. Perhaps it would be best not to make too much of it. "A sermon; that is it. A sermon next Sunday. That will serve. They can't all have been Methodists and Baptists."

"No, no, my Sweet. They were acting morally."

The rector was momentarily silenced by these words.

"How can scaring the wits out of my wife be moral? How can a drunken mob be moral? My dear, this will not do." He was the leading resident figure in the village, in the absence of the squire: he knew his duty.

His wife, apparently, did not. "Simpkins says that they did it for you: for us. I told her they had no need to and she said that she had told them as such when she had heard gossip amongst the village women."

"Gossip, about what? Tittle-tattle amongst the lower classes is not to be given weight. They look to us, people of higher station for moral leadership. My dear, you must understand..."

"Simpkins said that they did not like the attention that Mr. Rodolfi seemed to be paying me in your absence. There was no basis for such vile allegations, my dear; you know you can trust me to the end of the earth. Nay, beyond."

Thomas suddenly felt humiliated. It was none of their business, damn them all. His affairs were his own. First his mother stuck her nose in, then his grandfather. All the villagers. And his grandfather had spread the news amongst those vile boat people: Mr. Happy. The Bishop. Mrs. Happy. He was on the verge of invoking the Lord of the Old Testament to smite them all.

Then it struck him. Mrs. Happy. A Longbottom of Littleborough. He was not sure how, but he was sure that she lay at the bottom of these events. All he could say was, "It may be for the best to forget it happened."

Two days later, Thomas was back into the routine of his parish. On his way back from visiting Mrs. Jenks who was in confinement for the eighth time, he saw a stout woman marching purposefully up the high street. She was striking up dust with each step. He was sure that he recognised her, though he could not summon up any memory of where he had seen her before. However, he did not have to fathom further. She hailed him.

"Morning Vicar. Mr. Happy sends his greetings and thanks you for the beer." Mrs. Happy smiled broadly.

Thomas was not sure to reply. So he muttered some general greeting. He wanted to question her, but recalled the strong and steady sound of this formidable lady wielding a cleaver. "Are you here to visit your relatives?" That was the best he could manage.

"My cousin and all the others. Just bringing them a few bits and bobs. Have a bit of a gossip too. Must let folk know how things go."

"Things? Any things in particular?" Thomas did not want his affairs spread even further afield. He especially did not want any news of a riot seeping out to the Bishop or to his father-in-law.

"Have no fear," Mrs. Happy looked at him with a peculiar squint that was meant to show her discretion.

Thomas decided that he would ask her directly. "Did Mr. Happy organise the mob that assembled here a few nights ago and conducted itself in such a vulgar and threatening manner outside the rectory?"

"Heaven, pardon, no, Sir. He was safe in The Boat and then on the boat, so to speak. Along with me and young Septimus Severus." Thomas knew that she was telling the truth: the canal was too far away – even if Mr. Happy were a prodigious walker.

"Mrs. Happy, your husband predicted that Mr. Rodolfi would leave before I spoke to the Bishop. He advised me to tell the bishop that he was gone. Now, how did he organise it all?"

"He didn't organise no mob! You should be ashamed of yourself, insulting a hard-working soul like my Vesuvio." She smiled. "No, Sir, he did not organise anything. Bless you."

"So how did he know that Rodolfi would go?"

"Ah, Sir, them gipsy folk have some powers the rest of us are unpossessed of."

"I do not believe in second sight or any such superstitious nonsense. How did he know?"

"Well," said Mrs. Happy, "perhaps he didn't. Perhaps all he knew was that you was to be from home that night. And now I must be on my way. Good day, Sir." And off she strode to visit her Longbottom relatives.

Thomas was about to call after her and demand a clear answer. Then he thought better of it. After all, he had not, when all was done, told the Bishop an untruth.

Class

That Sunday morning the vicar had begun another crusade. This one was even less relevant to the villagers than the last. It was not that he was a fool or an uncaring martinet intent on marching his flock in chains through the Gates of Heaven, it was probably just that he had never laboured a whole day in the stifling heat of late August or ditched along the headlands and hedgerows in the freezing wetness of January days that never saw the sun. Men who had done so had truly earned their pint of mild ale in the summer and their winter warmer. Mr. Doddrington's abstinence crusade had been stymied, despite the formidable support of the respectable ladies and gentlemen of the village, by the reluctance of those who drank for sustenance to give up the necessities of labouring life at the request of those that drank at leisure. In truth, he knew that there was little drunkenness within his flock and that when matters got out of hand there were ways in which the villagers righted matters. Despite this, he had been particularly disgusted that Mr. Oaktree, Baptist Minister, who had been opportunist enough, in the eyes of the established Church, to preach the virtues of temperance over total abstinence, thus gaining a lead in the close run rivalry between Church and Chapel. Mr. Doddrington said that he was only surprised that Mr. Oaktree had not taken to serving intoxicating liquor at those frequent teas that the Baptists held to celebrate every anniversary they could dream up. Mr. Oaktree replied to these charges with a pleasant smile and the assurance that, as in the days of John Bunyan, the non-conformists stood with the ordinary man.

Mr. Doddrington had learned his lesson. It had been suggested, in several missives he had received from groups of well-meaning middle-class moral reformers who might have been better off spending an evening in the village inn, that gambling was a great offence and a major cause of poverty amongst the lower orders. Indeed, the good vicar knew that on meagre wages to gamble was to invite hunger and poverty through the cottage door. Yet he could not believe that the pennies that exchanged hands amongst the labourers when playing at cricket or ratting were really such as to offend against God or undermine the well-being of their families. This was, he felt, in any case, not the field upon which to renew his battle with sin. His common-sense had got the better of him.

There were, he felt, more fundamental matters: matters that, if they were not removed from the land, would challenge the whole structure of society, the Empire, the Monarchy. Thus, he had preached upon the order that God had created for man; how the great prosperity of the British depended on this; how futile it was to listen to those who would upset this equilibrium; finishing off by expressing, on behalf of the Good Lord, the sincere hope that all would seek the sure and certain wealth that was offered in Heaven and not adhere to ungodly doctrines that sought to overthrow the social order that had served them so well.

In the congregation the farmers assented: there was prosperity. The labourers agreed that attempts to change would be futile for it was surely the seasons and the weather that laid them off from work and slashed their pay for day labour. For the good weather they should be thankful to the Lord; and for their Harvest Home; and Christmas Box they should thank the farmer. There may have been some who did not agree, but they communicated this only by glances and frowns, as one would have expected from men who had enough for their families to live and wished to keep that happy state.

At the end of the service that morning Mr. Doddrington felt pleased that he had struck a blow against the monstrous forces that placed political reform above moral rebirth. Dangerous men they were, men who would see the lower orders misled into the hands of demagogues and Republicans, to the damnation of their eternal souls and the confusion of their life on earth.

It would be unfair to make too much of the faintest of glows that warmed his heart still further. Indeed it troubled him to think on it. Yet even he would have confessed that the possibility of having put one over on Mr. Oaktree ensured that his heart was full of the love of God as he cleared the vestry with the sun shining through the window as it had cleared the stubby boughs of the ancient squat yew. This old tree shaded a corner of the Churchyard and covered some low, coffin shaped mounds with its venerable limbs. Mr. Doddrington could not help but be reassured that the Baptists might be noisy, but they were new: the true Church would stand as strong as God's order that had created it.

He had heard how a visiting Baptist preacher, from some part of Birmingham, had bemused the gentler souls of Mr. Oaktree's Church by stating that the Lord would rather have proper sewers and decent wages for his people than wealthy men salving their consciences with gifts of beef and pudding to the workhouse once a year. Indeed, he had said that if the entire host of Angels had descended onto certain parts of Birmingham it would be less of a miracle than if cholera did not strike again. The rural artisans, smaller farmers, workers on the canal and railway, and handful of particularly brave, often poor, labourers, that made up the people of God, as they saw themselves, assented to the general idea, but were perturbed by his more radical ideas. Indeed, so alien were these to most of them that they had protested to Mr. Oaktree that they were feared of being murdered and robbed should such men as the visiting preacher have their way. Mr. Oaktree had done his best to calm them and point out that life in the cities would seem as odd to them as the things they had heard from the preacher. In this he had not met with complete success and it had reached his ears that some of his flock had even spoken to Mr. Doddrington. Mr. Oaktree was a man powerful in the word and a fine preacher and that Sunday he had done his best to settle his flock once more. It was exhausting and emotional stuff, and so, leaving the afternoon Sunday School in the hands of Mr. Cleaver he set off for a walk by the canal to prepare for evening service. Likewise, Mr. Doddrington, enervated by his own sermon, left the Anglican Sunday School in the hands of Mr. Strong – a fine young curate and much better at keeping the Boys Improvement Class in order – to stroll by the canal and perhaps talk with that collector of local intelligence, Mrs. Jagland.

Mrs. Jagland was washing the pots following an excellent Sunday lunch, or dinner as her father called it. The little meat that there had been was cooked to tenderness beyond compare and the rich gravy mixed with the floury potatoes and mopped up by pudding had filled them all to the ribs. From the cottage garden had come young carrots and fresh-shelled peas. A fine meal of just the sort that ensured her ascendancy in the house: one that she would have denied. She, staunchly conservative, would have let it be known that it was Mr. Jagland who was master of the house, had you asked her. This was true, though the husband of the excellent cook and housekeeper, might have smiled. Yes, he was master, his wife chose him to be.

If you had asked her father, he would have beckoned you across the garden to his chair under the apple laden tree where the scent of honeysuckle hung in the shade, and asked you if he had ever told you about the time he was taking a load of coal down to London and how it had spontaneously combusted and the boat would have been lost had it not been for them shovelling it all into the cut until the water steamed.

Just as she finished her washing up, Mrs. Jagland heard the knock at the door as Mr. Doddrington poked his head round the parlour door. She was always pleased to see this man of the cloth and, given that her father had failed to infiltrate one of his acquaintances from his boating past into lunch, she was in a fine, cheery mood.

"If I'd have known, I would have invited you to share our lunch – though I know Mrs. Blackwell will have done you proud, better than our humble…"

She was cut off, just as she hoped to be, by the vicar. "Most kind, but Sunday lunch is something I should not like to intrude upon. Besides this is the day I am busiest."

"Well. At least I can offer you a cup of tea." The kettle whistled, as if by appointment.

"Now, Mrs. Jagland, have you heard…" Thus Mr. Doddrington and the lady of the house began to exchange information about the spectre of socialism amongst the Baptists.

Mr. Jagland did not hear them, being asleep in a chair. Lest he might be thought lazy, let us remember that he had but one afternoon when he did not work and he had every right to spend an hour of it asleep.

Out in the garden, the old man, looked as if he were asleep, but was merely "resting his eyes" and keeping a sharp ear out – his faculty for hearing was only sporadically limited by his age – for any familiar voices along the canal. It was strangely quiet that afternoon, the sluggish water sitting unmoved as blue and red damsel flies provided the only movement, the flash of colour adding to the silent hum of tranquillity.

As he drowsed, he heard footsteps on the other side of the wall that separated the garden from the towing path. Both were hefty boots belonging to men who were used to walking. That was not unusual, but these were not boatmen for they were not accompanied by the soft plod of a horse. Then he heard their voices. He recognised them immediately. One was Mr. Oaktree. The other belonged to Joseph Boot, who was, strangely enough, a cobbler or shoemaker, depending on whether you asked his customers or him. He lived in a village a couple of miles off along the canal and often walked by to collect and return shoes to people in the villages around and, on Sundays, to go to Chapel. He was a Baptist and a Deacon and the only one of Mr. Oaktree's flock who could be described as a radical. Typical of a shoemaker, some said; typical of a Baptist, said others; intelligent progress, he said.

"Good afternoon, Brother Oaktree," began the cobbler, "A powerful sermon this morning – and I look forward to this evenings even more so – though I did wonder if we might have that Birmingham preacher back again."

"A powerful sermon."

"It was, Praise the Lord for his Word, Brother Oaktree, and we should act upon it."

"It offended some."

"So, I heard. It will be raised at the next Church Meeting."

"I fear it will," said Mr. Oaktree with an understandable air of resignation, "a number amongst our Church will wish to be critical."

"I shall raise it." Mr. Boot had fire in his eyes. "I shall raise it, brother. Some of our number should count themselves fortunate for the blessings of country life and be ready to act for the benighted and oppressed not just across the sea. To act." The emphasis was strong. "To fight with giants and not to relent."

"Yes, Brother Boot, I am sure you will raise it. Some will see it differently."

Before Mr. Boot could reprimand Mr. Oaktree further, a voice was heard coming from the other side of the garden wall.

"That Mr. Oaktree, there? Care to step into the garden?" It was Old Job.

Mr. Oaktree had not the easy access which Mr. Doddrington's acquaintance with Mrs. Jagland gave. Yet he was as determined to achieve the salvation of the Old Man's soul as his counterpart. Indeed, he was firmly of the opinion that he was better placed to achieve this goal, as he had not spent as much time perplexing the poor fellow with assaults at every opportunity. In any case, it was an increasingly urgent matter. The Old Man could not live forever, and he already appeared to be the Methuselah of the towpath. Mr. Oaktree knew that Mr. Doddrington held the strong ground in this battle, but he hoped to capture the full house that the funeral of such a man would guarantee. The rafters of the Chapel should be raised, not the rotten beams of the Parish Church. Hardly the right attitude, you might argue. Mr. Oaktree would have replied that the power of his preaching would lead to converts and that would be God's Will. In any case, Mr. Doddrington would have argued along the same lines, and Mr. Oaktree knew it.

Thus he abandoned what was becoming an awkward discussion with Mr. Boot, excusing himself with a brisk farewell and explanation that he had intended a pastoral visit all along.

Mr. Boot stalked off, looking little like a threat to Her Majesty the Queen. Rather, he resembled a rural shoemaker out for a walk on a Sunday afternoon, the only outward sign of treason against the state an old Bible that poked out of his pocket.

Mr. Oaktree headed for the gate to the garden. He hoped that he might be able to make an impression on the Old Man and win him for true religion. Equally, he knew that he was more likely to get a good story. What he did not know was that the Old Man had called him only when Mrs. Jagland and Mr. Doddrington had entered the garden. Years of experience had taught him that a dull Victorian Sunday afternoon could be brightened-up by some jousting between the established Church and the Dissenters. He closed his eyes and waited. He heard some pleasant greetings. No fireworks to be expected for the moment, but give them time. There followed some polite conversation about the weather, the progress of the harvest and the health of Mr. Hannah, who would not see that Harvest Home. The Old Man kept his eyes resting. Disappointing stuff it was so far, no doubt, but it was Sunday and these were religious men. Wait a bit longer and they'd get going. After all, as far as the Old Man knew, Mr. Oaktree still thought it was the vicar who had tried to pitch him into the canal by hoiking his left leg from under him with a walking stick. Sadly, for the Old Man, Mr. Oaktree knew that Mr. Doddrington had not been his assailant. He would have been even sadder to know that despite recent events neither man was willing to stir things up that afternoon. Mr. Oaktree did not want to provoke his foe, being on the weaker ground, and Mr. Doddrington did not want to waste his opportunity by appearing to take it unfairly – or when there was so small an audience.

However, patience can be one of the things that age teaches us, and the Old Man had many years of it. So he sat: eyes at the rest. He heard them discuss the new constable, the new timetable for the branch line, the lack of boats on the canal and the delicacy of the embroidery on Mrs. Jagland's tablecloth. Patience ran out.

The Old Man jumped awake, as if surprised to find others present. Blinking, he glanced around. He greeted each by name, finishing with his "Dearest Daughter" and asked if Mr. Oaktree and Mr. Doddrington were now going a-visiting as a pair.

Greetings were returned, most politely. The Old Man said that he was surely soon for the next world and what should he best do, having been such an awful sinner when he was a younger man.

The reply, disappointingly, came in unison. "Open your heart to the Lord," said the two men of God.

"Surely so, but which one?" He smiled innocently.

"There is but one, though there may be different ways of approaching Him," said Mr. Oaktree in unison with Mr. Doddrington. Both were as nonplussed as much as the Old Man.

However, ecumenism was clearly the order of the day. "Indeed, for the Lord is merciful and as…" Mr. Doddrington glanced at his new found colleague, "…I believe that the great Dissenter, John Bunyan said, surely we should not let a few drops of water divide us."

Mr. Oaktree smiled cherubically at the Old Man, who looked from the face of the Baptist to the face of the Anglican and saw them glowing in perfect harmony.

"Perhaps I should turn Papist or Quaker?" That would do it surely. But no. The men of the cloth continued to beam at him, biting their tongues behind their amiable smiles.

"Find the Truth," began Mr. Doddrington.

"Open your heart to the Lord," added Mr. Oaktree.

"Let him lead you into the land of the Righteous."

"Listen to the Shepherd calling in his sheep."

"He will comfort you as you walk through the dark vale."

This was not at all the kind of Sunday that the Old Man had hoped for. What was ailing these two fellows?

Matters got worse. Mr. Oaktree asked the Old Man if he would join in a prayer with Mr. Doddrington and himself. Mrs. Jagland was ready to join in, so the next twenty minutes were spent asking for forgiveness for this and that and for blessings and all the rest of it.

As soon as the last "Amen" faded, the Old Man reasserted himself. "I didn't say I was off now, just as how I would be one day."

"So will we all, following the way of all earthly…" With the prospect of all this starting again, the Old Man decided to nip it in the bud before the next twenty minutes went the same way as the last. No longer on the offensive, he resorted to an obvious ruse.

"I have a story for you gentlemen." He noticed them look at each other. "Not one I've told to any before," he added. Both were reluctant to be distracted, but neither was willing to be the first to break away. To increase the appeal, the Old Man added that it was a moral tale. "Sin of gambling, Mr. Doddrington, and the wastefulness of privileged men, Mr. Oaktree."

"It was like this," he began.

Mrs. Jagland said she would fetch some tea and cake, though she doubted that Mr. Oaktree should have any. He could have the cup with the crack and the saucer with the chip. The one she saved for the gentlemen of the road who sometimes cut wood in the yard in return for a bite to eat and a pot of tea. She could not approve of him, but nor would she be rude if Mr. Doddrington was on such amiable terms. Mr. Doddrington, she would have words with him later on.

"What do you know of bears? No need to answer an old 'un like me, for you're educated men, but I know little of them and knew less then. You know Tommy Twitchell who gets coppers by making his bear dance, tramps round places hereabouts from time to time? Well, a bear like his, except bigger and not so tame, not by a long chalk. That's what I mean."

The educated gentlemen assimilated this information readily and with a glance the story could continue.

"Now, I couldn't tell you the year exact, but it was a good while back. It was when I had a boat of my own, well someone else's that I worked. The horse was mine and the rope and harness. Well, it was early one year, round about January or February. I remember the cold morning air as I stuck me head out to see the sun rising over a copse and lighting up the hill opposite. That clean cutting air that fills your lungs and heart. Glorious, I thought. So I give the boy a bit of cold pig – gentle-like – woke him - and says, come now we've a fine day for a good step down to...now where was it...not my usual neck of the woods, you see. I have the job in mind. Load of stone for some rich doctor who had a place for curing sick gentlefolk. Wanted to build a lake in the grounds or some such thing. Any way I was well away from home so to say.

"Out in the borders on the Shroppy it was. Yes, I have it we was on the way to Ellesmere or close by. That was it. See, I may be for the grave but I still have it fresh as a daisy if I sets my mind to it *(ed actually he hasn't – see note*)*. Now I think we'd moored up at Whitchurch. That is me and the lad who followed the horse. Peetie Harris. New lad then, thought he was quiet because he was shy of me. Turned out he was just one of those gentle lads that wants no more than to follow a horse. He'd have been just at home as a plough boy. He was happy enough offling along. Looked so weak you'd never have thought he'd make it to pudding time. Careful of the horse too, but no company for a human."

"A boy who knew his station in life," Mr. Doddrington spoke up.

"We are all God's children, Mr. Doddrington," responded Mr. Oaktree.

"Very true, and we owe our filial allegiance to the order our Father created," Mr. Doddrington replied.

"In His image was man created. In His image. Not as a servile wretch, but as one of His children." Mr. Oaktree raised his voice a little.

"Any road," the Old Man raised his voice louder, "We was at Whitchurch or was it Prees. No Whitchurch."

Mr. Doddrington lifted his voice above the Old Man's. "A man in your position should not encourage the foolish and self-destructive ambitions of those who would ride roughshod over the ordained order of things."

"I would only have all men treated with the same respect that is paid to some of that order."

"Gentlemen, don't you want to hear my tale. You both might learn something from the moral." The Old Man shouted at the top of his voice. The volume had not been great but the strange crack that sounded as he tried to outdo the rival gentlemen had the same effect as firing a cannon. Now he'd got started he did not want to stop so they could argue. They had had the opportunity for that earlier.

"Thank you, sirs." Having got the argument he had wanted at first, he now wanted only to tell his tale.

"Any road, I give Peetie the toe end of my boot and in no time we was off. Few miles afore breakfast, best part of the day. After an hour or two we stopped for a bite of ham and bread, but not for long. Peetie didn't argue, but he did look tired. Mind, that was him. Still, I was eager to get a move on. We was short of money and was best heading-home for another load. Not much use travelling empty, which was what we'd be doing. Besides, if that weather got colder there'd be snow and ice and maybe we'd be held by it. I didn't care much to be holed up for a few days in a strange country with no money. So, we was getting ready to push on.

"Then, never known this before or since, a fox leaps from the top of the bank, we was in a little cutting, and lands on the boat. Springs away onto a boat heading the other way and lands on all legs on the far bank. The captain of that old boat stares at me and I at him and then we watch him disappear into some scrub.

"As he passed level with me, he called out, 'Where's the hounds?'

"I laughed. Then I found out as a dozen of them came flying over the bank and gathered on the towpath and on the boat. One big one even had its snout down into the cabin. It was as I was dragging him out that I heard a voice. The voice of a gentleman.

"Damn you. You, Sir. You damn navvy. Hold your hand with that hound, I say.

"I thought to myself to take care. I'd had dealing with gentlemen before and had nearly ended up in slavery. So I pulls his dog out all nice and gentle, returns him to the towpath, and looks up to the gentleman."

The Old Man noted, with disapproval, Mr. Doddrington's approval. "I had to look up for he was atop the bank and I was stood on the boat. He was on horseback too. He threw his mount forward and teetered over its head as it dug its hooves as best it could into the frost hard towpath mud. Peetie was staring too. We waited for him to go head first into the cut and serve him right. But he didn't. He held on, sat back in the saddle and smiled broadly. In fact he beamed.

"He must have seen us staring, for he dismounts and says. 'Finest sport ever was had. Blast these navigations. I expect the fox was away up to that copse. Would wade across, but no cottages I know of to take the horse to for warming up after. Don't suppose you know of any? Only I'm a bit away from my usual country.'

"I told him that I was away from my usual country too. And, yes, his fox had been away up to that copse and would either be holed up there or a good way further on by now.

"He didn't seem too downcast. Then he asks if he can stop and talk a while. Well, I told him he was most welcome to talk, but we weren't stopping. So he hands his horse to Peetie and tells him he's as gentle as a lamb. So off goes Peetie, one horse in front and the other behind. As for this fellow, he steps aboard without a by your leave, grasps my hand and introduces himself as John Mytton of Halston Hall. I introduces myself, Peetie and the horse. I tell him I know nothing of Halston Hall, but he tells me it's a few miles further on the other side of Ellesmere. He then pulls out a flask and asks me to drink to our well-found and fortunate acquaintance. I drank. Fine brandy it was. Cold day, you'll understand gentlemen.

"I asked him how far Ellesmere was and he said he could reach it in no time at all, but I'd take a good deal longer, but should be there easy enough by dark. He asked me what my business was. When I told him he asked if I was prospering. Generally, so, though this had been a bad few weeks. He asks if I'd like to earn a bit of extra money by doing a simple bit of carrying beyond Ellesmere. Not far he said. I pondered, for whilst the pay was tempting, there was the likelihood I'd miss a cargo if I didn't get back, and then there was the danger of the cut freezing over and an even longer delay. I thanked him, but said that going further on into strange country was something I didn't like to do at that time. He only turns round and offers me twenty guineas. I was dumbfounded by such a sum. He took my blank face as being refusal and adds another five for the lad. I frowned for I was sure I hadn't heard him right. He takes this as me digging my heels in, so says he'll pay me another ten for the services of the horse. I should have stayed puzzled longer, but I was still young and leapt out of my skin at the offer of such wealth.

"Out comes the bottle once more and he drinks my health and we seal the bargain. He calls out to the lad, 'I say, what's your name.' I tells him it is Peetie. 'I say Peetie, your master...' Captain, I says. 'Your Captain, Peetie is a sportsman for all his clod-hopping boots.' He then turns to me and says that if I moored up, we could take our horses a-hunting Reynard. Then, he changed his mind and said that we should push on.

"His word 'sportsman' stuck in my mind. I wondered what I'd come across and what I had promised to do. I wondered if he had a pack of hounds to carry back to his country or had some strange idea that he could hunt by boat. So, I asked him.

"He told me that there had been a meet of the hunt up here and he was taking the hounds back that morning to Halston Hall. Long old way, he told me, but faster at the trot than at the walking pace of my old nag. Straighter way too. So, no, he did not want his hounds to go by boat. As for hunting foxes, no, we were after bigger game. When I suggested deer, he shook his head. I couldn't think what else there was, so I told him that I wouldn't wager much if he and his hounds were to go after Farmer Jones prize bull. He laughed but said he'd have a go if I'd take his odds. But no, he said, we are after a bear.

"Now, some of these gentlefolk are as near to mad as makes no difference. So, I asked him if there were bears to be had thereabouts. He said there was one. So, he was going to hunt a bear from a boat and he wanted me to carry the carcass to his Hall. Well, I'd never heard the like, but I told him that I had made a bargain and I would do it. He slapped me on the shoulder. He then said that the hunting was easy for he knew where it was. It was my part that would be hard, because he would have it alive and healthy.

"My jaw must have dropped. 'Alright, a few more guineas, but you will do it, won't you. You will keep your word?' I said I would, but he'd better tell me what was behind all this nonsense and then let me know exactly what I must do.

"'Happily,' says he, 'Look here, I am a sporting fellow. A few days back, after a fine run, some of the chaps wagered that Tom Harbottle would not ride his hunter into dinner. Of course, good old Tom did. One fellow then suggested that we have a wager on whether he could leap the table before it was cleared. So he did. Then, some other fellow says to me, Jack Mytton being the man to take on anything, what I thought. So I said that Tom had ridden bravely and such a leap had not been seen at many tables, but that I thought it could have been done riding a bear. Well, amongst the laughter, it seems that a wager was made and that now I have to find a bear, ride into dinner and leap the table. I will admit that I am confident of finding it and of riding it, but getting it to Halston and leaping the table are less of a certainty.'

"I said that if he told me where it was I'd carry it, but best not to say too much to Peetie at present. Now getting the poor creature was easy. Mytton says we can collect the bear from a farm, some mile or so from the canal, this side of Ellesmere. Since there was space for a cage in the bow, we agreed that he should ride ahead and get all prepared so there'd be no delay. So, off he trots, hounds following along. I wondered what I'd let myself in for. What Mytton had let himself in for I cared not a fig. For men like him it's all or nothing, so there was no telling him. I told poor Peetie that we'd be stopping to pick up some livestock for the gentleman and he should say nothing about it.

"The sun was well up by then. Out of the cutting it was as warm as a spring morn: in the shade of the banks, it was still deep winter. The air was clean and I remember thinking to myself that I could get used to that neck of the woods. Different from Brum, that was like sticking your head up the chimney. In the sun there were tiny pit marks of light green, the first sign that spring would be along. No more than a freckle on an elephant, but there if you looked hard. In the shade the dark ivy crept across the bare earth or sagged amongst the crisp leaves that lay dry and brittle as if frozen. I like that sort of thing. Surprising how hard work in the air can be a pleasure. Mind, not the sort of pleasure you want every day, but better than none.

"At least I made the most of those last few hours of peace.

"As the sun began to dip towards its early setting, I spied Mytton, still in his scarlet, standing on the towpath. As we neared, he shouted a greeting and began to wave his arms. As we moored up a man with a rope in one hand and a stick in the other appeared out of a gateway. Behind him lumbered a bear with the other end of the rope about its neck. No, don't ask me what sort, except to say it was middling big and had a sorry look in its eyes.

"Don't see many of those in Shropshire, says I. The man with the stick and rope, said to his certain knowledge it was the only one. Well, I said, let's fetch his cage and then well load up and be away.

"The man with the rope looked at Mytton. He turned to me, and smiled. Mytton pipes up all blithely, 'We'll manage without a cage, bear don't like 'em. The beast will sleep most of the way: no need for you to do more than throw him some food and keep him covered. Hibernate usually, bears in winter. He'll sleep all the way, won't he Lew?' Lew smiled and added that it was likely as not. His accent was Welsh: soft, it was. Should have thought I'd talk like that with a bear about.

"I must have looked doubtful. Mytton told Lew to poke the beast with his stick. He gave him a good sharp 'un and the poor creature hardly stirred. Poor beast, I thought. Mytton just says, 'Very sleepy'. Then Lew shows me the way the animals claws had been clipped short. Looked painful, worse than fingernails down to the quick. Reassuring though, I'll admit.

"'See, here,' says Lew, 'wouldn't harm so much as a fly would you Sampson. Gentle beast, he is. Never so much as growled, for sure. A lamb, he is.'

"'You'll do it in a dish, my friend. We'll have Sampson at Halston all ready in time for dinner in two days.' Mytton sings at me and claps me on the shoulders. 'Sportsman, a sporting boatman, that's what you are. God's speed.'

"With that he wheels away, ignoring Lew's calls, and rode off with his hounds.

"'Bastard,' says Lew.

"Thought you were friendly, says I.

"'Not you, him. Riding off and left no money for the bear nor his feed. Pay me later, if I can catch him first. What's he promised you?'

"I told him and he replies that I'd be lucky, 'specially as I wasn't about that way often enough to get into the mad huntsman's purse. 'He would pay if he ever had any money, but his fortunes gone. Make sure you get your money before you hand over the bear.'

"Shall I get yours too, and bring it? I'll go back this way in a couple of days.

"'No, he said, 'don't trouble yourself. I'll have my payment. Want to see how? See when I give old Sampson a jab with my stick? Sits still as a statue. But - I'll not do it - kick him here and he'll bite. No claws and a gentle manner. Fine. But what does that wastrel want him for? Did he tell you?'

"To jump over the dinner table with His lordship in the saddle.

"'Well, have you ever tried to make a bear jump? Nor has he. Where'll he kick him? Just here. What with? Come on. Hunting man like him?'

"His spurs?

"'There you have it. He'll not pay me my money but I'll have my pound of flesh – or Sampson will have his, more like. And he's no Lord.'

"Lew smiled. It was not a pleasant smile and I can't say I liked him much. Mind, I'd not been swindled yet. But I was curious. So why not leave him to lose his money? All this is for a wager, after all.

"'Because he'll not pay anyway. He'll forget. He might pay you, because he'll be happy when you get there.'

"But why not just not give him the bear? Only one hereabouts you say. No bear, he loses the bet.

"Lew paused. 'Not so simple. I makes my living with that bear in spring, summer and autumn. Fair old dancer he is and us Welsh are a musical nation. Fine pair we are. But winter I stay and do a bit of labour on my cousin's farm.' He pointed to some nondescript buildings a couple of fields away. 'Well, I decided to add a little extra to the table. I'd been down towards Frankton, with a message, and it just happens that these pheasants came into my hands. His pheasants. Hauled off to Halston by the bailiff. Turns out Mytton reckons he can give me two weeks in jail. Then he persuades me to help him out by letting him borrow the bear and he'll forget all about pheasants, in fact he gave me another brace to carry back here. Goodwill, he says.'

"I made no comment. 'Best be off, he says. Night'll be here soon.' He was right.

"I noticed that Peetie was still standing and staring and not knowing what to do. So, I told him we'd set the bear on him if he didn't look lively with that old horse. The bear was loaded with no trouble at all. Good as gold, he was. Tied up and curled away under the sheets. Not even a whimper or a snort.

"Jump aboard then Taff.

"'I'm not coming.' He looked at me as if I'd gone in the head.

"No offence. Jump aboard Lew.

"'I'm not coming.'

"But he's your bear. How do I know what to do with him?

"'You'll learn. Good night, to you.'

"And with that he was through the gate and away into the gathering gloom of the evening.

"I liked Mytton's 'we'll manage'. I thought he meant that Lew, whoever he was, would be coming along. What did I know of bears? What if it ate Peetie?

Worse, what if it ate the horse or bit a hole in the boat? Best just get along and keep the beast sleepy and get him off as soon as we could.

"Though we hadn't made Ellesmere by dark, which was my fault. I wasn't too concerned. We came to the stone wharf as a man, muffled against the cold, seemed to be locking up for the night. I called to him and he told me it was the right place, but we'd have to wait until morning. Fine, I thought. We'll do it ourselves and be off. A lot of work and trouble with the canal company – didn't like you going at night, not in those times – but easier than explaining the bear.

"So, we sweated and strained and steamed as the night pressed on. By ten we had done it and so pushed on until about midnight, before we moored up. Poor Peetie was too tired to eat and my belly was roaring for sustenance. So, I has some ham and bread and a swig of something good. Then it struck me how we'd heard nothing from the bear. So, I wakes Peetie up and we go to take a peek at our passenger. Well, I lift the sheet, getting ready to leap backwards. But the creature doesn't do so much as stir. Peetie asks if we should prod it. I give him a look and he went quiet. We slung in a bag of rank smelling meat that Lew had given us. Not a movement. Deep, contented breathing and a smell of brandy. Dash it, I thought, forgot that little bit of contraband we'd had as our right.

"Peetie says, 'Is he alive?'

"Not so you'd notice. Think he's content, though I shouldn't like to upset him in the morning.

"But when morning came, the bear still slept. And, you know, you'd not of known he was there if it weren't for the odd grunt and the way he stuck his head out and rested it. Got some odd looks. Course the smell was pretty strong. Well, I couldn't get young Peetie to go in there with a bucket and shovel. Nor could I do it myself. After all, I had to be in charge.

"So, what Lew had told us was true enough. He'd poked him sharpish with his stick and there was never a movement. Not a twitch. And I had learned fast. Good dose of brandy and you have a happy bear. And while the bear slumbered we headed on. Good speed we made too. Then it struck me that I wasn't any too sure how far we had to go. All gone well so far, but I didn't like it above half – and the thought of having a bear on board another night I liked a good deal less. And it had affected poor Peetie. I saw he was walking in front of the horse. I called out to him what he was about. Said he thought the bear'd eat the horse before a little chap like him. Turned out he's seen a dancing bear when he was a proper little nipper and it had broken the chain and killed a farmers dog, gobbled it up, he said.

"So, I hailed a passing boat and the skipper new that country well he said. Told me Halston was out of reach tonight and it was a long old stretch the next day. I cursed under my breath, I'll tell you. Still, nothing to be done except lay hands on some more brandy. The boatman said there was an inn in the next village. The Gate, he said. That much was right. I sent Peetie to fetch brandy and he got hold of a small cask. I told him to get a flagon for us too.

"So, when we moored up for the night and threw some more of that rank meat under the covers – should have heard that bear gobble it up. Knew what Peetie meant about that dog. Trouble is that it's not so easy to chuck a small cask of brandy, 'specially when you've had the bung away for a taste. So, I told Peetie to lift the covers and drop it in nice and gently. Well he mutinied. So I lifted up the cover and just as I did the creature lifts its head with a lump of meat in its jaws and sticks its nose in my face. Peetie screams and I jump like a stuck pig and the bear lets out a roar and tugs at his ropes. Up come his clawless pads. For a moment I was feared that he'd broken his ropes. 'Chuck him the brandy,' I yelled at Peetie, who'd run off down the towpath. So he runs back a few paces, throws the little cask and heads back down the path towards Lord knows where, with me not more than a yard behind.

"After a bit we turned and ventured back. And there we saw a sight that we'd never thought to see. The bear had not broken free. He had not set off to gobble up more farm dogs, cats and children. In fact he was stood on his hind legs, stretching the rope to the limit, fit to snap. In his paws is the little cask, with the top broken in and the creatures licking and sucking at it.

"I told Peetie to take a closer look, being as he's given the bear the brandy I thought he might see him as a butty. More mutiny. So we crept closer together. The bear lifts its eyes, stares at us, and a great rumbling growl comes up from his guts somewhere. And as we get ready to turn tail again, or Peetie does anyway, the beast sinks down into the hold and there are sounds of liquid being lapped up and by the time we've seen to the horse – I thought it best to help Peetie that night as he'd had a bit of a fright – there were snores from deep within rising into the night air. We'd learned alright, and so had the bear. We even went and looked in to see the great bulk of fur curled up. We covered him over and pulled the top cover down. Peetie looked dumbfounded.

"'Stop gawping,' I said, 'Not seen a sozzled bear on a boat before?'

"Then we went off. Next morning we had a bit of a shock. Turned out that this Frankton place was no more than a short step along from where we'd moored up. So, I says to Peetie to wait a while I go and find Halston Hall and find out what Mytton wanted us to do with the bear 'til later. Thought I see if I couldn't screw some money out of him too. Pricey stuff brandy. But Peetie was afraid the bear would wake up and I'd be gone a long time. He was probably right enough on both counts. Well, would you want to keep company with a bear with the vapours? So, I said to Peetie there was one sure precaution and if we took it he's be fine to stay there alone. I sent him off to wake the landlord and fetch another little cask. So afore the bear so much as stirs we have his breakfast ready and served.

"Peetie still wanted to go to Halston. He'd not have got money out of Mytton though. Not that I did, either, though I didn't go unpaid. After all, all that liquor was getting beyond my pocket.

"I used to love those late winter mornings, but I'd not gone far when the cloud began to blow in and there was the spit of cold sharp rain pricking my face. Not much, just a spitter of a shower. So, at the Hall I bangs on the door and some fellow in knee-breeches tells me to sling my hook before he sets the dogs on me. Didn't like it above half when I told him I had business with his Master. He told me I couldn't have and I told him that his Master stood to lose a good deal of money if he didn't see me. That changed it of course. Wonder how long it had been since this chap had been paid? Still he scuttled off and hardly a minute or two later Mytton comes bounding into the entrance hall, slaps me shoulders like I was a gent and is all hale and hearty. Knee-breeches scowled at me, but I was just the chap Mytton wanted to see.

"'Have you brought the beast?'

"I wanted to look around me and make out it had snapped the rope, but I thought I'd better humour this one. So, we arranged that I should lead it up to the Hall and put it in the stable, where the lunatic Mytton could mount up and charge in when the port and cigars were doing the rounds.

"Thought I would bring up the question of money. I explained the extra expense. All I got was a promise of cash on delivery, but he told knee-breeches who was smouldering shruddy by the door to fetch me a couple of bottles of brandy and look sharpish. 'Don't believe it's for the bear, but I know what you boat chaps are for medicinal spirits.' I didn't set him right, good job as it turned out. He'd not have attended to my words anyway.

"Back at the boat, Peetie was near frantic with fear. The poor old bear was sleeping away in the bow making a fearful snoring, but Peetie didn't care. He was magging away like an idiot, telling the bear little stories like a mummy lulling a babe to sleep.

"So, I told Peetie what we had to do and said that I'd stow the brandy in the locker while he woke the creature up. All this time he's muffling on to the bear, making little comforting noises. He stopped when I told him to wake the creature and almost burst into tears. At that moment, as Peetie turned to look at me with an expression on his face that mixed fear, anger and plain amazement in a way I've never seen before or since, the bear opens its eyes.

"'Well done laddo,' says I.

"Peetie looked puzzled.

"'He must have taken a fancy to your voice.'

"'What do you mean?'

"'You stopped to look at me and he woke up.'

"A paw slapped the cover. Peetie leapt toward me. The bear didn't stir more.

"'Look, Peetie, he likes you. Tell him stories as you lead him to the Hall.

"I never knew Peetie to swear, but he looked at me all watery eyed and red faced. 'Come on then, my boy, let us go together with him.' I took the rope and gave it a gentle tug. The bear yawned. So I said to him to come along nicely; he opened his mouth wide and let out a sleepy belch. I pulled hard on the rope. The bear lurched forward and I ended up sitting on the towpath. The bear lay back down.

"'Clever creature.' It was unusual for Peetie to speak, but you had to give it to him. The bear was a clever fellow.

"'Rightly said, my boy.' It was clear that brains and not brawn would help here.

"'Try giving him a poke with the barge pole,' I called to Peetie.

"'Won't work.' Heaven, pardon me gentlemen but it was so unusual, thought I, four words in fewer minutes and he'd disagreed. I wondered if it wasn't just the bear who'd supped that brandy. No, Peetie was never even market day merry.

"I wasn't used to him telling me what would and wouldn't do. 'Why?'

"'That chap prodded him and he never moved a muscle, Captain.'

"The boy was right. 'Well we can't fill him up with more spirit or we'll have to have a cart to carry him. I'll put me mind to it.'

"'I have a way of moving him, maybe.'

"'And what may that be?' Peetie looked hurt by my sarcastic tone. Well, as far as I knew he'd never had an idea let alone tell a soul that he had. Yet something must have passed through his head when trudging after that old horse. 'Come on Peetie,' I said trying to sound more enthusiastic, 'tell us what it is you have to say.'

"'If you'll hold the rope, I'll sing to him.'

"I must have looked downcast for he went on. 'My Dad said that his granfer always sang to his horses when he went ploughing.'

"Well, this wasn't a horse, but it did come to mind that I'd heard it said that singing to the animals was something men did in the old days. 'Peetie, five minutes ago you were so scared of this beast when he slapped his paw on the cover. How you going to manage to walk all that way singing with him coming after you?'

"'I trust you to hold him, captain. I know you'll not let him slip away.'

"That was responsibility. No wonder he hardly ever said a word. Poor lad put his trust in me to steer the boat and organise things and in his mind getting a load of nails from Brum to London qualified me to tame a bear.

"Mind you, must be said that poor old bear was scarce kin to a wild one. So I held the rope. I could hardly wait to hear what Peetie was going to sing. He started with some old tune that I can't remember – mind, nor could he, for he soon started with another. The bear first stirred his head, then fixed Peetie with a stare that made Peetie look at me wide-eyed and caused me to pull tight on the rope. Then the bear raised itself up and with a great heave and pulled itself onto the towpath. Peetie stepped away and the bear put a paw forward. Then another. Peetie smiled hopefully and commenced to sing a hymn. The bear liked it and with a heave of its bulk began to lumber after the boy. From the way Peetie became calmer and just walked slowly along I could tell that it must be working.

"I waved directions to Peetie and the bear kept on going. Painful slow it was. That suited me, though Peetie was running out of songs and had to start some again. Our friend didn't mind. After all our fuss it was turning out to be all done nice as nip. It was a slow walk, but there was no incident to speak of, though we did get enough odd looks to make it a relief that we did not have to go through a village.

"Knee breeches had been sent to keep watch at the gate. He asked us where we'd been. The bear bared his teeth at this interruption to Peetie's singing. Knee breeches showed us straight to the stables, which were set off to the right at the end of the drive. We stowed the bear all ship shape, though as soon as the singing stopped he stood on his hind legs and bellowed. Must have been saying thank you to Peetie for he then lay down and snored. Poor old creature, I thought.

"So, I asked Knee breeches for our pay and said we'd be away. Some hope. He said his Master was away for a few hours and had left no such instruction for payment. The Old Devil, pardon me once more, had pocketed it. He suggested that we try again when we came to fetch the bear tomorrow morning.

"That was a new one on me. I said so. Knee breeches says that we surely didn't expect a gentleman to take a bear all that way. I said that I didn't expect a gentleman to let a man do a day's work for him and leave him unpaid. He said that I obviously did not understand polite society. I said that I understood his Master. He said that I clearly did not frequent the company of gentlemen. I said I'd seek them out a good deal less if this was the manner in which they carried on their business. Knee breeches said we could have some ale in the kitchen before we left. I told him we had work to do. Truth was though that we didn't. I told Peetie that we'd have to come back tomorrow as we were so far in to this that we could not afford not to get something for our trouble.

"We set off discontentedly. I was discontent. Peetie was beaming. I'd never seen that before and it stuck right in my ribs that he chose that time to look so pleased with himself. But I couldn't begrudge him. I asked about how he knew about singing and he told me all about the days he'd spent walking with his father – a ploughman – and scavenging the hedgerows with his mother as they gleaned the grain and plundered the berries. Then how he'd ended up on the parish and found his way to boats because he liked horses. He was a good lad. He spoke all the way back to the boat, where I treated him to extra rations. Never heard him say so much again in all our days on the boats together. He slept all afternoon and I rubbed the horse down and made up fodder, cleaned round and swept up. When he woke he found all his work done.

"'Well you were sleeping you idle fellow. And you did save the day this morning.' He beamed again.

"'Will we get paid,' he asked.

"'Don't you worry, my boy,' I tried to sound confident, but I wasn't sure how. I should have just trusted my betters. As it turned out they could not have done better by us. Or that miserable Taffy who wanted his pound of flesh. He even cheered up, when I told him as I handed the bear over."

"You had a ruse in mind?" Mr. Doddrington asked.

"Splendid," chimed Mr. Oaktree. "A cunning device to get your due."

"I am sure the money would have been forthcoming, Mr. Oaktree. Why must you take so against the better people in society?"

"Of course he would not pay. The man was a drinker and a gambler. You heard how he exploited these poor men?" Mr. Oaktree shot back at Mr. Doddrington.

"Come now gentlemen." The Old Man liked playing the peacemaker. So happy was he to be yarning and provoking that he even called out for more tea. His daughter dutifully went to fetch it. If only, she thought, Mr. Doddrington had not been there.

"It was none of my planning, but, as you might say, the Lord did provide. The chance came and all it needed was a sharp mind to get Peetie and me our due. And this is how it happened.

"A day of rest was pretty rare on the boats, even in those days before the railways came. So we caught up on drowsing by the little fire. The day merged into night as it does when a working man has no purpose to his day. We woke early and as the bacon sizzled I had still not the foggiest idea of how we were going to get our payment.

"We were just about to head off to the Hall, when a little way ahead a horse and rider appeared on the towpath. It was just light enough to see him. The rider looked either way and then galloped towards us. He pulls up right by our door, all snaffling and steam in the morning air.

"It was not Mytton, but it was one of his friends, I guessed.

"'I say, are you the man with the bear? You are? Well, come to the Hall now, if you please. We are in need of your assistance, please. Come as fast as you can.'

"Then he turned to ride away as if I were at his beck and call. So, I called out to him to come back and tell me what was happening. 'Bears aren't so easy as to rush things.'

"He returned and even said that he was sorry for his ill-manners. This is more like it, thinks I. So he told me what had happened. Mytton had won his bet. Taken a hundred guineas from them. But there had been a cost. Lew had been right. Mytton had stuck his spurs in the lolloping old beast and the sleepy Sampson had taken umbrage. Reared up, twisted and turned, with Mytton hanging on for dear life. In the end the bear got him half off, slewed right over one side, and bit a chunk out of his calf. The bear had then gone off to terrorise the house and Mytton had gone to bed to await the surgeon. The bear was now terrorising the hounds, having sent the humans scurrying to their rooms. Fortunately there were no ladies in the house, only maidservants and the housekeeper.

"Well, I said, I wanted the money I was owed up front and a bit more. Hundred guineas I thought? 'It'll cost thirty above what I am already owed.' The gentleman agreed and turned his horse back toward the Hall. Once more I called him back and he handed over the twenty guineas. I also told him to wait. Best to seem to know what I am about, so I'll ask him a few questions and give him a bit of eye-wash about bears.

"I first went down to the cabin and poured a bottle of brandy into an old pail. I called Peetie to get the boat hook and whispered to him to think up something to sing about when we got the bear quiet. I told him that he should be a bit mysterious about his skill, but he didn't quite understand.

"As we went I asked the gentleman about what the bear had been doing. Little enough it seemed, but they were in a far old panic about it and I didn't want to discourage their fears. We went along at a fair old rate. I'd got money from this man and I wasn't letting him out of my sight.

"When we got to the Hall we were greeted by Knee breeches, who was sitting in the boughs of a big old oak. He gestured wildly and screamed out some nonsense. The bear, it seemed, was in the orchard. There were some ten or twenty men looking at the bear which was standing under a tree scratching itself.

"'At last, Bagley, where have you been?' They chorused. 'This the man? Are you sure?'

"Have no fear I said, I shall save you from the savage beast. None of course was afraid, but were keeping their distance so as not to provoke it.

"'What will you do?' asked one.

"'I'll have my fee up-front to start with and then we shall get to work.'

"They didn't seem to like this much, but they were in no position to argue. One tried to beat me down with promises and assertions about my betters. His friends soon did for his objections when I made to walk away.

"'Don't be a Damn fool Harry. The man is worth his pay. Dig in your pockets. Come on.'

"So, I had fifty guineas all told in my coat pocket. And I had a bear to tame. I looked at the poor creature and, with Peetie at my side, advanced into the orchard. For some reason I was confident, though I can't think why. I should have been petrified, but I looked on that poor old bear as a fellow and somehow knew he would not hurt me. I looked the bear up and down and saw matted fur and blood all down one flank. That fellow hadn't just pricked him, he'd hacked into his hide and torn away at the flesh. I must have looked sympathetic. I know it cannot be true but I still maintain that the bear looked me in the eye and winked as if to say, 'Both me and you too.' I told Peetie to hold his tongue until I said otherwise. After all, those gentlemen would want a bit of a show for their guineas.

"We stalked all a-tiptoe towards our quarry. I gestured quietly with my arms, drawing big circles as if to mesmerise the creature. Dead still he stood. 'Good Old Sampson,' I whispered and the bear gave a low moan. I placed the pail on the ground some six feet from Sampson and stepped back. He sniffed the air, stretched forward and shoved his snout in. You could hear him slurping and snorting. Right old soak was our Sampson. Mind there was only what was left of a bottle – no good giving him the whole he'd have collapsed snoring. I hoped that Sampson would be merry and well-humoured.

"When Sampson came up for air and breathed a deep sigh of soporific contentment, I told Peetie to start singing and to make it a jaunty tune. Sooner we were out of there the better. So Peetie strikes up some kind of march and Sampson lumbers toward him. Round of applause there was from the assembled throng, as the papers used to say, and three times three for the hero, when I slipped that rope round poor Sampson's neck. Well, it was a bit heroic, even if you knew how pot happy the bear was.

"Sampson was no trouble, but I think we were all pleased when we moored up and fetched his rightful owner. He was happy when he heard about Mytton.

"'Discover his liking for brandy did you? Thought you would. You'd not have believed me if I'd told you.' He was cheerful.

"He was right, of course, I'd not have believed him. After that I'd have believed anything. Except what happened when we got back to Watkins' yard. There was a packet for Peetie.

"'Brought by a gentleman in knee breeches riding a fine hunter.' Watkins' was suspicious. 'Said young Peetie had done his Master a good turn.'

"'Good lad, Peetie is. Must have been that hunting gentleman whose hound you saved from the cut,' I butted in. Watkins didn't approve of men on his boats doing a bit of work on the side and he'd have had it out of Peetie quicker than spit.

"As it was, he wandered away. Peetie opened it up. There was a note. We called across Joe Blandy, who could read better than Peetie and better than I cared to let on. The note read:

'Young Fellow, I know what Devils these Master's can be when sharing their bounty, so here is five guineas for you to keep safe from him. Mytton.'

"And there was too. He was wrong. I'd shared out our bounty as was appropriate. 'Breeding will out,' I've heard it said. Well, gentlemen can have their airs, but if I come across him I shall give a piece of my mind to him. Never did. Heard he fled to France to escape the hoard of people who were his creditors. Came home to die.

"Now, there's a moral tale for you men of the cloth." The old man finished and looked from face to face.

"Indeed, there is," Mr. Doddrington assented, adding, "The faithful servant is rewarded."

"The wealthy man is a fool and a wastrel if he uses not his talents in God's work." Mr. Oaktree was less sympathetic to the squire.

"Now, now, Mr. Oaktree, surely you have had your fill of Baptist Jacobins," Mr. Doddrington landed a blow.

"I trust you do not consider the squire a fitting example of a religious man in a position of social responsibility, Sir?"

"Indeed I do not, I merely point out that to undermine God's ordering of our lives is unfair to those who will be ruined because their hopes are raised and then cast down."

"Neither," said the Old Man.

The vicar and the pastor looked at him, as if to inquire what the moral was.

"Something to do with the bear...or Peetie...brandy? Can't remember. Old Age?"

Note – The Shroppy, or Shropshire Union canal was formed by the amalgamation in 1845 of a number of canals under the official title of The Shropshire Union Canal and Railway Company. This story could not have taken place after that date. The main protagonist dies in 1834, almost certainly having been away from his Shropshire home since 1831 or 1832. Whilst the Ellesmere and Chester Canals had penetrated the area, there was no link to the Trent and Mersey until 1833. There is little chance that the encounter could have taken place in 1833 or that a canal boat could have run down the Mersey between Runcorn and Ellesmere Port. The exact explanation for this is unclear, but might be that Carter and his boy had vacated their usual country for some reason and the old man superimposed this onto a journey after 1833.

Three Captains

"Good for Mr. Gatti. Clever man for an Italiano."

"I heard he'd walked all the way to Paris and then come on to London."

"A man of intelligence and judgement."

"Better off amongst honest folk than in Paris."

"Dare say. Mind you, I've seen the huge well where he keeps the stuff. Deep as the pit and a sight colder."

"Down on the Regent's ain't it?"

"Aye. Just along from Hampstead Road."

"Call them Cockneys honest? Tricky bunch, I reckon."

"What do you say old 'un?"

"If you wish, I shall tell you a tale that will answer your question. But hold a while 'til I finish. This'll warm you up good and proper and no doubt it's needed."

"Never was a truer word said. Never was such icy-cold weather. I can't remember worse than this."

"Nigh on a week we've been here about. If that old ice-boat don't come along soon then I don't know what I shall do. Mind, it freezes so quick, even at day."

"Bleak days." The old man looked away from the pot that he stirred with a long wooden spoon. "Mind, I remember one winter when it was like this at the end of March – a whole week of ice in March."

The five boatmen sitting around the fire, letting the warmth of the logs as they glowed, sputtered and were stirred into flame, seep into the marrow of their chilled bones. All knew that the old man would have known a worse winter than they could have known. After all, he had been alive for so much longer.

"Brought you all to a halt, has it?" The old man knew the answer. "Well very handy for us all. If you must be halted, you may as well make the most of it. Can't last much longer, but we'll do our best to make merry while we may."

He took a jug, dipped it into the iron pan and filled his pot. The cinnamon and sugar wafted around the room with the strong smell of old ale and apples in its wake. The assembly each took their turn as the jug was circulated. There was not such dignity as attends the movement of port or claret amongst gentlemen, but there was more anticipation. The wind whistled around the isolated house at the old wharf, in the moments of quiet the sharp crack of splitting ice could be heard and the snap of sparks from the fire. The men knew that what they were about to receive would be something to be grateful for; there would now be stories, but gratitude would be unnecessary, even offensive. What else was there to do? And the old man was a notable feature of the waterway. As was his third daughter.

"Where is she?" The old man answered a young man, probably fearing the lady's reputation. "She has had the fortune to be taken to lectures in Birmingham, along with all the pious interfering old battle-axes in the entire village. The Lord moves in mysterious ways, though they are good ones for the poor oppressed that is their husbands. Heaven help the folk of Brum if they step out of line. Dozens of them there are from all over Warwickshire, Stafford and all around. And she has taken that poor old husband of hers, to help the vicar shift the bags about. Trunks that is."

"I expect you can remember when the railways first came along, old fellow," A man of some forty years, who had swallowed his drink so quickly that he had gone red in the face, piped up.

There followed a discussion about how the railway had changed things. Speed and strength united. Life was hard now on the boats. Many of the men shifted their families with them, crammed into the tiny cabin or sleeping under the tarpaulin, until the children could be sent off into service or found employment.

"They'll be the end of us", was the general opinion.

The old man said, "I do, Joe. Every man should have the chance to earn a fair day's pay by the labour of his hands, nor should he have to worry himself about the Workhouse."

"A crime to be poor," said Joe.

"My mother told me that immoral women was sent there to save decent folk's money," spoke a youth, Joe's boy.

"That don't mean you need find your way in – there's immoral women for you elsewhere, I should say." The Old Man, didn't approve of such talk.

"Your mother – my dear wife –," added Joe, to explain and add to his son's embarrassment, "should know better than to say such things. We've had hard times and there's more on the way for the likes of us."

"I remember when they first come along too." The Old Man didn't want to see more joshing of the lad who had only just bucked up enough courage to say anything because of the steaming pot he had taken two mouthfuls of. "Bad places: bad places. My loving daughter threatens to send me, but she's too good a Christian soul to do that to her poor old father in his twilight days."

"It's the shame of going to the Union. I was there as a little 'un. My dad, he ran off and mother had no choice. They sent us one way and her another. Worse thing was the little babbies. Oh, your ma's right, me lad. Immoral women: litttle babbies with no father, or not one you could get at – gone to sea or hiding in the manor house. I can still hear them: winter morning, they washed those little 'uns in a trough by the yard wall. Broke the ice and plunged them in."

" 'ope your mother weren't no immoral woman." Joe was only joshing the speaker, a man in his fifties by the name of William Hammond, who was a newcomer to this stretch and had introduced himself as Hammy. There was nothing to distinguish him, save for an eye of blue and grey. A stranger? No boatman was unwelcome in the Old Man's house when his daughter was away.

"So, how come you ended up in there? Don't you worry about shame. There's many an honest man who finds times hard. Mr. Happy, do you know him? He says 'tis only the dishonest that never has to worry about money." The Old Man was incurably curious, despite being of an age at which he should have known better, or maybe because he did.

"I can only tell what my mother told me. I suppose I was about five years old, with a sister a little older. As far as I know, we just had no money. We must have been some of the first ones in it: a huge new brick block. My mother always told me that me dad had run off. Could never get more from her, but he'd been long gone, for I never knew him: I don't believe he knew me either. Mother always said that he'd have been proud to have a son. Miserable bastard I say. Leaving his family, deserting her and us. That's what's wrong with those places, we had no choice. My mother, she worked as best she could, but with two kiddies and no home. So, in the end, when she'd worked herself nearly to the grave, we went."

"Mean Devils, some of these clever men." The Old Man could remember a more generous age. "Got worse too."

"What was it like in your day?"

"Don't know. Never went to the parish. It was all the parish then, not all these Workhouse Unions and Boards of Guardians and this and that. There was guardians, guardians of the poor they was called. In each parish, shopkeeper, churchwarden, farmer. Depended on them, honest folk, but fearful of raising the poor rate and offending the pockets of their neighbours."

"So I heard," said Hammy. "Mind, they did give me a few letters and numbers. And they 'prenticed me to a carter."

"To save paying for your dinner," derided Joe.

"No doubt," said the Old Man, "But leastways they set you on the road."

"They did. Still like to scrag my father, should I come across him. He's the one I blame." Hammy emptied his pot.

The Old Man sprang to his feet using just one stick and refilled the pots with the warm, spicy liquid. "Your old dad might have had good reason for doing a flit."

"He should have stuck by us."

"You must have been born about 1830 then." The Old Man pursued his own line.

"That would be about it. Mid-winter, I believe, though it could have been the next year."

"What did your dad do for work?" The Old Man remained curious and was not yet sated.

"He was a labouring man, farm labourer, so my mother said. Worked hard too she said. Then he just ran off. Deserted us. Always seemed to me that she had one fault – loyalty to him."

"Where are you a native of? Buckinghamshire, somewhere round Aylesbury way? Wendover? Well, I weren't so far off. Not seen you up here much before?" The Old Man had a memory for accents and dates, as well as faces and tales.

"No, I spent years working up and down the Lea to Hertford. When the old carter got too old, he sent me to work for his cousin who had boats carrying barley and such for the brewers in London. Last year, I had a feeling to see my home county again, so I found work for Mr. Watkins." Hammy liked to talk about himself and held out his pot, which was duly refilled. "I can only tell what my mother told me", said Hammy.

Joe's son snored.

The Old Man passed judgement. "Hard year that was for the labouring man, 1830. Bad harvest the year before, little work in the winter, costly bread in the spring and summer. Not that they were better than hard done by in the first place. I had cause to go to a cottage about then: needed to fetch some old bit or bob that I hadn't got. Autumn it was, late autumn and harvest all done. Cold and wet. You know how miserable it can be in a little boat cabin. Well, you know nothing of discomfort and hardship by comparison."

The men seemed to doubt this.

"You may look like that, but today a farm hand knows nothing of the hovels those folk tried to raise their families in. Things has got better that way! Much better. This place had no floor but the mud, there was a sorry fire that wouldn't warm a mouse, and this poor lass was kneeling at it with a pot of greasy water with some bits of leaf floating in it. There was a baby wrapped in a rag, held against her mother for warmth. And she was plumped up with another. That's what I saw, when a man pushed open the rackety old piece of wood that served for a door. I asked if he had, whatever it was I was after and offered him money for it, more than it would be worth. He pointed at a stool, he pointed at the pot and he pointed at some sacks in the corner. That was where they slept and that was the total of their goods.

"Well, I asked him, if there'd been no work at Harvest. He said there had, but that pay was low and the farmers now hired by the half-day, there'd been a bad crop the year before and this year weren't much better. I told him I was sorry for the plight of his family. He said I should be sorry for the plight of all the labourers around there if there were valuables on the boat. With that I headed back to the boat, though he said it in a kindly way. Well, I needn't have worried then, but he was a desperate-looking man. His eyes full of shame, so shamed that he was at the end of his tether. I'd looked on his wife and children afore I went and offered sixpence for something they didn't have and left. That were hard to see but not so hard as for him. He'd to lay there under a sack and listen to his child weep with hunger. Not for an hour, but every night and day. You'd have said he'd either take his own life or someone else's, if he hadn't been so scraggy that he hardly appeared to have the wherewithal.

"Were things that bad, you ask? Don't doubt it my friends. Bad harvests, little work. And then there were the threshing machines. Now men of your generation have seen machines all your lives, but back then the farm labourer earned his living after harvest by threshing: threshing by hand. But the machines took that away. Bad harvests meant bread was beyond his pocket, at least enough to keep your belly full. Now some of the old-thinking magistrates tried to keep the cost of bread within the labourers pocket, but what chance when he had no pay? The vestrymen helped as best they could in some places, but there was a general turning against the old way of doing things: help the poor and you made them poor and you made more of them — the sort of thing men such as you have been told all your lives. Well it hadn't always been that way. All that autumn, as I navigated up and down to London, all through Northamptonshire and Buckingham and Middlesex there was discontented talk about the machines and how the farmers were depriving the poor man of his livelihood.

"Then one night, on my way back to Coventry, I smelt it. I'd had a bite and stuck me head out for a bit of a breath of air. And I got a breath of air that roughed-up my throat and made me retch and splutter. The air was weighed down by sorrow, full of damp smokiness, hanging there. At first I thought there must be a fire in the hold, so I leapt out and went to see. I never got to look. My eye was caught. Away across the fields I saw fires. Dotted about. Some close, some on the horizon. Radiating around, patches of orange. The closest threw light on a farmhouse and some barns. There were a few figures in the flickering brightness, fetching and throwing water and making not one whit of difference. The ricks were burning.

"What I'd seen a couple of weeks before in that man's eye was now made real: desperation and despondency in that cottage had boiled over. In hundreds of hovels like it, hatred of the machines had come to a head and the farmers, the villains as far as those poor folk took it. They were going to pay.

"I kept the door tight closed, but when I rose next morning, I could see a smouldering pall from the nearby farmyard. Most hard to the nose, despite all that wretched smokiness, was the stink of hatred and fear in the country. Hopeless and one-sided it was and it would turn out more so, of course. I pushed on. I stopped at a wharf to pick up some hay for the horse. There was an old farmer there, complaining about threats to his machines and to his family, while he supervised sacks of grain being loaded onto boats. Said he could not trust his men at that time. Damned the government long and hard, he did, and hoped the Justices would send for the yeomanry: not the militia, he said. Too many ordinary men: Jacobins who'd slice the throats of the folk they were meant to protect and pillage the farms they should defend. He looked scared to me – and I did not blame him one little bit. He saw a French Revolution in his own rickyard and he'd heard what that meant. Clever man, no doubt, though looking to France was looking over what was obvious. Trouble for him was that farmers were alone: they were surrounded by men who they expected to do their bidding, and would had they not ceased to treat them as worthy of their proper attention. Yes, they'd get the yeomanry or even the real soldiers in and the rick-burners would pay for their carrying-on. But that could take days to be organised. Until then or until the rick-burners went back to treating their betters with the respect they thought they deserved, they had a good deal to be scared of. I won't say all the farmers were at fault: they had families and they had livelihoods too. And maybe hunger in the land was but a part of bigger things, but I, for one, can understand those men, and I won't condemn their burning of what they believed to be the source of their torments."

Held hard in the ice were the men around the fire and they knew there would be the ice-breaker before too long to rescue them and get them on their way. The boy snored away and the men looked at him, wondering if he'd be following in his father's wake.

The pots were filled again and bread cheese and apples placed on the table. A bottle of plums was put on the table and a jar of pickle that would slice through the muzzy cinnamon and clove of the medicinal concoction that had smothered their bones in a blanket of warmth.

"Hard times", said Hammy. "You had a family then, Job?"

"Yes I did", said the Old Man. "Had this house too from my parents, who had both passed away. Neat little place it was too, even then. My little girl may lack the respect she should have for my age and wants – we all know that if you had not brought around a bottle or two I could not have treated you with anything more fortifying than tea – but she can keep a tidy house and cook like an angel."

The others agreed, that the house was tidy and, as the pickle burst upon their taste buds with elegant piquancy coupled with the force of a charge of hussars. All lauded the good woman and wished her good listening in Birmingham. They heaped blessings on the assembly of the Evangelical Women's Society (though all the lecturers were male) for Witness and Mission in Benighted Lands, agreeing that it should long continue, especially while it coincided with such freezing weather, amiable company and was at such a suitably good distance off.

"As I went on that day," the story-teller continued when the celebration of the domestic virtues passed into silence, "There was destiny in the drizzly mistiness – and always the smell of smoke. It was in my throat, in my clothes. God only knows how it must have been choking a few of the farmers that day. Away from the wharves there was quiet. A long day waited for a busy night. Dragged along: can't recall a time I liked less, on the boat that is. The few folk I saw looked fearful and said little. The progress of the boats was as normal, as if the troubles of the villages and farms were none of its concern, while the country folk ignored us, as if we were alien men. I wondered if they were jealous or saw in us a new world as their old way of life struggled against changes they could not hope to stand against. They'd be off to the city soon, I thought, like so many others. All the blazing lights and bustle. They'd have been best off staying where they were, if you asked me, in the long run. Mind, what man can live where he can't eat, even if he is surrounded by good things?"

"My boy, at that time was a quiet lad by the name of Harris, Peetie Harris. Nice lad, but no match for a sharp wit and not much company for a sociable chap such as I was. Said little: let me do the talking. You felt lonely in his company."

"Don't imagine he suffered the same in yours, Old Timer," one of the fireside audience spoke up as the prophet took time to wet his whistle and wipe pickle from his beard.

"True, very true, though I don't know if he blessed me or cursed me. Good lad, I hope he found a good wife to give him guidance because that was what he needed. Well, I said to him that we would keep ourselves to ourselves that night and would open the door for no-one, but would keep half an eye out. Truth was I didn't fear for the cargo overmuch. These men weren't after us, though some might see the chance for pilfering, but I thought it unlikely if we stuck out of the way. In the long run, I wasn't bothered if a hungry man took a bit to sell, because he couldn't eat our cargo that time: cloth and trunks of goods we had. So, I told Peetie that we would keep our heads down and let what happened that night pass us by as best we might. Wise for us to stick to the world of trade and not get mixed up with either set.

"The evening passed quietly away as dark fell early. Whatever was going on in the wider world, we heard nothing and saw less.

"Then, come about midnight, we were woken by banging on the side of the boat. Peetie looked afraid, so I told him to get behind me and went to look. I opened the door and let the cold autumn moonlight into the cabin. The cloud had gone and the smoke was on the breeze. At first I saw nothing. Then, a woman appeared on the towpath, with two little children at her side, all looking scared out of their wits. Before I could say anything, she begged me to let her take shelter and she would explain, or at least, let the children in. She was fair panicky and all of a flush. I looked at her in her warm cloak stout shoes. Well, thought I no mistake that you wouldn't be seen dead with the likes of us if there weren't some good reason for it. Too prosperous she looked. Not rich, but healthy and kempt. Strange women aboard, what would it say for my reputation or hers? She didn't care she said, just let her take shelter from the cold and she would tell me then, but let her off the towpath and inside. She hadn't the first idea how pinched it could be with two of you in that little cabin. Still, damsel in distress – and she was – cold night, too; so I told Peetie to go and bed down in the bow. Good lad that, not a word of complaint.

"So, in they came. All three of them and squeezed themselves in. Looked terrible uncomfortable, not being used to having to make the most of little bits of space. She looked around. I wondered what she was thinking and asked her so. She told me that she'd seen the boats passing the farm before and wondered how we did for living space. She asked where the bedroom was. I told her she was in it. The children clung close to her; they looked ready to sleep, but seemed to be awake out of confusion and worry.

"She told me what she was doing about that time of night. It turned out that she was the wife of a farmer, not wealthy, but prosperous enough. A go ahead young man with a head for business. Like me, you'll see where this was leading long before we get there. So, to cut it short, she'd received a letter that day. I say she had, her husband being away from home and though she was sure he was hurrying back as news of the troubles spread, she was on her own with the children and the servants – a maid of all work and a handyman.

"She showed me the letter. It was scrawly writing sure enough and I could only make a few of the letters out. The writer was not an educated man, as far as I could tell, but he was a sight more educated than I was. She noticed that I didn't read it. Without saying a thing about that, she read the letter aloud. Most polite, I thought.

"The letter read, as best I can remember, 'Hannan' – that was her married name – 'sins you chewz to starve the poor men and prosper as thay do go hungry now that we shal come by to burn your ricks and smash your infernal mashins that do our work and that we intend to drain your blood for your meanness. Signed Captain Swing.'

"She looked at me and made to explain. But I held my hand up and she fell silent. I think she was wondering what I was going to do – after all, she must have been desperate to ask help from the likes of us. Truth was that I was wondering, but not what to do. I was thinking of that poor hovel and its inhabitants. The ones I'd seen but two weeks since. Hereabouts too. The gist of the story was obvious, but she told me more. At first, she had decided to stick it out. The servants had run off, before even she had the letter. It had been stuck to the farmhouse door with a nail, as darkness fell. She did not know where her husband was, though she was sure he would be on his way. Then she had heard steps in the yard and heard the crackle of lighted straw and the flames of the ricks had danced upon the wall of the room where she had taken refuge with her children. Whether the brutes knew the man of the house was away or not she did not know, but when they called out for those inside to show themselves for they would have blood as well as fire, she decided to take the children and try to find safety elsewhere. They'd left by a little used door and climbed over the yard wall and run across the stubble as fast as the children could toddle along. Then she had realised that there could be no safety at any other farm and that the children would never walk to her uncle in the town. The night air being unhealthy for her children, she had reached the towpath and seen our boat. She then begged that I would not turn her out. Nor did I, though I confess that at first I thought a good dose of damp smokey air would do her beloved children a world of good and that a good long walk along the cut to the town would make her a bit more sympathetic to those poor brutes who cut her husband's corn for a shilling a day when he favoured them with work. No, I couldn't do it. So I asked what she wanted of me. Shelter for the night and, if I was willing, a ride into the town the next morning. I could see nothing for it. Then she asked where I would sleep. Fool I was, up I got and went and bedded down next to Peetie. Good lad. Not a word of complaint when I took the sacking he was under and told him to fetch himself some more.

"Sleep didn't come much. Fitful I was. It wasn't that I'd become too grand to kip rough. No, it was more to do with a feeling that the night's doings were not yet at an end. Strange how imagination plays upon the mind at times. I never thought the rick-burners would really want to do murder to the woman and her children, though I was less sure of what fate would have awaited her husband had he been home. I got my answer the next morning, when I spied out how the land lay. Right on the horizon, just in view, was the skeleton of a roof, charred timbers festooned with a gauze of smoke. This was more than rick burning and machine wrecking. But as I lay trying to fall asleep, I did not know that.

"I drifted in and out of a light, uneasy sleep. A low voice was saying, 'Here, get under here.' Whether it was a dream or not I did not know, but there was a gasp of surprise when whoever it was saw me half asleep as the first light of dawn fell on my face and I opened my eyes. They were surprised, but I was struck dumb. For looking me in the eye was none other than that same man from that hovel. He spoke first, saying sorry for waking me. I told Peetie to stop trembling and go and feed the horse and prepare to be underway. Then I rose; course I had slept in my clothes. Yes, it was him alright, and there was his wife and her little 'un. And there was another, wrapped up in some old cloth and cradled in the man's arms, held tight close for warmth, half covered by his shabby old coat, new-born I'd have said.

"'I know your eyes,' said I. 'You do,' he replied. 'I could ask what a man and his family are doing sneaking about my boat and spying in the hold, at first light,' said I. 'You might justly wonder, as I might wonder what you're doing sleeping here,' said he. He looked me in the eye and I guessed at his story and told them to get aboard.

"No sooner did he get cosy as it gets in the bow of a boat on a cold autumn dawn, than he says he would like to explain, lest I thought him a common thief or a vagabond. I told him to be quick with his tale, for I wanted to be away. Truth was, that I guessed that he was running from the law and it struck me that he might have been one of the burners of the farmhouse which my other passengers had fled from. 'Speak low,' I said. He told me that he wanted his wife and child to be taken away up the country, to where her family were. Could I take them? He had no money, but I said I would, for I had not the heart to turn them out.

And what of him? Well he said that he'd come a little way and would then set out alone to find work and call his wife to him when he could support her and the children. I looked him in the eye and asked if he had been busy in any of the past nights doings. He fixed me with a gaze and asked me if I really wanted to know. He was right. My question was a foolish one so I decided it might be best to know as little I could.

"So, we were underway, with Peetie plodding along with the horse and me steering. In the cabin the wife of a mean old farmer who had been burned out, most probably, I thought, by a gang including the man who, along with his wife and babies were sheltering up at the bow. Now, the folk at the front knew to be quiet, but the others didn't. So, shortly after we started to move, the door opens and the lady smiles up, asking how long it will be to the town and what there is to breakfast on. Would you credit it? Fresh air and three hours or so, I said. She puffed a bit, but thanked me pleasantly. Yes, I thought, you'd not give me the time o' day if you weren't on the run. Mind you, at least she weren't on the run from justice. So I told her to keep quiet and to make sure her kiddies did the same. I told her it would not do her reputation any good to be associated with the likes of me – even tugged my forelock, though she couldn't see – and we'd let her off a bit before the town, when no-one would see her. She was happy to agree to that.

"It was a dull morning, cloud had blown in again and there was cold drizzle. The stonework of the bridges, so bright when the sun shone was no more than washed-out grey. Every step the horse made seemed eternity itself. A miserable pace, though no slower than was the usual, on a dirty day, with a sheet of cloud hanging over the country pressing down on the dirty air as if it would burst your lungs. After a while, just by a copse we came to a bridge. As we passed under, I heard the splash of hooves on a muddy track and the jingle of spurs and bridles. I looked over my shoulder just in time to see a man, standing tall in his stirrups, wearing uniform of the yeomanry, bring a dozen, uniformed figures, all on horseback to a halt by raising his hand. He then cupped it to his mouth and yelled to us to hold where we were in the name of the King. And so I did. Never does to offend Royalty.

"He trots down onto the towpath and rides directly up to the boat, along with a pair of his troop. 'You,' he cries. 'I require information on the whereabouts of a woman and two children. Have you seen a woman and two children last night or this morning?' Well, I was in a fair old quandry about what to say, but I needn't have bothered because two things happened at absolutely the same moment. The door to the cabin was thrown open and there were cries of, 'Here, here, my dear: father, we are down here.' So, here was the ambitious young farmer come to rescue his family. 'What's the meaning of...' But he had not time to ask.

"If only I had had the wherewithal to tell Peetie to come to my side when I first saw these men. Then the farmer-soldier and his wife could have had a happy reunion and all the explanations could have been civilised. We could all have gone on our way and nothing more need have been done. But I had been too slow and poor old Peetie was too scared of the uniforms, though I guess the men had never seen shot and certainly had never taken part in a real battle with an enemy of equal strength. Well, they had scarlet tunics and looked for all the world like the fanciest cavalry – to the eyes of Peetie, anyway. Well, poor lad, he calls out, 'Down here, in the bow!' My heart sank, for I was sure that this man was taking himself and his family away because he'd played a part in events. And though not forged in battle the mettle of these farmer soldiers would stand bravely against half-starved Hodge, his wife and two babbies.

"Two of the yeomanry trotted the few yards to the bow. Thank fortune, thought I, the fugitive had good sense. They'd asked for a woman and two children and that was what emerged from the bow before the brave boys could make a search. Bright lad, I thought. Peetie helped her onto the path. The gentlemen did not dismount. They looked her up and down and sneered. 'A silly slut and her bastards, no doubt: nothing to us, I'll warrant,' said one. The other turned to Peetie and said loud enough for all to hear, 'Is she yours or the skipper's?' Peetie shook. I told him to hold the horse steady and lead it to feed. He needed something to think about.

"The farmer had been intent on his re-found wife and children. There were embraces and, I'm pleased to say, she told him how I had given them shelter and acted like a gentleman: given them the cabin, small and dirty though it was. Dirty! I thought, keep quiet and look humble and he might tip you a sovereign.

"Just as things were looking up, events led him to catch sight of the woman, baby on one hip, new-born, slung in a shawl knotted over her shoulder. Rain had started to fall. The scene at the stern sheltered the family with happiness: the farmer's joy may as well have been a warm cloak for all the notice they took. At the bow, the poor lass, in fear, I guessed over what her husband had done, stood head bowed and back turned. The warriors towered over her as the trees in ranks by the field stood above them. 'Your name, woman?' One of our brave boys was demanding of her. 'Speak up, slut!' I don't know if she answered or not, but the horseman was getting angry. 'I'll teach you to mumble to your betters, your name?" He reached for his sword, drew it, raised it and swept it towards her face. She pulled her babies close to her, as the soldier turned the blade and caught her a blow with the flat. She screamed. It must have broken her cheek bone and blood flowed from her nose.

"I exclaimed and the farmer stops attending to his domestics for a moment and calls out, 'What are you about Matthews?' Then his eyes lit up, or rather burst into flame. Matthews shouted at her again, demanding her name and once more raising his sword. 'Hold' shouts the farmer. Thank God, I thought. But her troubles had just begun. 'Stay your blow, Matthews, old chap. I can save you the strain to your sword arm. I know her name. And it will be useful to have her conscious. This, my friends is Mrs. Keach.' It obviously meant something to them, for they let out a whoop and cried Tally-ho or something like. Good soldiers as they'd hunted foxes, as some old boy once said, I heard. The farmer, who, it seemed, was what passed for an officer amongst the gentlemen of the County Yeomanry, turns to two of the three horsemen who had hung back. 'Be good enough, Mr. Owen and Mr. Jenkinson to escort my wife and children to Mr. Arthingworth's. Wait for us there, we'll be back before dark.' The men dismounted, placed the two children on one horse, while the farmer's wife mounted side-saddle. Very neatly she did it too, considering. They gave them their cloaks and lead them off to Mr. Arthingworth's dry, warm house and plenty of grub and clean sheets no doubt. Their adventure was over.

"I said that we needed to be off. But the officer says we should wait. He wanted to know what the woman was doing on my boat, when had she boarded and where was I taking her? Well, I was stuck for what was best to say. But, he said he could wait for my answers and strode to where the woman stood and heaved her round by the shoulders, so she faced him. He stared at her, with not one whit of compassion. The rain fell and washed the blood down her cheek. She'd catch her death alright. But there was not one jot of feeling for her plight – or even the sorry state of the little 'uns. If this was the man who the letter had been meant for then I knew what they meant by meanness. He didn't have to drag it out, but he did, whether for revenge or for spite.

"I told him to hurry for I must be gone. 'You'll wait. Search the boat. Keach'll be here. Just the sort to bring his wife and brats to this. Search it gentlemen. Or let us see if our quarry can be drawn out by another stroke of your sword Mr. Matthews.' Well, there was nowhere to hide and Keach was, he proved, not the man to see his wife suffer violence more. So, he reveals himself and hands himself over. His face turned to the ground and not even a look at his wife and children.

"The gentlemen of the Yeomanry were delighted. 'Skulking in the hold of a canal boat has made sorry affair of your uniform Captain. I'd hope to appear up to scratch if ever I were held captive. And your soldiers? Have they deserted? A shame this silly slut had not the wisdom to do the same. Don't protest. We took a whip to Henry, William and a few others, when we caught them blacked up this morning. Oh yes, they confessed and they told us all. They'll be off for judgement, but you...you will hang at the next Assizes. Come Captain. We won't bind you, for if you try to escape I shall shoot you, and should I miss, we will hunt you down until you are exhausted and have our horses trample you into the ditch in which you'll die. Maybe your brats and this whore will stagger to the same one as we leave your carcass to rot in. Let them wander where they will. Walk ahead of us.' 'No farewells.' They turned and shoving the desperate, hapless, helpless man to the front, mounted up and took him off to face judgement. He did hang, at the next Assizes, just like the gentleman said he would. I wish a poor man such as me was blessed with such foresight. Nothing like education and breeding – and he was only a gentleman farmer too.

"What happened to the woman, Mrs. Keach, and those sorry littl'uns? No word of them ever came my way after they left the boat a few miles on. At least when they left their rags were dried out and they had a bit of something for the rest of their journey. Strong woman, though weak in frame and worn away by scraping to give her kiddies some hope when there was none: I hope those babies lived, though pitiful start in life they'd had."

"Now," said Hammy, "I expect you're going to tell me that the gotch-eyed man was my father and I was that baby, but my name was never Keach."

"No, no, I wouldn't say it could be you. The name means little. A woman on the road would need a story. No, it couldn't be you. After all, your father ran off, didn't he?"

The boy stirred, looked up and asked, "When will you tell the story?" The company looked puzzled. "You know, the one to show what tricky folk those Cockneys are?"

"Best have another pot, my boy."

With a gulp and a sniff he was soon lost to the world of his heartier seniors. Reflections on the state of the next generation were given, but he would not have heard the story, for it was not told that day.

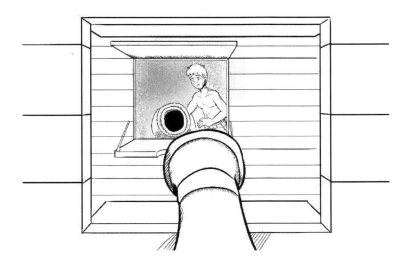

Me and Horatio

"Well, when I was eighteen, and scarce of age...do you know that one? I ran a roaring trade, and many a sly trick did I play on many an unsuspecting maid...Not that I ever did, in truth. Maids weren't so unsuspecting as some of them like to be nowadays...But my parents saw that would not do, for I soon would spend their store...If they'd have had a store of anything more than spuds...And they resolved...That would have been my mother...That I should go aboard a Man o'War..."

All around the fireside looked in amazement. My great-grandfather was not given to singing though, I have been told that it was not unknown for him to strike up with "Who Would True Valour See?" when Mr. Boot, the zealous dissenter, passed-by along the tow-path, or some unmentionable ditty when my grandmother hung out her unmentionables to dry.

He looked pleased that the attention had been shifted away from our discussion of the benevolent fund for the dependents of the county militiamen.

"What has that to do with it?" My grandmother asked.

He sung again. "Well, the bold press-gang surrounded me and their warrant they did show. They said that I must go aboard and face a deadly foe so la de de and la de da, I then did learn my fate, that I must float aboard a ninety-eight." His voice cracked on the higher notes. "Man o'War, that is. The wooden walls of old England."

"Very good father, we know that. Nothing."

"No, my dear, let your father finish his song. You know how he beats all-round the bushes." That was my grandfather, who was always sympathetic when it came to changing the subject from questions of moral welfare.

"Well, when first I did set foot on deck, I just did stand and stare, but the admiral – the Hero, no less

– he did give word, there was not time to spare, so away I went all on the sea...ah da de da de da da, to fight the French in storm and gale, aboard a ninety-eight."

A pause. My grandmother opened her mouth to speak and the singer recommenced.

"Well, right well, I did my duty do and da de da de da. I could climb aloft to the topmast and value not a scar, and right well I did my duty do, I soon got bosun's mate, then Damn me soon got bosun too aboard a ninety-eight. You'll understand this is only a song."

"No need to..." interjected my grandmother, but too slow.

"Well, at Trafalgar and da de da, Bold Nelson he fought and fell, and when they capsized that hardy tar I took a shot as well, so to Greenwich College I come back, because I'd my duty done, and served my King in storm and gale aboard a ninety-eight."

"Perhaps, your memory, great-grandfather, is..."

"So, here I stay in comfort fine because I the King had served. With my three-cocked hat and my baccy-pouch I'm happy as a Lord. For I done my duty and served my time all on the salty sea, but I'm too old to sing no more for I'm nearly ninety-eight. Didn't quite fit that, did it?"

"Thank you father, as we were..."

"No, daughter, my point is that those who serve their time get looked after and so should the widows and orphans. All I got was grape-shot in my arse and not a penny to show for it. Where's fairness there? Where's morals?"

"But," my grandmother butted in as if she meant to checkmate him, "you did not serve your time. As I remember, you deserted as soon as your ship got back to port."

"Throw that in the face of a hero who defended his land against Old Boney? I weren't cut out for a life at sea. Land-lubber and proud of it, that's I. Mind, once I'd spewed a few times and we'd caste off...Besides all that, I never wanted to go in the first place, did I? I was pressed, was I not? Still did my duty. I could have jumped overboard."

"No you could not, father. You never could swim." Grandmother was ever practical.

"When I was a lad, I could do many things you'd not believe my girl. For a start..."

"Tell us about the press gang great-grandfather," I said, deciding that here was a chance to find out more on a subject that I found interesting and maintain some decorum in the presence of ladies.

My grandfather joined in the appeal. "Yes, Job, tell us more, you never did tell me of you and Trafalgar but what you say in passing on to something else." He found anything more interesting than the moral welfare of orphans and widows, with the possible exception of missionary expeditions to the benighted heathens of far off lands.

"Press gang? You know what they were? Aye, so thank God you live in your age and never met them down some slummy alley, when you'd taken refreshment and weren't too nimble on account of your new boots. Don't suppose they ever got so far as Southam on market day. Mind in the old days they'd of found some slummocky old wenches doing as lively a trade as the taverns and plenty of poor fellows ripe for dragging off to sea. Wonder they didn't try."

"I expect your seamanship was so renowned father, that they despaired of Warwickshire men and took against them."

"Indeed grandmother, it was the Warwickshire men and others of the inland counties that stood against Ship Money in the time of Charles I. These counties have little to do with the sea and less desire to increase that little they do have." I felt some erudition was required.

"Just shows how it was unnatural like to send me aboard. If we'd have been born in Cornwall or some such place beyond Gloucester the sea would have been like our second home, but God saw fit to place us here and so 'tis against His will to set us upon the waves. I expect that even Mr. Oaktree and the Reverend Doddrington would be agreed on that point." The old man winked.

"What Mr. Oaktree might think I would not waste my time with, but Mr. Doddrington would certainly not trivialise the Lord's intentions in such a way." Grandmother could be quite put out by mention of Mr. Oaktree, the Baptist Minister, and God in the same breath.

"God created Warwickshire men to be labourers on the land, or squires at the hunt. Same with folk from Northampton, even the snobs, Oxford too."

"So, how was it that you of all this land-locked breed was to be found holding centre stage in one of our great naval triumphs?" Best to get back on course soon I thought.

"Skulking in his hammock, like as not." Grandmother again.

"Would happily have done so, daughter, all being how the sea took my belly all queer. Yet what man would upon Crispin's Day have been abed – the bard of our own county, that is, Henry or Richard or some such tale."

"Vanity, father, does you no credit, though you doubtless did you part as best you were able."

"What I was meaning, child, was that as my country lay all exposed to the tyrant of France, so did I gird myself up and set too with the Froggies and no holds barred." Great-grandfather turned to flowery language often, though he claimed to have little education apart from what he had from Sunday School and had heard read aloud in the taverns and coffee houses. Strange is it not, at least to the ears of an educated man in the great age of progress, that the ale-houses of the past must have been such different places to those of today. Albeit the tracts he heard were no doubt mostly radical news-sheets or bawdy ballads, at least there was an improving element to be found, where now there is little but excess and the debasement of humankind. Even so, there were times when I, shame it is to say, doubted his veracity when he claimed so little education that he was illiterate.

I was thinking this on that winter night in those days between Christmas and the New Year, when one visits, as weather permits, one's nearest and dearest. It was mention of Lord Nelson that reclaimed my attention. The story was moving on. So, I decided to give it a bit of a push in the right direction.

"Did you ever see Lord Nelson?" I expected him to reply with a stern "No", being somewhat wary of the aristocracy.

"Indeed, my lad, I did see him." I was surprised by the reply, but also by the fact that he added no detail. So I asked, where and when?

"He was easy to see. So was Collingwood and all his captains too. The sailors liked that. Thought he was sharing their troubles. Liked him they did. Thought he felt for them. You know he told them to lay by their guns before action began? Made them safer. Bunch of idiots to my mind. I didn't need telling to keep my head down." He hadn't answered my question, but this was not unusual.

My grandmother had left the room, declaring that she had not the time for idle tattle, thus admitting that she had lost the field.

The old man looked round waiting for someone to comment. My grandfather broke the silence. "Well, what would you tell them Admiral?"

"I'd tell them that they'd best watch for the press and heed their mummies and not go to sea."

"Bit on the late side for that weren't it?"

"True, still, Sammy, my lad." He continued, "You've not been at sea have you, Sammy, nor you Jonny Boy?" He called most of the younger family members who visited the house by the canal Jonny Boy. He had even been known to apply the epithet to his great-grand-daughters, though they were more often called "Becky". He liked to pretend that he did not know their names or could not be bothered to do so or was too aged to own a memory for such trivia as other people. This annoyed my grandmother, but she rarely saw the wink he made to the young ladies and the smile that was returned.

He was right that neither I nor my grandfather had been to sea. Nor had we been to war, as he proceeded to point out. Nor had we heard the roar of a French broadside and felt the timbers quake when it was returned. Neither had we witnessed solid shot crashing through wood and the gunners made limbless or stuck in the guts with splintered wooden daggers. Not the gun-deck awash with gore, nor the screams as the surgeon or carpenter took off bloody limbs as the vessel rocked and the victim struggled. We had to admit that we had witnessed none of this and that thus we were ignorant and comment would be uninformed and worthless. It was clear that he had seen all this. There was a sharp tone in his voice that those capable of recognising it knew to be the signal that no opposition or comment would be brooked on a point. It generally steeled his otherwise casual conversation when what he perceived as injustice was under discussion. He was, I suppose, a socialist, though he would have baulked at such a label and had anyone mentioned such a thing in my grandmother's house they would have been the victim of the kind of scowl that only the Baptists or a drunken boatman – her interpretation of drunkenness was an unusually broad one - might expect under normal circumstances.

"Hold on there, father. Now you fought to save Old England, so how would that be done if no one had manned the ships? We'd all have been lost and oppressed."

"Well, I did fight and so did so many others, but it didn't stop us being put-upon, did it?"

"Oh, how can you say so?" My grandfather was being extraordinarily vocal. The cause of this was almost certainly that he had been allowed a second and third pint pot of beer after his day's labour. It had been a condition of my grandmother consenting to marry him that he would abstain from excessive strong drink. He had become comfortable with one pot, a suitable quantity for the head gardener at the great house, at least according to the lady of his house. After three glasses he became unusually fond of conversation. "Free born men all of us."

"Free enough to have a third pull of ale once a year? Man of my age, Sammy, hero of Trafalgar, don't get that unless the boat-boys sneak a flagon over the gate or through the window."

"I think grandfather was referring to political and legal freedom."

"Rather have good liquor than either of them. Parliament or Monarch never filled my belly so much as their own Jonny. Never. Knife and fork. That's where freedom's to be found. 'spect Boney would have treated us the same, and I'd take French brandy over that piss they brew today."

"No you wouldn't old 'un. Not you. Hero of Trafalgar, that's you."

"Green I was. Green. Not just sea-sick. Green and a fool."

"But surely, you are proud to be a British subject, with equality before the law, the best of Constitutions and the root of the leading nation in this age of progress. No despotic..." I stuttered to a halt as the old man stared at me with the strangest look in his eyes. A combination of pity, disdain and laughter, mixed with love for someone as green as he had been.

"Eight bottle men, each night they said." That was his obscure response. He liked to invite a puzzled-look and a request for clarification. Knowing that it was necessary in this case he explained, just enough to invite further opportunities to hold the centre of this cottage stage.

"Pitt. Younger. Saw him too. Eight bottles a night. Fox too. You'll know them from history Jonny. Politicians, Sammy, when I was setting out on life. Big drinkers those gentlemen in those days. All of them. Mind there was proper beer then. Turned their noses up at honest drink of course, but had enough of their claret and port to keep 'em warm at night if their mistresses were away."

He paused whilst my grandfather and I politely expressed a desire for elucidation.

"Take a ploughman. Is he a wastrel and what's the word they use for folk who have no money? No matter. Were he to drink his fill, what might happen to his furrow next day? The worst? And what would be the worst were the great men to be befuddled?"

"Things have changed since your youth," I said. He was failing to understand that the age of progress was underway. "Mr. Gladstone is a model of moderation."

"Shame, I say. Hey Sammy, shame." My grandfather was a Conservative. "When a man who labours takes ale or a sailor goes a-whoring, he is a dissolute – that's the one – and drunken man. Great men have mistresses, poor men have whores. Haven't the money for a mistress. Still, Gladstone has more virtuous intentions no doubt."

"Did you ever see the Hero?" I returned to the heart of the matter I thought.

"I did. At least he stuck by his Emma. Saw him come aboard to dine with the captain. He did, that Nelson. Invited them to dine a little after he turned up off Cadiz. Expect he told them all what they were to do. Loved him, they did. The tars were the same. Knew there would be things happening. Better than sitting there in all that heat waiting for the day your head'll be blown away by some Frenchie ball-shot. That's what the men thought, so did the captains. I hoped they'd get fed-up waiting or get homesick, but no such luck with these sorts. Itching they were to be set to work clearing the decks and cleaning the guns and to have a pot at the French. There were lots of Spanish, but they hardly got called dago. It was all damn the frogs and kiss my arse Boney."

"True patriots. The spirit that made Britannia rule the waves. You would not denigrate that would you father," said my grandmother, who had returned.

"Nor would I ever. Damn them as wanted to take my country from my masters. No, the spirit of the tar was something to hear and when they went into battle it was even more to behold. I have often wondered since if the French were so bold as us brave boys."

"Were you not denigrating their bravery a little back and did you not say you would rather not have been there? It seems that you have changed your mind great-grandfather."

"Course I'd have played at skittles with Jean-Pierre or seen Pitt and Boney have a mill, than have been there. Don't mean I can't spot a brave man when I see him and don't mean I wasn't heartened by it all. Some of them had been sitting off Cadiz for weeks after they drove the French and Spanish in and bottled them up. Scandal it was they didn't destroy them. Admiral Calder got into a scrape with a court-martial for that. Not enough slaughter for the men in Parliament, I should say."

I explained some of the background to my grand-parents, pointing out that Calder welcomed the court-martial in order to clear his name. I concluded by proposing that if there were to be war then it were best carried out with a view to bringing the enemy to book as soon as maybe and that the criticism of Calder was, thus, justified.

"True, my boy," agreed the old man. "If there is to be war then best to fight it fiercely and have done. Should think the Frenchie's would say so too. Sooner some are blown to bits the sooner the others can go home."

My face must have shown that I thought he had misunderstood because, before I could expand on my point he mollified me with a smile and began again. "No, no, you have the right. If you must have war then get it done with for it is an affront to honest trade, except the munitioner and the surgeon, as well as the limbs of men."

I smiled. He continued. "War at sea makes it hard to escape so there was little to be done but join with my mess-mates and make the best of it. Like your kind grand-mama has reminded us all, I never was a swimmer. You know the song that goes "tis fear the coward slaughters', well it's about correct, I should say. So, puff out your chest and do and die for old England. We were ready to do our bit, which was to do as we were told and slit the throat of any Frenchie who came into our grasp. The officers were the same, except they thought the slaughter counted only for the enemy men, not their officers. Killed them of course, but when they struck their colours we were ready to tip the lot into the sea, but not our officers. Do you know, and this is so, that one of our officers, don't know who, for I heard this told when I reached Portsmouth, that this chap found the skipper of a Frenchie that had struck her colours and when this fellow gave him his sword in surrender, he gave it back to him and told him to keep it 'til he met the captain of the victorious ship. Another went aboard an enemy vessel as he believed it had struck, strolled, calm as you like up to the captain, only to be told that it hadn't. Walked back as calm as you like.

"Tell you this; our officers played a cool hand. Maybe there was their like amongst the French, expect so, but some of ours took the biscuit. Nelson himself stood there for all to see in the height of battle, so did Collingwood – headed for the enemy line crunching an apple he did. You know Nelson covered his face with his kerchief when he was carried below? You lay beneath the guns my brave boys, see how I put you above me? Fine men. Few years later you could have seen them giving a poor cripple begging by the quayside either a sixpence or a kick up the arse."

My grandmother said that she felt this was unduly cynical, even by the standards of her father. Unusually, he agreed.

"Indeed, you speak truly. Had the officers run the land the ordinary sailor and his type would have been better served. Don't know if the same was true of the soldiers. See in land battles the general can sit away back from the brunt. At sea even the Admiral had to face shot and ball as much as his men. Still, it must have been their cruel uncles that were in Parliament when peace came. Thank Heaven they thought of the workhouse to spare the poor folk's suffering."

"Not all men were pressed, surely," I said.

"True, my lad, true. There were plenty there by choice or by poverty in the hope of a bounty. And off we all sailed in two lines straight for the enemy rank and burst right through it. That's what we wanted to do, well that was our orders."

"We're you scared?" That was an unusually direct question from my grandfather, who was still enjoying his third festive pot of ale.

"Indeed, Sammy. Scareder then I ever was before or since. See, the Hero's plan, as I heard it, was that we was going to burst through the enemy in two columns and then blow them up willy-nilly. Mind, the Frenchie's was agin it, and the trouble didn't end with that. The wind was low and we had to amble along towards this long line of ships who peppered us with shot as we came on, and all we could do was sit there and put up with it. That was enough for me. Sitting ducks, hoping for the best, knowing that the best might be that you get done-in before you know about it. I was sacred then, but when we hit the line and followed the Hero through it was like entering the pit, or some bits of the country round Dudley – fire and flame and the roar of their guns and the roar of yours and the screams and groans and everything disappearing in smoke. I'd peeped out of the port as we ran toward the line and saw how Collingwood's broke it and how everything went up in smoke."

"The fog of war," I summarised.

"You have it, my boy. The fog of war was just it. Mind, when we sailed into the fog we found two lines of Frenchie's who weren't in hospitable humour."

"You must have seen the heart of the action. Do tell me more. Which ships did you see strike, what heroism amongst our men?" I so wanted to hear more.

"Not the first thing do I know of any of that." He saw I was disappointed. "See, it might be like that for the officers, but all those between decks know in battle is to load and fire and clear away. Don't matter what the name is, all you see is the wooden wall in front of you and you hear the order to fire. To tell you truly, I can hardly remember what went on round me when we first burst into battle."

"Is the scene not etched onto your mind? I find that most odd." I wasn't so much disappointed that he could not remember it accurately as surprised that he did not offer a general impression, however fictional. Yet he was serious, I could see it in his eyes.

"No, no memory of that. Peculiar, isn't it? Don't even want to make it up. Fighting like that was just bloody slogging it out like two drunk brawlers in the street, I suppose. You didn't think, I just did what the rest did. Didn't have the guts to hide away. Mind, on a man o' war there never was anywhere to hide. I'd worked that out long before. Ball, grape or chain could find a mark anywhere; a mast come down atop of you; splinters of wood flying; sharp-shooters; fire, oh I feared fire. Stuck you are floating past your foe. What counts isn't if you are hit, but how hard it is."

He paused. Not even my grandmother spoke.

"I do remember one thought. It comes back to me now. As I peered out of the port, down the barrel of our gun, I saw hard by us the enemy ship as, for a moment the smoke cleared. Directly ahead was the line of ports that marked a gun deck, that and a red painted line. To this day swear that I caught a glimpse of some crapeau behind his gun. Was he as scared as I was? The barrel of his gun gaped. I can't truly say that I thought this at the time, but I have pondered often since on who he was and where he came from and if I did see him in truth."

"You felt compassion for your foe? You felt empathy for his situation, as a common man. Very philosophical for the heat of battle." I made it clear that I was impressed. "Perhaps you have hoped to meet the man who you think you saw that day?"

341

He smiled. "Not too soon, I hope most sincere, for we were good gunners, or my mess-mates were, and we got two rounds off. Don't suppose he saw home." A pause. "Nor so did my mates, and I know not how I was spared with nothing more than a splash of brains on my chest – we all stripped off our shirts, such hot work."

Again there was a pause. "It was then that I feared for myself and did the most foolish thing. See, it is fear the coward slaughters, or nearly does. For seeing it was all up with my mates, I left the gun which was off its mount in any case, grabbed a jacket and went above. My God," and the fact that my grandmother did not condemn this blasphemy is testimony to our captivation, "there was a scene like I had never seen since."

We waited. "There was a tangle of mast and rigging brought down in a pile, the mast resting on a Frenchie laying hard by, or it might have been his mast laying across our main deck. There were spars at all angles and turmoil with corpses hanging here and there, all twisted. There was a stink of powder and the sticky reek of blood. It was even worse than what I'd seen below. Here I could see slaughter rather than a gunner who was to fire his gun when ordered and clear away and load as the commands came. Up here it was all around you, not that little square of your gun port, all about murder and destruction.

"What woke me was a whistle. Then a crack a musket ball striking the post on which my head rested. I ran forward. Up in the rigging opposite were some French sharp-shooters, peppering the quarter deck and the half of the main deck. A little way below, I saw some of our marines repelling boarders. Now I know I should have run back below and looked lively, but I ran forward and grabbed a musket and ball that lay by some corpse. We'd all been taught arms. So I hid, dived behind a barrel that had somehow stayed upright, and loaded my weapon. I poked my head round the side and sized one of them in the rigging. I pulled the trigger. A flash. A man fell to the deck."

"Well done old 'un. Hurrah for old England, Strike home, Britons," cheered my grandfather, who was ever the patriot. His wife scowled at him, not so much because of the sentiment expressed so vigorously, but more because she felt that its origin lay in a surreptitious acquisition of a fourth pot of beer.

"Thank'ee Sammy, though, in truth, half of them fell all at once. May have been my single ball, for it was well shot, may have been chain shot that took down the rigging they were perching on. Any rate, as we battled away I set to fire again. Before I did though, I ran up onto the whatever that deck is called that is high up at the back. I ran past the officers who were standing around as if nothing were happening and giving orders like it was some sort of parade. Waved me on with a hearty cheer, one of them. Away jack and aim true or some such stuff. You see, I wanted to get a better shot and get a look from above. See the French ships, Spanish too, were bigger than ours on the whole. I peeped from where I hid. Below and away were billows of smoke and tumbled messes of rigging. Masts shot away, fires burning and sailors dowsing. Hundreds of men running and shouting and firing guns and repelling boarders. Corpses lying here and there. And in the midst of it all there he was, like in the paintings, pacing about and giving orders."

"You saw the Hero? The Hero himself in the storm of battle? I can scarcely credit it. Why have you never said this before?" That was my naivety.

"Father. This does you no credit, though I expect you care little for that. You take unfair advantage of folk who wish to hear what you have to say." My grandmother looked at me.

I blushed. She continued. "I doubt that you were even there."

"Better had I not." The old man glanced at her. "Indeed, daughter, best it were had I not witnessed it."

"Did you witness it?" My grandmother asked the question directly.

344

"I did."

"Then why, as a man who enjoys telling a tale, have you never spoken of it before. To me it seems most..." she did not finish. I interrupted, which was unusually brave.

"Perhaps great-grandfather feared we should compare his courage to that of the Hero. After all, he was hiding whilst Nelson was calmly giving orders." I realised my mistake and apologised for doubting his bravery. His answer should not have surprised me as much as it did.

"Doubt my courage? No offence there boy. Always one for skulking when the cannons roar. Other men can be brave. I wouldn't so much dare as vex your granny." She did not like 'granny'.

"So why haven't you spoken before?" I asked with a plea that his tale should not be utter fabrication.

"'tis more shameful than being a coward. Which I wasn't in truth. No. Now I have little time left I must speak. To leave some things unsaid would be a great affront to history and truthful memory."

"Hurry and speak then father. What act of heroism have you been hiding from us?" Grandmother clearly felt that he was not making sufficient speed for the allotted time that God would grant him.

"I shall. Indeed, my girl, I shall speak truly and say what I know to be truthful and no more, for now I'm old and not long for this world."

"So what happened," I asked.

"Oh, my boy, you shall hear. To leave our progeny in as much ignorance as that in which they presently wallow would be little short of a sin against the ever-living memory of our heroic departed." He halted, only to continue as soon as he saw my mouth open.

"Ah, hold awhile Jonny. All eagerness for bold adventure. Don't you be too happy to find it. I never was. Adventure is best for those who live on it after. So wait and listen to my tale."

I kept my mouth firmly closed in the hope that he might get to the point the sooner were he not prompted away from his set course, so to speak.

"Well, there was the whole scene of battle, or that which was close by and not hidden in the smoke, in my view. Truth be told it was not much, but the smoke cleared and there he was clear to all on the quarter-deck of his flagship. The Hero himself. Now he was a cool hand standing there and calling out here and there to those around him as if it were a cruise on the cut and he was at the tiller. He must have known the danger he put himself in by such conduct and dressing as he did. Sitting target for the Frenchie's up in the rigging I'd say. Still he knew best and he paid the price. Yet at that moment he cared not one bit, by the looks of him. Yet, as you know, he was in mortal danger. I saw that danger up in the rigging of the enemy vessel that had come along side and was battering the flagship most fearful. I saw them and knew what I must do to fulfil my duty, as he himself had called upon us all to do. Mind, you know, it was a long old shot to pot one of those chaps."

"'Specially with a musket in your hands."

"True, Sammy, fighting was never my best, and shooting has always been alien to me. But do my duty I had to try. Never be a-feared of failing. Let the Hero die with no man raising a gun to defend him? Not I. Not even I. So good was what I intended, so hard the doing of it. Still, do it I must, I said to myself.

"Up went my stock to the shoulder, up went my elbow to level the piece. A squeeze of the trigger. And as I pulled to fire a great shiver went through our vessel and she pitched, dropping my aim right onto the deck where he stood. What could I do? I could neither stop, nor hold my aim. And there it was."

"Away with you father. A taller tale than any you've told." That was my grandmother, who instantly dismissed the notion that before us was the man who had silenced the noble heart of Lord Nelson himself.

All others were silent.

I was more cautious. I did not want to believe that he had been so foolishly unfortunate. After all, he had tried to do his duty. I felt that sympathy should be our course. I did not believe him, but half wanted to. I had no famous ancestors, so an infamous one would have to suit.

I was to be disappointed.

My grandfather spoke up. He rarely made the leaps of inference that his wife made. He preferred to ask straight-forward questions.

"You say you shot Nelson?"

"Course I never did."

"But great-grandfather," I still hoped, "You say you fired the gun and Nelson fell as the ship lurched and you lost your aim. How are you so sure that it was not you?"

"Fired? Whoever said fired? I pulled on the trigger, but I never said I fired."

He was infuriating, but his meaning was clear. I looked at my grandfather, then at my great-grandfather. "Your musket did not fire?" My grandfather widened his eyes as all became clear.

"You speak truly and have my meaning exact." He looked at us in turn and explained. "Most unreliable. Nothing like things they have today, I shouldn't think. No, it never went bang Sammy. Though 'twas hard to hear distinct even a sound so close."

"So why are you ashamed of your action?"

"Failure to defend my Admiral, daughter."

"Telling-tales, more likely, father. That's your shame. If you were ever there you were hiding in some corner."

"Wrong, daughter. I did hide away when I flung that musket to the ground and gave my toes a fearful bruising. Black and blue they were. Then I scuttled away and hid my poor feet. But I was never a coward, proper."

"So where lies your shame?"

"As your granny knows, I have none, do I daughter? Just like those orphans of the soldiers who spend their days in the workhouse."

"Father, the welfare of the families of the militia and the county regiment..."

The old man rose slowly as she commenced to speak and, interrupting her, stated imperiously, and much satisfied, "Is an improving topic for tomorrow. Or perhaps young Jonny here should like to hear how I came safe home and left the sea for ever?

For me 'tis time to be away to my berth, my hearties."

In Hope of Resurrection

The storm clouds had rolled away, driven from the sky by the dawn of another late August day. In the village the men were already away to the fields, where they found their anxious masters studying the crop they hoped to commence to harvest. There had been much thunder but little rain and the weather seemed set fair. In the cottages, the women and children were readying to follow. All was alive and all was eagerness to be on with life. In the Rectory Mr. Doddrington snored in his bed, whilst the maid raked ashes from the range and fetched water from the well. Mr. Jagland was

351

already away from the cottage by the wharf, striding merrily away to chivvy the gardeners at the big house. Along the cut the boats had been passing along all night, but now, in the spreading light one or two had moored up and there was the smell of bacon and potatoes on the dawn air.

It was about an hour later that Mrs. Jagland would, had anyone been near, have been seen coming out of her front door. She walked as quickly as she could, her characteristically purposeful stride taking her rapidly up the cart track towards the village. It was unusual for her to be away from her home so early in the day, but her stride was the same stride that had carried her towards the Church twice each Sunday and on all her other errands to the village. The expression on her face was the one she usually wore; her dress matched it in modesty and tidiness. Whether she was contemplating on how often she had walked along this track in her sixty-two years or whether she was wondering how many more times she might do it, she was in thoughtful mood. Unusually, there was what appeared to be a tear in her eye.

The countryside was awake and the harvest was to be begun as it always had been. That morning, her father, Old Job Carter, had not awoken. For the first time in nearly a century the world would be without him. He had died without pain or fuss, to be found by his daughter who had entered his bedroom when she had seen her husband on his way to work. There had been no wailing: that was not how she treated troubles, and she saw no reason to deal with death in any other way. She shed a tear and got on with what needed to be done. She was not callous; simply practical in all things. She knew that all life was mortal and when a man had lived such a long life it was no surprise when it came to an end. She had laid him out neat and tidy before she left.

So now she was away to fetch the doctor, call upon the carpenter, summon the family and make arrangements with Mr. Doddrington, the vicar.

When the doctor sent his maid up to the Hall to fetch Mr. Jagland, Mrs. Jagland felt a little affronted. She had no truck with those few misguided women who were demanding to do the same things as men: she knew she was eminently better at managing domestic matters, death included, than her husband. She was, however, happy to see him, when he found her at the carpenters. Mr. Jagland appeared to be shocked. He was all comfort for his wife, but he had a closer affinity with the dead man than she had. Mrs. Jagland loved her father so much that she had been frustrated to the point of surrender by her inability to make him understand the error of his ways and recognise that, under Queen Victoria, life had changed. She had not, however, stepped-back from her duty to reprimand the old man when necessary. That had been often.

The carpenter said he would follow the doctor down and measure up. As the Jaglands walked down the village street women and children, off to the harvest, had already heard the news and made their condolences.

"Sam, we shall call on Mr. Doddrington to arrange the funeral, then we shall go home," instructed Mrs. Jagland.

"I have the day off: his Lordship said." Mrs. Jagland was unsure whether this was a good thing. Her Sammy was soft-hearted and would need to comfort her.

"You must write letters to the family." A useful task to occupy him. "If we make arrangements with Mr. Doddrington this morning you can tell them all."

"He wasn't much of a Church-going man." Sam was right.

"All the more of a reason why he should have a good Church funeral and a safe burial place." Mrs. Jagland was equally sure she was right.

"I wonder if that is what he would have wanted? Though I know it is best, as you say, my dear."

"He would, though he would have said he'd happily be thrown in the canal, just to be provoking towards decent folk. He should thank the Lord that Mr. Doddrington is such a good Christian man that he will take no account of all the rudeness and obstinacy with which father rewarded all his good offices." Mrs. Jagland was right, Mr. Doddrington did not hold grudges.

Mrs. Jagland expected that to be that. When Sam continued on the same topic she was, consequently, to say the least, surprised. "Indeed, Mr. Doddrington is a tolerant and Christian man, but your father had a last wish."

Mrs. Jagland was horrified. She knew her father well, but surely she had not been correct regarding his wishes regarding the disposal of his corpse. "He will have a Christian burial, whatever he wished."

"Be calm, my dear," said Sam. "He wanted a Christian burial. I heard him say so."

"Well, what are you fussing about then, husband? For once, we are as one."

"I fear otherwise, my Love. I heard him say to Mr. Boot only two days ago that he would have Mr. Oaktree."

Mrs. Jagland froze. "He wanted a Christian burial, so he cannot have wanted Oaktree. Oaktree is a Baptist." Such was her logic.

"Well, my dear, he didn't say he wanted a Christian burial, but he did say he'd have Mr. Oaktree do it."

"He will have a Christian burial and so he won't have Mr. Oaktree. When did you hear this?" She was determined to have her way, but sought to confound any objections.

"As I said, just the other day. Mr. Boot..."

"Boot is not desirable company even for an old Devil such as my father."

"...was standing at the gate to the towing path and your father was leaning on the wall chatting. Well, I needed a pair of boots mending, you know the one's I was trying to cobble the other night that I could not make good, so I went across to them. And as I got there I heard him say that he would have that Mr. Oaktree send him on his way, when the time came."

"He might have meant anything." She did not convince even herself. "There is nothing written and you should have a care for his soul and be quiet about what you think you heard. I do believe your ears are not what they were. You have said as much yourself."

Mr. Jagland did not speak again. His ears, he thought, were not what they once had been, though he could not recall having heard himself say so.

Mrs. Jagland knocked on the rectory door. Mr. Jagland stooped to inhale the scent of the sweet peas that clambered up some poles by the porch. He stood up as his wife prodded him to attention. The door was opened by Mrs. Blaymire, the widow who kept house for Mr. Doddrington. A rosy cheeked woman in late middle-age, known for her hearty constitution, she did not smile.

"Good Morning, Mrs. Blaymire. Is Mr. Doddrington home?" Mrs. Jagland was always formally polite with her social equals.

"Dear Mrs. Jagland, my condolences. I have told Mr. Doddrington your news," she said.

Mrs. Jagland thanked her. Mr. Jagland scratched his head at how word ran round the women of the village.

"Mr. Doddrington is expecting you. Come through to his study." Mrs. Blaymire continued, "Despite his age, it must have come as a terrible shock to you."

"He was an old man, and a trial, but he was my father." Mrs. Jagland spoke truthfully, as ever.

The door to the study was open. Mr. Doddrington looked up from the paper on which he was making some notes in preparation for the funeral. He sprang to his feet and came to the door, drew Mrs. Jagland in and showed her to a chair. Mr. Jagland followed her in and stood by the chair. Mrs. Blaymire was sent for tea.

"My deepest sympathy is yours my dear Mrs. Jagland. Likewise to you, Mr. Jagland. He was a wonderful character, with such spirit and such a memory. Shall miss his many gifts."

Mrs. Jagland did not spend more than a moment pondering upon which ones the reverend gentleman had in mind, but spoke up for her husband, as well as herself. She thanked Mr. Doddrington. "You are more than kind for he wasted many an hour of your time."

"Not at all, not at all, no, his tales of the old days could be most enlightening." Mr. Doddrington had easily been diverted from his purpose by tales of the old days, told under the apple tree where, in summer, the old man held forth.

"Some grain of truth may have found its way in, no doubt..." Mrs. Jagland thought the vicar unduly soft-hearted, but baulked at telling him so.

"No, indeed, I am positive that he spoke with veracity on many subjects!" Mr. Doddrington saw no point in speaking ill of the dead.

"You are a kind man, Mr. Doddrington, but I meant your efforts to bring him to salvation. He stuck his heathen heels in more than once with those tales he beset you round with." Mrs. Jagland was beginning to wonder why everyone seemed to think that her father had been such a fascinating man.

"Well, now I hope that I can aid him on his journey to the next life. When will the funeral be held?" Mr. Doddrington knew how much Mrs. Jagland appreciated the practical tone.

"We thought that two days, that is Thursday, would be more than enough time to prepare. Sam will write letters this morning and we'll have them to his family who live away as soon as we may." Mrs. Jagland aimed to make the arrangements for the first date which would not seem unduly hasty. She also wanted to sort things out quickly in case Mr. Jagland got a fit of courage and started once again on his silly story about Mr. Boot.

Fortunately, all her husband said was that he would write the letters as soon as he got home. Of course, he hadn't thought that two days was about right until that moment. There seemed to be no need to dally, though. So he said so. Both these interventions surprised Mr. Doddrington, who had forgotten that Mr. Jagland was there, though he stood with his hand on the back of the chair on which his wife sat.

"Very, well. Shall we say eleven o'clock? I shall tell the sexton." At that moment the passing bell began to toll. "There, I shall go to see him at the Church as soon as we have finished. Now, we must choose some hymns suitable..."

The interview ended shortly after this. Business-like and to the point, as Mrs. Jagland liked all her dealings to be. So rapidly had the crucial decisions been made that Mrs. Blaymire drank the tea she had prepared.

The Jaglands walked away from the sound of the bell which rang out ninety-eight times. In the fields work halted briefly as the chimes floated over the rank of scythe-wielding men and the army of women and children who followed them. A moment's pause, and then back to the sweat of hard labour which was their lot. Mr. Doddrington hurried up to the Church to find the sexton and make the necessary arrangements.

Mrs. Jagland was pleased to see that the trap belonging to Dr. MacKay stood outside the front door of the old house. From the top of the track the broad frame of the doctor was easily picked out as he stood in conversation with the nimble little carpenter, with his lad standing close by.

"There they are," Mr. Jagland pointed out, unnecessarily, to his wife.

"No point hanging the whole affair out." But she spoke with the sound of sorrow in her heart. Sam took her hand and pressed it gently. That was enough to restore her self-control. Wouldn't do for the carpenter to see how sad she really was. Besides, she meant what she said.

As Mr. Jagland and his wife were half way down the track, they saw Dr. MacKay, carpenter Thomas and his lad all look towards the far corner of the wall that enclosed the garden. They had clearly heard something, but there was, for a few seconds nothing to see. Then two figures came around the corner. Two men, who Mrs. Jagland recognised immediately. Her stride became even more purposeful, her eye glinted and her nostrils flared. Had the two unfortunate men been close enough to look her in the eye, they would have anticipated an assault. Mrs. Jagland had spied Mr. Boot and Mr. Oaktree and she was ready to do battle with them.

When she reached her own front door, she greeted the doctor and the carpenter and the carpenter's lad by name. A pause then ensued before she invited them to enter and do the things that had to be done. During this pause she stared down her nose at Mr. Oaktree and Mr. Boot, combining distaste with a warning not to interfere in proceedings: she knew what their business was, but she was not about to allow them to escape without having to explain themselves.

However, it was Mr. Jagland who broke the silence. "Excuse me, I have letters to write. Urgent letters. I shall be indoors. Yes, indoors." his words petered out as his resolve to write letters gathered strength. He slid around the door.

Mrs. Jagland was not perturbed by his withdrawal from the field of battle. She loved him and knew that he belonged amongst the greenhouses and flowerbeds: his reasonable gentleness would only have served to undermine.

"Good morning, Mrs Jagland. We have come to offer our condolences to you and your family, sincere sympathy." Mr. Oaktree opened the contest.

Mrs. Jagland replied with her thanks, though she adopted such an aggressive tone that Mr. Oaktree was left in no doubt that his sympathy was unwelcome and irrelevant.

He was pleased to know that he had hit his mark with his ranging shot. "Might we be of service at this time of sadness? I knew your father well and would happily offer the succour of the Lord's Word to those in need."

This probe was repulsed with a powerful volley to the effect that Mr. Doddrington had provided all the words of comfort that were needed in that household and would continue to do so when more were wanted.

Mr. Oaktree tried a new tack; had not Mr. Carter had an affinity with the Baptist rites and ways? He had never been an attender at the Chapel, but nor had he been to the Church since the time of his children's baptisms.

Mrs. Jagland was derogatory of any suggested affinity with any form of religion. Mr. Oaktree might say what he liked, but to her mind her father was an unreformed sinner from a past age who was little better than a heathen, her shame being that she had failed in all her attempts to turn his mind to the Lord in his old age. Then, as Mr. Oaktree seemed about to mount a counterattack, she informed him that her father had, he knew, attempted to turn him head over heels into the cut on more than one occasion, thus demonstrating his contempt for the dissenting sects.

Mr. Oaktree recoiled momentarily, but regrouped and would have pointed out that the vicar had also only narrowly avoided being pitched into the muddy water by the outstretched walking stick. Of course neither case demonstrated respect for clergymen of either hue, but they had been treated with equanimity.

However, Mr. Oaktree never began his rear-guard action, for the cavalry, in the form of Mr. Boot, charged onto the field to set the advancing forces back on their heels. A true inheritor of Bunyan, he swept onto the attack, as if fighting a giant, lion or foul fiend.

"Mrs. Jagland, your father asked Mr. Oaktree to conduct his funeral. He told me so himself and your own husband was witness to his words." He paused to admire what he believed to be a decisive intervention.

Mrs. Jagland's response was swift. "You may say so, though what his words signified I cannot say, nor indeed do I believe that you have his true meaning. My husband told me of his words. They might have meant anything. As for my husband as witness; he freely admits that his hearing is not as good as it once was. Even you, Mr. Boot, should know better than to twist the words of an old man; words that he spoke but a few days before his death."

"I seek to speak the truth and to see it done, Mrs. Jagland, that is all. So, your husband told you of his words? Did he also tell you that I wrote it in my notebook?" Mr. Boot turned a few pages of a board bound pocket book. There, amongst the money paid and received and the minutiae of a rural shoemaker's business, he pointed to a sentence that read, "I, Job Carter, do wish and desire that my funeral and burial be conducted according to the rites and practice of the Baptist Church." Beneath this, in the scratchy hand of an old man who wrote but rarely, were spindly pen strokes that, combined, made the words "Job Carter". He shoved the page under Mrs. Jagland's nose, without the least delicacy, for closer inspection. He stared earnestly and triumphantly at her.

"Please, please, Mrs. Jagland, do not be offended by Brother Boot's fervour. I am sure you understand how it would have been disrespectful of your father had we not brought this to your notice." Mr. Oaktree felt the need to intervene.

"You need not concern yourself, far be it from me to doubt his fervour, Mr. Oaktree, nor to be offended by an opinion for which I care not a fig." Then turning on Mr. Boot, "As for him writing his name, I assure you that you are mistaken, though how you could mistake your own forgery I do not know. You know, surely, that he could not write."

"No, I do not, Mrs. Jagland, for he could, when he wished. He could read too, when the fancy took him." Mr. Boot was, as ever, following the straight and narrow path of truth.

Mrs. Jagland knew that he could, though he and she, for different reasons, preferred not to let others know. She hazarded, though half-heartedly, that the writing was not his. And then, added simply that the funeral was already arranged, so their attention was not only unwanted but also unnecessary.

Nor was she overly concerned when Mr. Oaktree declared that he would, for one, ensure that the old man's wishes were fulfilled as far as he could manage and that the tyranny of the established Church would not reach into the grave. Wishes might be ignored, but he would ensure that Job Carter did not go to meet the maker of all things unheeded by those he had turned to in the name of the Lord.

With that he and Mr. Boot left the field.

So preparations were made.

The day of the funeral was close and heavy. By mid-morning it had become oppressive. There were dark clouds on the horizon. The days since the old man's death had been hot, very hot. In the churchyard, the sexton had prayed for rain to soften the ground. The harvesters had sweltered and dripped even in the shade of their short breaks. That morning they broke an extra time: the harvest must go on, but they could, at least, watch the small cortege pass up the village street. The bell tolled laboriously, as if smothered by a pillow of heavy air. The wheels of the cart rumbled over the sun-baked street. Those apart, the only sound was that of the footsteps of the mourners, melting in the heat of their hefty black clothes.

The close relatives followed the hearse. After they had passed the harvesters turned away to return to their labour. Only a few followed on to the Church. Only those who were truly faithful in their beliefs and those who did not harvest, though they relied, as did all in the village, on its success. In a few minutes all had passed under the lych-gate and entered into the cool certainty of seven hundred years of obscure, forgotten history.

The service must remain private, as is only proper. Outside the Church the still was broken by the hammer of the blacksmith. This ceased as Mr. Hartley mopped his brow and stepped out into the roadway: for him the burning sun and breathless air meant relief. All was quiet. He looked down the street and was surprised to see, coming around the corner by the rectory, a group of people marching purposefully. Mourners, late, he guessed. They'll be warm, he thought.

Then he recognised the men at the front. On the right strode Mr. Oaktree and on the left was Mr. Boot. Behind them were some twenty or thirty of their Baptist adherents. As they passed the smithy Mr. Hartley saw the sweat streaming down their faces. Mr. Boot's stiff collar seemed to be particularly troublesome to the radical bootmaker. Yet, onward they marched, as if to war.

They did not, of course, enter the Church or the Churchyard. Instead they followed the wall round until they came under the shade of an aged oak tree. It was the same tree that shaded the fresh dug grave. Gnarled and broad, with the sun soon to be at the zenith, it could cover them all. They were welcome under its boughs.

Mr. Hartley, who professed no religious faith whatsoever, was further encouraged in his atheism by the odd behaviour of these religious folk. He noted how, despite the obvious distress caused by a rapid walk in formal dress in hot weather, they did not sit down and quench their thirsts. Instead they formed into a semi-circle. Mr. Hartley then heard Mr. Oaktree, a man powerful in the scriptures and the lungs, boom out a prayer. When he finished, Mr. Boot carried on, though his voice was not audible. Mr. Hartley knew he was praying by the whirling of his arms. They then struck up with "I hunger and I thirst...", which, at least, struck the non-believer as appropriate.

Indeed, he was so impressed as to take himself off to the parlour of the ale-house and refresh himself. The only other customer was Constable Jenkins. He tramped the roads of the local villages, this being in the days before police bicycles, and rarely found much to do but fail to catch poachers, apprehend the odd participant in a drunken brawl and refresh himself at the inns and ale-houses. He and Hartley looked out of the window. A fine view of the Baptists was theirs.

The singers had just begun "The Lord's my shepherd..." when the door of the Church opened and Mr. Doddrington, fully robed for the special occasion, chasuble and surplice shining in the sun, followed by the coffin borne on the shoulders of six men and the mourners.

Whether Mr. Doddrington heard the singing or saw heads of the rival congregation poking above the wall first, will never be known. To his credit he did not miss a step or bat an eye-lid. He steered his course to the appointed spot with unerring dignity and purpose. The same could not be said for all of those that followed him. Mrs. Jagland was more stirred than anyone else.

When the party arrived at the graveside all settled to quiet. Mrs. Jagland stared menacingly at Mr. Oaktree's hair, which was all that was visible above the wall.

She was awakened from her unchristian thoughts by Mr. Doddrington's quiet voice. He began to speak the age-old words. He got no further than the first sound when Mr. Oaktree was to be heard speaking what appeared to be a eulogy. Mr. Doddrington raised his voice in firm pursuance of his purpose. Yet Mr. Oaktree was not outdone. He was accustomed to speaking outdoors and easily increased the volume. Mr. Doddrington, tried heroically to maintain his primacy, but was no match for such a voluble Dissenter well-accustomed to outdoor meetings.

Around the graveside there were looks of distaste, disgust and general puzzlement. The sexton strode to the wall and called upon Mr. Oaktree to desist out of respect for the deceased man and the grieving family. Finding himself ignored, the sexton, said that he would fetch Constable Jenkins, whom he had seen go to refresh himself across the road and knew well enough had not been there the hour or two it usually took for him to slake his thirst. Mr. Oaktree continued, with voice raised even higher to Heaven. Mr. Boot told the sexton that they would face the wrath of the leviathan state that had so long been the persecutor of Truth, in the same spirit as Bunyan dismissed Hobgoblins and Foul Fiends, so the sexton might happily rush to the forces of worldly law. In fact, had the sexton done so, he would have found no-one in the parlour. Mr. Hartley genuinely had better things to do, whilst the Constable decided, with great prescience, that he would walk to the Red Lion, some two miles distant to ask about stories of disorderly conduct that he thought he had heard rumours of.

The sexton did not go for the forces of law and order, however. Not that he did not stand solidly with the established Church and State, but because he was struck by a sod of earth. Mr. Boot pointed out that there were sods conveniently situated at the graveside, proving that the projectile was launched from inside the Churchyard. He had, of course, been unable to see the culprit, but was thoroughly disgusted by such conduct. Mrs. Jagland was furious, but neither had she witnessed the casting of the first sod. It seemed unlikely that it had been thrown from the graveside. Everyone there was respectable, even a great-grandson of the deceased, who was now a student at Oxford, could not be suspected. As he said, he would have cleared the wall and struck the vile Mr. Oaktree. He was perfectly insulted by the notion that he might have hit the sexton, who, though a common man, was 'on his side'. He later offered to summon his college dining companions to vouch for his aim.

As for the theory that it had been hurled from outside, this seems equally unlikely as it hit him squarely on the side of the head. It remained a mystery as no-one saw a small boy scuttling back to the undergrowth and out of the Churchyard through a hole in the wall. Later, the talk in the ale-houses and the supper tables was of the mischievous spirit of Job Carter having his bit of fun. There was life after death.

If the origin of the event was obscure, the course was inevitable, though confused. The sexton, on being struck, cried out accusations in a most un-sexton-like fashion, using words that were thoroughly unbefitting. It was Jeremy Collier, candlemaker, who decided that the sexton would be well-served if some substance were given to his baseless calumnies. His aim was true. The sexton, provoked beyond endurance, returned the stick that had hit him, with such inaccuracy, caused by his fury, that he hit Mrs. Balding. A lady of conviction and valour, she removed her hat and threw the apple she kept thereunder, blindly over the wall. At the same moment her husband, who had come equally well prepared, hurled his apple.

Back they came.

In the exchanges that followed it would be pointless to describe who threw what and with what fortune they found a target. Fortunate they would indeed have been, for even the Anglicans, from behind the wall at the top of the bank, hardly ventured close enough to see the foe. As for the Dissenters, they fired blindly in the general direction of their opponents.

In the battle a remarkable number of blows were suffered by good Christian folk of both persuasions. The fact that the numerous hoard of victims openly avowing the injury they had suffered at the hands of the enemy was not matched by equivalent claims of marksmanship can be explained by the sure fact that all were of too sturdy Christian character to stoop to such conduct on such a solemn occasion, as much as to poor lines of sight or willingness to suffer blows for the sake of the Lord.

When Mr. Oaktree and Mr. Doddrington had regained control of their erring sheep, which, to their credit, they attempted from the start, the two sects sidled away. The sexton filled the grave. And the heavy weather raised anvils of black in the sky.

About ten o'clock that night the weather broke. The village street was like a river, the stream gouging shallow channels in the packed mud and stone way, the cottagers on one side of the street wondered what had become of their neighbour's opposite, while those folk strengthening themselves after a day's labour in the fields were unanimous in declaring that another pot of ale was called for as there'd be no work in the morning. The rectory window panes rattled under the rapid fire of the summer deluge and the yellow roses around the window of Mr. Dodrington's drank deeply as their petals were scattered on the ground. They window framed the peering face of the vicar, looking like a rather dingy portrait. No more dismal than the trepidation with which Mr. Doddrington looked upon the task he had set himself that night. Nor was it the rain that filled him with worry, though the storm did little to improve his view of the prospects. Yet there he was, umbrella, lantern, coat and hat at the ready, some sandwiches stuffed in his jacket pocket. He had determined to face the storm and anything else the night might bring.

Initially he had sent a lad to find the Constable. The boy has searched and sweated in the heat of the afternoon for some five miles, but had no luck. He had given up after ascertaining that the forces of law and order had refreshed himself so well during his investigations at the Red Lion that there was little prospect of him doing any useful service to Mr. Doddrington even if he were to be found. A glass of lemonade and sixpence ensured the boy's discretion and he had told Mr. Doddrington, on his return, that the Constable was investigating some folk who had begun gleaning early at some hamlet over towards Bishop's Burton.

The vicar, disappointed by the Constable, thought of the sexton, but pitied his aching joints after the hard digging he had done. He wondered if the rain that, he correctly, predicted would come, would aggravate the sexton's rheumatic pains. In any case, the old man would think him foolish for suggesting the possibility that one of them should mount guard in the Churchyard that night. He half thought the same himself. Why should an intelligent man be put upon so because of a remark by his housekeeper. A chance remark. Yet the idea had burrowed itself into his reason and addled it. He knew this. At the back of his mind lurked the possibility, the merest chance, that she might be right.

If Mrs. Blaymire, the guilty housekeeper had seen Mr. Doddrington's preparations she would have regretted the innocuous words that had formed only a fraction of their brief conversation at afternoon tea. All she had said was that, "of course, such an old corpse of such a remarkable old fellow would no doubt interest the surgeons." She had simply meant to recognise that there weren't many folk like Job Carter. And that, until he sat down to write his next sermon, had been how he had understood it. But the sermon was uninspired and he was tired after the heat of the day and upset by the despicable behaviour of the Baptists during the funeral. He knew of his own propensity to build mountains out of molehills. He knew he was probably being foolish, but what if the resurrection men were active still? In his Churchyard! Poor Mrs. Jagland. That paragon of the working man's wife, she who had so often been his counsellor. Indeed, were it not for the fear of adding to her grief, he would have consulted her upon the issue currently agitating him. No, he had decided, he had no alternative. He must mount guard that night.

So off he went, into the tempest to do his duty.

On arriving at the Church, he first thought of setting up his camp under the shelter of the lych-gate. Yet, what if folk were to see him? The villagers would surely make merry with their vicar sitting in the pouring rain. They would ask why. They would speculate or have to be told the truth, neither of which were relished by the vicar. So, on reflection he settled for the porch. No one would come up into the Church at that time of night and he could sit and keep his vigil before slipping off before first light. He reached his shelter and sat down. He patted the small spirit flask he had secreted in his inner pocket and stared out into the rain.

The curtain of water became less dense, stopped briefly, returned as drizzle and then came down, once more, in a sheet. He took a medicinal sip. He had another as the clock struck one. He opened his sandwiches. And then his hungry gaze was drawn away from sustenance to the far corner of the Churchyard. He was sure he had seen a movement. And then he saw a brief pin-head of light flicker and he heard a squelching footfall moving across the yard.

If he had thought at all, he might have wondered why a grave-robber might come single-handed. At that moment he did not think, he just stood and moved slowly towards the light, thinking to intercept the intruder before he could reach the grave.

Mr. Doddrington, even in his youth at School and University, had never been a vigorous athlete.

Quite the opposite. He had not begun to think about what he would do when he had stalked his prey. He hoped, in the back of his mind, that discovery would make his quarry flee. He was soon to discover whether his hope was justified. He had gone little more than ten yards, stepping carefully on the uneven stone path and reaching the grass, when, forgetting the ancient grassy coffin shaped mound some six inches high that marked the grave of some long departed and unknown parishioner, he fell. As he did so he dropped his darkened lantern sending a shaft of light across the faces of a row of stones and illuminating a figure draped in a long coat, with a hat pulled tightly down.

The vicar exclaimed, without making an oath, fortunately.

"Mr. Doddrington?"

The vicar looked at the man, who was now advancing towards him. The figure repeated his question.

Mr. Doddrington screwed up his eyes. "Who is it? And what are you doing in my Churchyard at this time of night?"

"Your Churchyard? By what right do you call it that? Consecrated ground I grant you, but robbed from the people by the established Church."

Mr. Doddrington was not pleased by this, but was relieved that the intruder was clearly Mr. Boot. Not even Oaktree went on like that.

"And I might ask you the same, Mr. Doddrington? Have you taken to sneaking about in the hours of darkness? I jest. Here take my hand." Mr. Boot was unusually amiable.

Mr. Doddrington thanked him as he rose to his feet. "Though," he added, "I am loathe to touch the hand that began an affray at Job Carter's funeral today. Indeed, I am."

Mr. Boot 's amiability disappeared. "A slur. T'was not I that caste the first missile. Nor, I say, any."

Mr. Doddrington was in no mood to bicker. He was relieved that Mr. Boot was not in fact a pair of burly criminals. He knew he should be grateful for the hand of friendship. So "Thank you, Mr. Boot," he replied, without apology.

A flash of forked lightening caste shadows all around. A mighty crack of thunder shook the air. Mr. Doddrington, retreated to the porch. Mr. Boot followed. They settled down opposite each other on the stone seats, smooth from five hundred years of like use.

Silence in the rain. Mr. Doddrington pondered if it were worth observing that it was pleasing to see that even the most ardent Dissenter might seek the shelter of the Church of England. He did not. Mr. Boot was wondering if he should ask the vicar if he had been locked out of his own Church. He did not.

Both knew that conversation would mean explanation and neither wanted that. This induced civilised conversation, or something of very close resemblance, between the two opponents.

"How long will this rain last?"

"Very like it will keep on for an hour or two."

"You think so?"

"Indeed, we are here together for a good while, lest we brave the tempest."

"We are. I think you are correct."

"Very wet."

"Yes."

"There is now something of a chill too, I fear."

"The closeness is gone. The rain does follow the closeness."

Mr. Doddrington felt the need of a medicinal swig, to fend off a summer cold. He knew Mr. Boot was a strong temperance man, most like an abstainer. He did not wish to provoke a quarrel. However, he could feel a chill creeping into his head, so he reached into his jacket and removed the small flask. He held it and bit the bullet.

"Would you care for a nip for medicinal purposes, of course. To drive away a chill."

Mr. Boot looked most grievously offended. Inspiration surged through his veins. He hung on the edge of a sermon. And then he calmed himself. Perhaps this was not the place or the time. He did not want to pick a quarrel either.

"It is not my habit to sip from the Devil's bottle whatever circumstances I might find myself in. If you wish to pollute your soul as well as your body it is your choice. Yet, it is a now a chill, wet night and you must protect your health, Mr. Doddrington. I will not partake, but, under these circumstances, nor will I object."

"Most kind of you, Mr. Boot. You will understand that such is not my habit." Mr. Doddrington sipped enough to send a little warmth through his veins.

"I doubt you not."

Silence returned, though Mr. Boot seemed a little agitated. Mr. Doddrington feared his frequent antagonist was building a head of temperance steam. He braced himself, as Mr. Boot began to speak.

"No, I doubt you not. I have no doubt either that," he paused and struggled for words, "that you, personally, took no part in the sad, very sad, events that shamed Mr. Carter's funeral. I believe that you, as a man, and a man of the cloth at that, had no hand in it."

"I should think not," the vicar replied, rather hotly, "It was, after all, a member of my flock, who was struck first." He cooled. "And you, Mr. Boot, I am more than certain of your innocence in the matter."

"Though I offer hearty thanks for that absolution, I tell you that the first clod of earth was caste from within your Churchyard. I plainly saw one of our number hit."

"You are surely mistaken. Am I to believe that my congregation throw sods of earth at one another? Really, Mr. Boot. I..." But he decided that he must try to calm the waters before they became too rough. He looked at the rain. There was still a deluge. He paused. "Mr. Boot, I accept your word, though I find the whole business most mysterious, not to say deeply distressing."

"And I will accept your word, and a mystery it will remain." Mr. Boot was too much of a Bible man to believe in superstitious nonsense such as spirits, but he knew of some who had already said that the clod was hurled by Job Carter's ghost to have a last jest.

Mr. Boot explained some of the silly superstitions of the country-folk to the vicar, pointing out, with special care, that these were tales told by ignorant rustics. He told how, in his grandfather's day, away over in the fenland, from whence the line of Boot came, there were folk who would not venture out after dark for fear of an assortment of boggles and corpse-lights throwing their meagre glow on the still surface of mere and pool. Indeed, his great-grandfather had preached against such things as he tramped about the isolated hamlets and farms – even after nightfall.

"Most foolish was their belief that the graves of the recently deceased might be desecrated by spirits who desired to drag the dead into their marshy lairs to consume the flesh and thus maintain their bodily form. These creatures were so determined to do evil that no house where a body was resting before the funeral was safe, lest a guard be kept and lights burned brightly. Even, they believed from consecrated ground, so strong were the creatures of the dark to be found in those parts." Mr. Boot haltingly explained that he did not believe in such things, but there were always the superstitious folk who did.

Had it not been dark, Mr. Doddrington would have seen Mr. Boot's cheeks reddening a little as he declaimed his disbelief in such superstitious twaddle.

"There have been humans too, who have done much the same." Mr. Doddrington introduced a new dimension.

Mr. Boot agreed, but added nothing.

Mr. Doddrington had hope that Mr. Boot would have developed the new theme, as he tended to expound on most others. He did not.

Mr. Doddrington tried again. "I refer, of course, to the wild stories a few years ago of grave-robbing and body-snatching." No response. "The fantasies of Mary Shelley and all those others too. There were, of course, real cases." Nothing. It was Mr. Doddrington who was discomfited, but avoided detection in the shadows of the church porch. "I heard of a man from the workhouse who requested to be allowed out for a week to sit by the grave of his brother as he heard that the resurrection men were active again. Mr. Stapler the Chairman of the Guardians told me."

Mr. Doddrington's voice was showing signs of anxiety. Fortunately, Mr. Boot put this down to the clergyman's sensibilities. Not knowing this, Mr. Doddrington, flustered and embarrassed, stood and declared that it was impossible that such a thing should happen here, in this day and age.

At that moment the rain ceased. Mr. Boot breathed a sigh of relief, and agreed that fears of resurrection men were groundless in this age of progress. Indeed, they were fortunate to live in such an age. They bade each other goodnight and parted at the gate. To the east the faintest hint of dawn could be anticipated just below the horizon, while fast-fading stars commenced their retreat across the sky. Both thought themselves fortunate to live in such an age and to be amidst their Lord's creation in its dawn glory. And both were certain that whatever had happened that day, the next would be another reflection of God's will. Boot would cobble shoes, Doddrington would prepare his sermon, the sexton would rub embrocation into his aching muscles and joints, whilst many more would await order to march in ranks with swinging scythes or plod beside their horses or sit under a tree and make the most of the summer sun.